Previously published Worldwide Suspense titles by
L. C. HAYDEN

WHY CASEY HAD TO DIE
WHEN DEATH INTERVENES
WHEN THE PAST HAUNTS YOU
ILL CONCEIVED
WHAT LIES BEYOND THE FENCE
WHEN MEMORY FAILS

WHEN DOUBT CREEPS IN

L. C. HAYDEN

WORLDWIDE

TORONTO • NEW YORK • LONDON
AMSTERDAM • PARIS • SYDNEY • HAMBURG
STOCKHOLM • ATHENS • TOKYO • MILAN
MADRID • WARSAW • BUDAPEST • AUCKLAND

If you purchased this book without a cover you should be aware that this book is stolen property. It was reported as "unsold and destroyed" to the publisher, and neither the author nor the publisher has received any payment for this "stripped book."

WORLDWIDE™

ISBN-13: 978-1-335-00001-9

When Doubt Creeps In

First published in 2021 by Angel's Trumpet Press.
This edition published in 2023 with revised text.

Copyright © 2021 by L. C. Hayden
Copyright © 2023 by L. C. Hayden, revised text edition

Recycling programs for this product may not exist in your area.

All rights reserved. No part of this book may be reproduced or transmitted in any form or by any means, electronic or mechanical, including photocopying, recording or by any information storage and retrieval system, without permission in writing from the publisher.

This is a work of fiction. Names, characters, places and incidents are either the product of the author's imagination or are used fictitiously. Any resemblance to actual persons, living or dead, businesses, companies, events or locales is entirely coincidental.

For questions and comments about the quality of this book, please contact us at CustomerService@Harlequin.com.

Harlequin Enterprises ULC
22 Adelaide St. West, 41st Floor
Toronto, Ontario M5H 4E3, Canada
www.ReaderService.com

Printed in U.S.A.

WHEN DOUBT CREEPS IN

To
Fran Fletcher
The Best Critique Partner—Ever!

and

To
Honey
RIP: Nov. 2007–July 2019

HARRY BRONSON

ONE

BRONSON SLAMMED THE book shut and leaned back on the foldable chair. He reached down and patted his dog, Honey, a light brown Basenji. A cool breeze whisked by and Bronson rubbed his arms. Despite the cool weather, Bronson liked it here in Pennsylvania and especially the campground Carol and he had chosen. Set on the outskirts of Pittsburgh, each campsite was large enough to give everyone plenty of space.

The people across from him were getting ready to grill some steaks and the smell of charcoal reached Bronson, enticing him to get up and do something productive. But age was catching up with him, and he'd rather remain sitting and reading, or rather, attempting to read.

He'd been doing that now for what? Fifteen, twenty minutes? Yet, he hadn't gotten past the first paragraph.

Something gnawed at his brain demanding to be heard. But the harder Bronson tried to get a handle on it, the more the thought plunged to the bottom drawer of his mind. If only he could grasp the image lurking at the forefront of his consciousness. He could do it if he focused, but the deeper he concentrated, the more it became a distant shadow on the horizon.

Filled with frustration, Bronson opened his book and resumed reading.

Sweat oozed out from every pore in Mike's body.

Bronson stopped and laughed at the irony. The character in the book was named Mike.

Mike. Bronson savored the word.

Mike, just like Mike Hoover, his ex-partner for over twenty years. The best partner anyone ever had.

Mike, the ace detective. The one who'd never cross the line. Everything always went by the book. Always by the side of the law.

Mike.

His best friend.

His almost brother.

A strange sensation crawled across Bronson's mind, and an elusive image flickered behind his eyes.

Mike was in danger. Something had gone wrong.

Terribly wrong.

Before Bronson had retired—okay, *he had been forced to retire at the tender age of 52*, but who was counting?—and while he still worked homicide for the Dallas Police Department, he'd always relied on his gut instinct. More than ninety-nine percent of the time, his gut gave birth to the truth.

And now his gut was telling him something had gone wrong.

Bronson reached for his cell and punched Mike's number.

The call went to voice mail.

That was okay. When Mike had the time, he'd return the call.

Traveling around the country in your motor home as you do, Mike would tell him, *is causing your imagination to run wild*. Then they would both laugh at Bronson's gut feeling.

Bronson swallowed hard and bolted to his feet. Before stepping inside the camper, Bronson hesitated. What if Mike was in trouble? Bronson shook his head.

He had to let it go. This was silly. He stepped inside and closed the door behind him, determined to put his fears aside.

Honey followed close to his side.

MIKE HOOVER

TWO

MIKE HOOVER SCANNED the desolate area that surrounded him. He'd swear he was alone in this God-forsaken New Mexico desert.

But Mike knew he wasn't. Somewhere out there, Pedro, one of the head honchos of the *Los Muertos* gang, watched every move Mike made, but Pedro wouldn't reveal himself. At least, not now. He would wait for the right moment.

So would Mike.

He took a swig of water and set the bottle down under the shade of a creosote bush. Mr. Cool. That was him.

He'd watch and wait.

The lechuguillas and sotol bushes swayed in the hot, stifling breeze.

Still, no Pedro. What was he waiting for?

Worse, what if Pedro chose not to reveal himself? Then what?

Mike's forehead and armpits grew even moister. He needed to control himself. Stop thinking about these worst-case scenarios. Focus on something. Anything.

A desert cottontail scurried by, scaring a kangaroo rat out of its hiding place.

Mike remained perfectly still. Listening.

That's when he heard it.

Footsteps. Coming from somewhere behind him. They had to be Pedro's.

Mike's Adam's apple started tap dancing in his throat.

The sound of a gun's hammer being pulled back froze Mike's blood, but still, he didn't turn.

"Why are you here?" Pedro asked.

Mike raised his arms and slowly pivoted. He faced a dark chocolate-complexion man with coarse black hair that framed a square face with dark eyes. "I'm—"

"I know who you are." A smug smile spread across Pedro's lips. "Mike Hoover, the famous Dallas homicide detective."

Mike shrugged. That's not how he'd describe himself. "My partner is—"

"Herbert Finch."

Mike lowered his hands an inch. He waited for a heartbeat. Nothing happened. He lowered them another inch. When Pedro didn't say anything, he dropped them the rest of the way. "You could say that."

"I did say that."

Mike threw up his right hand as though dismissing the comment. Before Finch, he had a different partner. Bronson. Harry Bronson. Mike wished he could reach out to Bronson right now. "Herbert is not much of a real partner."

"That's not my problem." Pedro thrust the Walther PPK forward. "For the last time, why are you here?"

"You are expecting Finch."

Pedro's face remained impassive.

"I came to warn you that he's going to betray you." Mike studied Pedro's face, hoping for the slightest hint of alarm. Seeing none, Mike continued, "As agreed, he will come by himself. But not far behind him, a swarm of cops will descend on you as soon as the deal goes down."

"Why are you telling me this?"

"Because I want in. I want the same deal Finch had with one small exception."

Pedro stared at Mike. The minute of silence stretched into eternity.

Pedro bit his middle finger nail off. He spit it out. "I don't know anything about any deal."

Mike took a step forward. Pedro didn't flinch. "I'm not a fool. Any minute now my partner will come. Let me take care of him for you, forever. This will prove I have your best interest at heart." Mike looked past Pedro's shoulder. A trail of dust rose like an ominous cloud. "There he is now. Let me prove to you I'm the real thing."

Pedro withdrew his sight away from Mike long enough to peek behind him. He stepped aside and within seconds, like the rest of the *Los Muertos* gang, he disappeared.

MIKE MOVED WITH orchestrated steps. First, he checked on his truck. He had hidden it as best as he could behind a cluster of large desert bushes in the fold of the small hills off the main trail. From where he stood, he couldn't see it, which meant Finch wouldn't either.

Next, without thinking of what he was doing and moving as if he were following a script, he withdrew the Glock from the holster. For a long second, he stared at the gun as though something was wrong with it. Did it feel heavier? No, of course not. He dismissed the idea to nothing more than nerves. He swallowed hard and replaced it in the harness. He adjusted it so that it fit perfectly and comfortably.

He reached for the bottle of water, took a drink,

sloshed it around in his mouth, and spit it out into the dry, cracked ground.

He crouched down behind a small Mexican Feathergrass bush. There, he would be out of sight. From his hidden position, Mike squinted, studying the dry, hot desert. If Finch didn't kill him, the July heat would. He wiped his brow and checked his watch. Two minutes had crawled by. He wet his cracked lips.

Thirty, forty yards directly in front of him, Finch brought his black sedan to a slow stop and opened the car door. Nothing happened. He stepped out, remaining behind the open car door. He scanned the area. "Pedro?"

No answer.

"It's me, Herbert."

Mike waited and watched.

Showtime.

MIKE SHOOK ONE of the branches above him, immediately drawing Finch's attention.

Finch reached for his gun but didn't raise it. He stepped around the door and toward the front of the car. "I know you're there. I just want to talk. Show yourself."

Mike took his time straightening up. He kept his head hanging low, and his right hand wrapped around his Glock. He slowly raised his head. A shark's grin spread across his face.

Finch's eyes opened as wide as saucers. "You!" He raised his Ruger 9mm, but Mike was faster. A single shot rang out. Finch dropped to the ground, his blood saturating the earth's dry cracks with rich, red pools of blood.

Mike holstered his Glock, ran, and shouted, "Let's get out of here."

The five members of the *Los Muertos* gang deserted their hiding places and stood, mouths agape, staring at the detective's inert body.

Mike came to an abrupt stop and turned. "The cops are no more than five minutes behind. If you want to stay here and have them arrest you, be my guest. But I'm out of here." He dashed toward his truck.

Pedro looked up toward the sky. "We need to wait for the merchandise. It should be here any moment."

"Forget about it. When the pilot sees the place crawling with cops, he's not going to deliver. We'll have to reschedule." With that, Mike turned and continued to head toward the Chevy truck.

Like stallions escaping a burning barn, Pedro and the other men bolted after him.

THREE

THAT NIGHT, sleep was Mike's enemy. The dreams, its weapons.

Over and over again, Mike saw himself withdrawing the weapon.

He pulled the trigger.

Herbert lay in a pool of blood, his blood slithering toward Mike.

The gun slipped out of Mike's hand, landing with a loud thud that sent a bolt of lightning to Mike's heart.

Covered in sweat, Mike sprung to a sitting position.

It had only been a dream, he reassured himself. Just a dream. Go back to sleep. He did. Only to have the same dream return.

MIKE, NOW AWAKE and alert, waited three hours before he made himself available to Pedro. Let him squirm. It'd be good for him. That would give Mike the edge he was looking for—and at this point, he needed every advantage. But now he was ready. From here on, it would be an uphill fight.

Previous research revealed that Hobb's Auto Shop served as a sanctuary for *Los Muertos*. He drove toward the shop located on the outskirts of the city. Within five minutes, he sat in the car staring at the shop.

It looked similar to other car repair shops. Its two garage doors were wide open, revealing four cars up on jacks worked on by mechanics in greasy coveralls. Outside, a line of cars waited for their turn to be repaired.

Mike checked his watch. He was five minutes late, late enough to show Pedro he wasn't in any hurry, but not so late that Pedro would lose interest. Mike stepped out of his car and into the shop. When he entered, he squinted several times, adjusting his eyes from bright sunlight to semi-darkness. No one paid attention to him.

He strolled toward the small office tucked on the left-hand side of the shop. Its windows, so dirty that they were opaque, didn't allow him to check the place out before entering, but still, he detected movement inside. He braced himself and without knocking, he let himself in.

He spotted Pedro, perched at the edge of the metal desk which overflowed with papers. Two chairs, one on each side of the desk, served as the only other pieces of furniture in this room. Mike noted a closed door to his left, probably a small storage closet.

Pedro shoved a newspaper toward him.

Mike remained standing as he reached for the paper. He smiled when he read the newspaper's headline: "Dallas Detective Killed in the Line of Duty."

"You think that's funny." Pedro's nostrils widened like an angry bull's.

Mike set the newspaper down without reading the article. "If you're asking me if I'm glad he's dead, yeah, I am. He would've been a constant pain in our caboose."

"Yesterday, you said you killed him for our sake." Using two fingers in each hand, Pedro put imaginary quotation marks around the words *for our sake*.

Mike nodded. "For our sake."

Pedro tapped his chest. "No, not *for our sake*. What

you did will only bring a swarm of cops to our city. Explain how is that for our sake."

"You've got to look at the bigger picture." Mike raised his index finger. "One, the police are going to be so busy looking for the killer, they'll leave us alone. This is precisely why I chose New Mexico, and specifically, Hobbs. It is one of our country's safest cities. So for this kind of murder to occur in the desert right outside the city limits, it's a big thing. Everyone's going to be focusing on that."

Mike raised another finger. "Two, everyone thinks I'm heartbroken over my partner's death. They think I'm still one of them. No one knows I did it. They have no idea. I'm safe, and no one knows I'm associated with you. So you are safe."

"So you think," Pedro said.

Mike ignored him and raised a third finger. "Three, we can now bring in all of those priceless Egyptian artifacts, distribute them to the proper private collectors, and no one will be breathing down our necks."

Pedro sat up. "Egyptian what?"

"Artifacts."

Pedro unfolded his solid frame from the edge of the desk and took a step toward Mike. "Art-ti-facts." He shook his head. "I don't know anything about Egyptian artifacts. If you were to mention black pearl, white stuff, brown sugar, or even weed, I'd know what you're talking about. But you mention Egyptian artifacts. That, I don't know anything about." Pedro reached beside him and picked up a clipboard and pretended to busy himself with paperwork.

Mike smiled, a curvature of the lips that contained

no amusement. "Don't play me the fool. I know about the Egyptian riches you are bringing into our country."

Pedro set the clipboard down. "As I said, talk to me about brown sugar, then we can deal. But Egyptian artifacts? Not so much."

Mike waited to answer while he studied his opponent. "I understand this may be a one-time deal. You deal mostly with gold, jewelry, and drugs. But now you're expending into artifacts because you're smart enough to recognize the opportunity to make a lot of easy money."

Pedro's jaw jutted forward. "If you know so much, then you know we had a delivery date scheduled. Now we don't because you decided to murder your partner. How's that better?" The anger behind the words surfaced like a roaring lion.

Mike took three steps forward, invading Pedro's private space. "Yeah, you had plans." He backed off. "But your plan was faulty."

Pedro set the clipboard down and remained silent.

"Let me ask you one thing," Mike said. "Once you had your merchandise in your greedy little paws, how exactly did you plan to get it to the buyers?"

Pedro continued to glare at Mike.

"Just as I thought. That's where Finch came in. He was supposed to tell you when it was safe to contact your buyers. He was going to set up the meetings. But like I told you before, he was also going to betray you. Soon as you handed over those pieces, the police would be there to arrest you and the rest of your gang. You'd be doing jail time right now, and those priceless Egyptian artifacts would be making their way back to Egypt."

The door to the office opened and a mechanic entered. Without speaking a word, he took a key from the wall. Pedro used the distraction to go around the desk. He pulled out the chair and sat.

After the mechanic left and had closed the door behind him, Pedro asked, "How do you know this?"

Mike shook his head. "Think about it. *Detective* Finch. *Detective* Hoover." He pointed to himself. "We worked together, remember? Partners always tell each other everything. Besides, I've been watching him. What I've done is cleared the path for you."

Pedro leaned back on the chair and focused on Mike. "Why?"

Mike smiled, waited for a few seconds, sat down, and leaned back. "Because I'm interested in attaining two things. Cleopatra's. Two. Figurines."

Pedro paled and remained still. Then his color returned. He took a deep breath and ran his fingers through his thick black hair. "I don't know anything about Cleopatra's treasures."

"In that case, let me refresh your memory. The Ancient Egyptians considered the Lapis Lazuli one of the most treasured gemstones of their time."

Pedro's eyes widened for a fraction of a second, but still long enough for Mike to notice.

"I see you're familiar with this stone." Mike paused for effect. "You should be because it was considered to be of godly importance. Cleopatra knew this."

Pedro bit his lips.

Mike continued, "She ordered her slaves to make two figurines made from this gemstone. One was of Osiris and the other one of Isis. Each of these god statuettes is worth two million, but together, they bring a staggering price of five million dollars."

"That's a nice story, but of no interest to me."

"Oh really? Then let me add one small detail." He paused for effect and focused his vision on Pedro. "I already have the perfect buyer."

Pedro's face lit up with a grin that was as ugly as it was insincere. "You have a buyer, that's…" He straightened himself. "That is a shame. You may have a buyer, but you don't have any items to sell. I'd say you have a major problem."

Mike took his time standing up. "I don't see me having a problem. You know that what I'm asking for is small potatoes compared to what the other items you'll be fencing will bring." Mike leaned over. "Look what you're getting in return: a guarantee that the police will never hassle you. Imagine, you'll be able to do whatever you want when you want, and you won't have to sweat a bit." He shook his head. "No, not ever."

Pedro drummed his fingers on one knee. "I need some time to talk to my men."

"No, you don't need to talk to your men." Mike shook his head for emphasis. "You talk to *El Patron*."

Pedro's eyes widened as though Mike had stabbed him with a thousand needles.

"As I said, partners tell each other everything."

"I never told Finch anything about *El Patron*."

Mike shrugged. "Then somehow he knew, for he was the one who gave me the information."

Pedro remained quiet as though considering the possibility.

Mike plunged on, not wanting to give Pedro much time to think. "Tell *El Patron* that I will deal with him and him alone."

Pedro raised his head in an attempt to defy Mike. "As I said before, I don't know who *El Patron* is."

Mike let his eyes drop for just a second before he raised them and stared boldly into Pedro's face. "You really expect me to believe that?"

Pedro cleared his throat. His gaze bounced from the floor to the wall and back down to the floor.

Mike leaned over the desk, closing the gap between them. "You tell *El Patron* for me that he has my guarantee. No police will ever bother him. He'll be free to wheel and deal wherever, whenever he wants. If anyone sniffs in his direction, I'll take care of the situation personally."

"Like you did with Finch."

"Like I did with Finch."

Mike turned and walked away. Halfway out, he stopped and spun around. "Tell *El Patron* that I'm going back to Dallas. I need to be there when my partner is buried so I can comfort his poor, grieving widow." Mike narrowed his eyes as he focused his attention on Pedro's face. "Also tell him that I'll use that time to gather some information. Then I'll be back, and I want a guarantee from him that those statuettes are mine."

FOUR

THROUGHOUT THE ENTIRE Dallas police station, the hatred for the person who had killed Detective Herbert Finch erupted into a burning rage that permeated every inch of space. One by one, the police officers gathered to find out what they could do to bring the animal in. They spoke in angry voices, their lips tight with rage.

The din, so loud and so filled with revenge, hung in the room like stale black smoke.

Just outside the briefing room, Mike stood still, listening to them. He had no choice but to step in and play the role of the bereaved detective. After all, Finch had been his partner and a good friend. Mike had to pretend he was enraged even more so than any of them.

He arranged his features in what he hoped looked like sadness intertwined with fury. He took a deep breath and lowered his head just enough to show his sorrow but high enough to let everyone know he was one of them. Together, they would drag Finch's killer through the sewers while beating him within an inch of his life.

Soon as Mike stepped in, an absolute and oppressive silence hung in the room like dark, threatening clouds.

Mike walked to the front and flopped down on the seat. He placed his elbows on the table in front of him and covered his face with his hands.

Officer Nancy Grillett sat next to him. A few awkward seconds passed before she patted his shoulder. "So sorry, Mike. I guarantee we'll get whoever did this."

Mike nodded. There was nothing like the death of a fellow officer to bring cops together and unite them in a common cause. Hang, shoot, maim the enemy. Mike knew it well.

Chief Rudy Kelley, a man in his indeterminate forties, rapped his knuckles on the podium. His sandy hair had started to thin, but to his credit, he made no attempt to hide the fact. "Everyone settle."

Some nodded. Others whispered to their partners what they would do when the monster was caught.

The Chief raised his voice. "The sooner we conclude the meeting, the sooner we can be out in the streets searching for this killer."

Instantly, the noise level dropped as if someone had turned the volume on the radio way down.

"I'll begin with a prayer for Finch, his wife, and their son. Anyone not comfortable with that can do a moment of silence." He lowered his head, and Mike could have sworn he saw tears pearl in the corner of the Chief's eyes. That puzzled him.

After a brief pause, the Chief wiped his eyes. "May he rest in peace."

A few murmured *amens* filled the room.

Chief Kelley waited until silence once again filled the room. Then in an authoritative voice, he said, "Now, let's focus on catching Finch's killer. He was killed on the outskirts of Hobbs, New Mexico, so Hobbs Police Department has jurisdiction. But all of Herbert's ties are back here in Dallas. We will keep our line of communications open with the Hobbs PD. But whatever we do, we're going to follow proper police procedure.

There will be no vigilantes, and no matter how much you're tempted to, you will not *accidentally* rough up our suspect. I repeat, we will follow proper police procedures. That is Rule Number One. Rule Number Two is that we follow Rule Number One. There are no more rules. Is that clear?"

A few officers, including Mike, grumbled an *understood*.

"Good. Let's see what we can find," the Chief said. "Officer Thomas has a list of your assignments. I want every leaf turned, and if there are none to be found, shake the trees until they fall off. Is that clear?"

The room vibrated with the loud "Yes, sir" answers.

Chief Kelley stepped aside, allowing Josie to step up to the podium. Before leaving, he looked over his shoulder and said, "Mike, in my office. Now."

Mike bolted to his feet and followed the Chief.

FIVE

MIKE'S EXPRESSION DIDN'T CHANGE, but he eyed each of the individuals sitting in the Chief's office. Detective Dave De La Rosa and his partner, Susan Epp, sat directly across from the Chief's desk. It always amused Mike to see these two together. Dave always chose to wear fancy suits while Susan's wardrobe consisted mostly of jeans and a T-shirt.

To their left, Officer Gene Buckanan waved at Mike as he entered the room. Mike acknowledged each with a nod.

"Sit." Chief Kelley pointed to the empty seat reserved for Mike. The Chief walked around his desk and sat down. "I realize this is unusual, but I've worked out a deal with the Hobbs Chief of Police. As some of you might know, Chief Reba Schemmel and I have a special working relationship that we've developed throughout the years."

Each of the room's occupants eyed each other, but all remained quiet.

"All four of you will be temporarily reassigned to Hobbs PD where you will assist with the investigation. Notice the emphasis on *assist*. None of you will follow any leads on your own. You will report to Chief Schemmel as soon as you arrive. From there, you will follow Schemmel's suggestions to the *T*. Is that clear?"

Susan's eyebrows came together in a frown. She crossed her legs and then uncrossed them.

"Spit it out, Epp." Chief Kelley focused on her. "Do you find something wrong with the assignment?"

"No, no. Of course not. It's just that I need to make arrangements for someone to take care of the kids."

"Is that going to be a problem?"

Susan shook her head. "I'll call my mom. I'm sure she'll do it. For how long do I tell her I'll need her?"

The Chief's eyes narrowed. "As long as it takes to do the job."

Silence met his curt answer.

The chief took a deep breath. "Sorry." His voice was barely audible. He cleared his throat. "Finch's death has stretched me to the limits." He leaned back and raised his head as though fighting some internal battle. "If you think this is going to cause any problems with your family, I'll find someone else. Do you want me to do that?"

Susan sat up straighter. "No, sir. I'll figure something out."

The chief nodded. "You do that."

The quiet that followed forced Mike to take the lead. "Chief, why don't you just tell us what you want to say?"

Chief Kelley stood up and rested his palms on top of his desk. "I don't like giving up control."

"Everyone in the department knows you're a control freak." Dave slapped a hand over his mouth and turned red.

Susan snickered.

The chief blinked fast, but otherwise ignored the comment. "Here's the truth. All of the details concerning this case will be kept between Chief Schemmel and the deputy chief. I want—I need—to be kept current with the investigation. I want to know exactly what is being done. As your chief and as a personal friend of Herbert, I want to make sure that this criminal—more than any other—will be brought to justice. If I leave it all to the Hobbs police, I will lose that control. The four of you will keep me up to date on the latest developments. Do any of you have a problem with that?"

"No problem here," Gene said. "I am deeply honored that you chose me to go to Hobbs. But truthfully, I'm confused. Why me? I'm just an officer."

"Because you're Mike's new partner."

Mike and Gene eyed each other through wide-open eyes. Gene broke the silence. "You're pairing me, an officer, with a seasoned detective?"

Chief Kelley opened his drawer and retrieved some papers. He made it a point of studying them. "You just recently took your detective test."

Gene cleared his throat and nodded.

"Your test scores are better than anyone else's."

Gene's face lit up.

"In fact," the chief continued, "they show that you have a lot of potential. I want to see you move up in the ranks. As of this moment, you're a detective. Any problems with that?"

"No, none at all." Gene was all smiles. "But Mike might object."

Mike patted his new partner's shoulder. "I'd be honored to work with you, but seeing how I can't keep my partners, are you sure you want to partner with me?"

"I would be honored." Mike and Gene shook hands.

The Chief turned his attention to Dave. "How fluent is your Spanish?"

Dave looked at the brown skin in his arms and curled

a smile. "You're assuming that because my last name is De La Rosa, I can speak Spanish."

"No. I'm assuming that because your file says you speak Spanish."

Dave attempted a small smile. He leaned back. "My Spanish wouldn't win me any awards, but I can understand it and get my points across."

"Good. That's one reason why I chose you."

"And the other one?"

"You're dedicated and one of my best detectives. I know you'll put all of your energy into solving this case."

"I thought you said we weren't there to solve the case," Susan said. "We're there only to assist."

The chief bit his lip and waited a few seconds before speaking. "You are correct, Detective Epp. But even though I said you're there to assist only, that doesn't mean you can't discreetly work on your own."

"How would Chief Schemmel feel about that?" Susan asked.

"Did you hear me say *discreetly*?"

All four nodded.

"Good. That settles it. Now, let's talk about theories. Who wants to begin?"

Mike sat up straighter. "I'll begin. Finch was my partner, and we told each other everything." He shrugged. "Or so I thought." He massaged the bridge of his nose. "If I'd known he planned to go there alone, I would've never let him go and least of all, not by himself."

"Can you fill us in as to why he chose to go there?" Chief Kelley asked.

Mike shook his head. "No idea."

The Chief frowned. "Do you know if he was meeting someone?"

Mike shrugged.

"Looks like we don't have much to go on," Susan said.

Mike rapped his fingers on his knee, and then mentally slapped himself. Someone might read something into that simple action. He crossed his arms and nodded. "Looks that way."

Chief Kelley leaned forward. "I'm thinking that his death is related to a case both of you were working on."

"Precisely my line of thinking. But no matter how much I wrack my brain, nothing comes to mind. I don't know what possessed him to drive to Hobbs." Mike leaned back on his chair and rubbed his eyes. "I just thought of something. Maybe someone was in the car with him, and that person led him to Hobbs and killed him."

Dave shook his head. "I have to disagree with you, Mike. All evidence points to the fact that he was alone, which means he was there for a particular reason. We find out why, we might find the monster."

"What evidence? Do we really know he was alone?" Mike stared at Dave as though he had grown an extra head. "He could have been forced to drive against his will."

"Why do you insist that there was a passenger?" Dave glared at Mike with an intensity that left Mike feeling cold. "Do you know something you're not sharing with us?"

Mike squirmed in his seat. "No, I don't. It's just that..." He looked away. "If someone was with him forcing him to drive him to Hobbs, then I could have done something about it. And I didn't. I failed him."

Susan rubbed Mike's upper arm. "There's no way

you could have known something was wrong. You can't blame yourself."

Mike lowered his head and covered his face with his hand. He waited a few seconds for the right effect. "Maybe. Maybe not. It's just that I feel so bad that I wasn't there for Herbert. I was his partner. I was supposed to protect him." His hands formed fists. "I want to find this…this…" He closed his eyes as though fighting tears.

"I understand," Chief Kelley said. "That's why I assigned you four to Hobbs. If we work together with the New Mexico police, I think we can close this case really fast." The chief stood. "That settles it. I'm sure you all want to attend Finch's memorial, which begins—" He looked at his cell and pressed a button, "in less than an hour, so I'll release you. Have a good night's rest and first thing tomorrow morning, leave."

Without a single word, all stood and headed for the door.

"Dave," the chief said.

Dave turned around. "Yes?"

"Stay here so I can give you all of the credentials to take to Chief Schemmel."

Dave nodded. The rest left.

SIX

As Adela's house drew near, Mike's nerves took a nose dive. He drew in several deep breaths just as he had seen Bronson do countless of times when situations got sticky.

Remembering how Bronson always did this when something went wrong made Mike smile. He wished, not for the first time, he could reach out to Bronson. They'd talk things out and find a solution.

But that was impossible. This time, there would be no Bronson to rely on. Mike was alone on this.

Mike pushed the thought aside and concentrated on his driving. Soon, he'd be at Adela's. He needed to focus on that.

Unable to do so, Mike's mind wandered to what it would be like to be stationed in Hobbs. He liked that idea. It would definitely serve its purpose. But what he didn't like was being stuck with three others. True, they were good people who would dedicate themselves to the cause, and that's what created the problem.

He needed to work alone, secretly. How could he accomplish his goals with three others hovering over him? No, that wouldn't work. He'd have to find a way to get rid of them.

The car behind him honked, startling him. Mike had been concentrating on the current dilemma and had failed to notice that the light had turned green. He waved an apology to the driver of the car behind him and sped off.

Ten minutes later, he still hadn't come up with a satisfactory plan. He glanced at his cell. Bronson was only a call away. He reached for the cell.

No! Don't blow it now.

He forced his hand away from the cell and maneuvered a left turn. He frowned when he noticed the unusual number of cars parked by Finch's house. The same ones he saw every day at the police station's parking lot.

Poor Adela. She didn't need to be burdened with all of these visitors, but how could she send them away when all they wanted was to show her their support?

Mike worked his way up to the door and knocked. He had no idea why he had chosen to do that rather than ring the doorbell like any normal human being. Officer Nancy Grillett let him in.

Mike spotted Adela. He found her sitting among a sea of well-wishers, all whispering gentle things to her. Things she didn't seem to hear. She sat unmoving, her face frozen in an expression of dread.

Adela looked up and noticed Mike standing by the door. She ran to him and threw her arms around him. "M-mike." Her sobs wrenched her body as if a hand had reached down and grabbed her insides and ripped them apart.

Mike's eyes searched Adela's face. His mind shouted the unasked question, *Why don't you know?* He wanted to assure her. If he could, he'd whisper the words of comfort she so much deserved to hear, but in the end, all he could think of saying was "I'm sorry. I'm so sorry." He had screwed up. He wrapped his arms tightly around her and looked around.

Huge, unblinking eyes followed his every move. Mike recognized the look on his fellow officers' faces. Pain intertwined with rage, as though these raw emotions had walked across their faces and stomped out the light in their eyes. He backed off. Now was not the time to whisper those words of comfort.

Adele took a deep, shuddery breath. "I'm… I'm having his…his body flown to Michigan…for a family only funeral." Mike looked deeply into Adela's face. The perky woman he had often admired had been replaced by a wild-looking imitation. Her long reddish-brown hair was all over the place, and her face screwed up tight. Tears streamed down her cheeks. Her body shook with each sob.

She knows! Mike tried to read her face, but all he encountered was a deep sadness.

"You understand, don't you? This…" She swept her arm indicating her surroundings. "This is his police and local funeral. This is how he would have wanted it." Her eyes were sunken and her cheeks sagged. "Please, please tell me you understand." Tears leaked from her eyes.

Mike understood all right. He drew her in his arms and hugged her tightly.

SEVEN

MIKE'S PHONE BUZZED. He stretched out his hand and fumbled for the phone. As he did, his vision landed on the motel's alarm clock. Already past nine in the morning. He hadn't gotten much sleep last night, but there was nothing he could do to remedy that. He had to get moving.

He read the text message his new partner, Gene, sent him. We're at your house. All ready to head to Hobbs. Where are you?

Mike bolted to his feet. Dang! He was almost out of time. True, he still had about four hours before they arrived, but he needed every single second to establish himself as a strong leader of the *Los Muertos* gang. One way or the other, he would have to get his hands on Cleopatra's two god figurines. Five million dollars—amazing.

Mike answered the text. After we all left Adela, I felt really bad for her. I went back to her place. Not quite the truth, but they could never prove otherwise. If they went to her house, they would find an empty shell. Adela and her son would have already left for their 5:00 AM flight to Michigan.

By telling this white lie, Mike could buy a few precious minutes that he'd spend getting ready to go. He pushed the send button.

The answer came almost immediately. You're at Adele's???

Mike waited until he finished brushing his teeth before he answered. Nah. Since I was up, I headed to Hobbs and found us a place to stay. I got us rooms at the Sleep Inn.

You're in Hobbs? What the hell, Mike?

Figured if I got us settled in, when you all get here, we could immediately get started on finding the bastard that did this.

Good idea. See you at Hobbs.

Do yourself a favor. Stop for breakfast. There's no good place to eat between here and Dallas. I'm going back to sleep while I wait for you all to arrive. Text me when you're half an hour away so I can get dressed.

Will do.

By the time he received that last text, Mike was dressed and ready to face *Los Muertos*.

EL PATRON DRUMMED his fingers on his desk. He glared at Pedro, making him feel as important as a speck of dust.

Pedro sat up straighter and tried not to grimace. One wrong move and his boss would shoot him on the spot. He knew this because he had seen him do it before. Countless times. *"Yo te digo—"*

El Patron slammed his fist on the desk. "English. We must speak perfect English so no one will bother us."

Pedro swallowed hard. He should've remembered that. *Switch his thoughts away from me. Say something.*

Anything. "His name is Mike Hoover. He killed his partner, Finch, because supposedly Finch turned against us. Mike said he could set up things so that we're never in danger. He'd let us know when it is safe to schedule delivery of the goods."

El Patron walked around his desk and sat at its edge. He leaned forward, close to Pedro's face. "This Mike. He must want something. What is it?"

"He wants the Osiris and Isis statues."

"How does he know that Cleopatra's statues are included in the merchandise that is scheduled to arrive?"

Pedro gripped the edge of his chair so hard that his knuckles turned white. He didn't know the answer. Why didn't he know that? He should have asked Mike. Now, it's too late. Is this the time and place he'd die? As impossible as it seemed, he tightened his grip on the chair. "I…don't…know."

El Patron bolted to his feet and headed for the window. He gave Pedro his back.

Pedro's nerves at the base of his neck quivered as if he had ants marching under his clothes. Was *El Patron* at this very moment reaching for his gun? Should Pedro run out of the office while he still could?

El Patron took a deep breath and returned to his desk. "Maybe you're right."

Pedro had to keep from giggling like a child at a funeral. He was going to let him live. He almost smiled but thought best not to.

El Patron rubbed his chin. "I've talked to my contacts and they're spooked. They saw the place crawling with police so now they don't want to deliver unless I can provide them with a fancy, safe plan. Maybe Mike can do that."

"So I tell Mike he's in?"

El Patron nodded.

Pedro bit his lip and hesitated before adding, "Mike wants to meet you. He wants nothing to do with me. Just you."

El Patron's jaw stiffened and his animal-like eyes bored into Pedro's. "No. Can. Do. You know the rules. Only you know who I am. If Mike doesn't like that setup, then kill him."

Pedro nodded. He'd been prepared for this.

El Patron threw his head back and laughed, a sound halfway between a bark and a snort. "You tell Mike to set things up. If he can accomplish that, he's in."

"What do I tell him about the Lapis Lazuli statues?"

"That they are his."

"Both of them?"

"Yeah." *El Patron* placed a finger to his lips and gazed up at the ceiling, as though doing mental arithmetic. "I want to hear what he has to say."

Pedro nodded, pleased with himself. He had shown his boss his worth. "I'll tell him." He started to stand up.

"Before you go…"

Pedro sat back down.

El Patron's eyes drilled into Pedro's eyes. "Are you sure Mike was the one who killed Finch?"

Pedro raised his head, trying to show his boss his confidence. "Me and my men, we saw him do it."

"Good, because that makes my plan complete."

"And that is?"

"Tell Mike that he'll get what he wants after he sets up the drop-off."

"I will, but I think you have something else planned."

"You got that right. Soon as he gets hold of those

god figurines, he'll run to his contact and get his five-million dollars, maybe even more, and that's when we make our move."

Pedro wanted to hear what that move would be but decided to remain quiet.

El Patron continued, "After we know Mike has the money, we'll take it from him, and at the same time, we'll anonymously contact the police about who killed Finch. They will arrest him. We'll have the money from the sale, and at the same time, we'll be rid of that pest all in one smooth move." A faraway look came over *El Patron*'s eyes. Gradually, they widened as if a thought in the horizon had crystallized. "I'm thinking, if we're going to turn him in, we'll need proof. That's where you come in."

Pedro braced himself.

EIGHT

PEDRO COULD NO longer deny the whisper at the base of his spine. Every day, *El Patron* grew more violent. Today, he had thought *El Patron* was going to kill him. He needed to tread carefully, especially when dealing with Mike, and speaking of the devil, there he was, entering the garage. Several large droplets of sweat formed on his forehead, and he wiped them away. He couldn't let Mike know how nervous he felt.

"Did you talk to him?" Mike spoke even before he had completely entered the garage's office.

Typical Mike. Always all business. Pedro remained sitting behind his desk. He nodded and two mechanics stepped in behind Mike.

Mike side-stepped them. "What's with the clowns?"

"Relax." Pedro offered him a wide grin. We're *amigos*. "I don't want any trouble. They're here to frisk you. There will be no guns while we conduct business. You'll get your weapon back before you leave."

"That's new," Mike said.

"Not really. That's always been the rule. It's just that the last time you were here, I wasn't sure if we'd ever do business again." He nodded at the two men standing by Mike.

They turned toward him.

Mike took a step back. "You could just ask." Mike eyed the hoods and quickly shifted his sight to Pedro.

With a flip of his hand, Pedro waved the two guards off. They stepped back, away from Mike. "If I ask nicely, would you give me your gun?"

Mike hesitated as though considering his options.

"I'm just playing fair. I don't have a weapon. You don't have a weapon. We do business. We finish, you get your gun back. No sweat." Pedro opened his hands and held them out. *See? Nothing here.*

Without taking his gaze off Pedro, Mike removed his gun from the holster. He set the weapon on the desk.

Pedro's heart skipped a beat. *The Glock.* It had worked. Simple plans always did. He looked up and dismissed the mechanics.

Without uttering a word, the two hoods left.

"Now, we talk." Pedro indicated the chair on the other side of his desk.

Mike sat.

Pedro opened the top drawer and placed Mike's gun inside. "To answer your question, yes, I did talk to *El Patron*. He's not sure he wants to work with you. He told me to tell you to set things up for the delivery of the goods. If he's satisfied with your work, then he'll talk to you. Face-to-face." Pedro shrugged. "That's the best I could do."

Mike let the seconds tick by. Then, "That works for me."

Pedro stood up. "I'll relay your message."

Mike also stood. "My gun."

Pedro curled a smile. "I had no plans to keep it." He opened the middle drawer and handed him a Glock.

Mike holstered it and walked out.

Pedro kept his eyes glued to Mike's back until he was out of sight and then let out a sigh of relief. He sank onto the upholstered office chair. He opened the top drawer and eyed Mike's Glock, wanting to reassure himself that it was still there. He took out his cell and punched in *El Patron*'s number. "I have it."

HARRY BRONSON

NINE

THE BAD THING about vacationing with a camper was the constant driving, and that was something Bronson strongly disliked. Tomorrow, he faced more tedious time behind the wheel even though his lovely wife every once in a while drove long stretches of the road. The Bronsons had enjoyed vacationing in Pennsylvania and visiting with Ellen, Mike's ex, but now it was time to head to Canada to do a lot of sightseeing, absorb their culture, and do the tourist bit.

When Bronson was still a Dallas detective, he had always let Mike drive. But now there was no Mike, and he was forced to do his own driving. Nothing he could do about it, so why complain?

Instead, he'd take advantage of the lazy afternoon and lie in bed and relax. Soon as his head hit the pillow, his eyelids drooped. He gave in to sweet slumber.

The soft pitter-patter of feet on the carpet and the dip on the edge of the bed beside Bronson's head called him from sleep. He semi-opened his eyes and saw Honey staring at him. He snapped his eyes shut.

Soon as Bronson did that, Honey began to whine. Being mostly a Basenji, a barkless breed, Honey seldom barked, but her whine was a high-pitched sound that ripped the air and pierced the eardrums. Bronson smothered a groan, refusing to open his eyes and grant Honey the satisfaction.

Carol's accompanying stomps followed as she ran into the bedroom, grabbed Honey, and pulled her back. "Hush. You're going to wake your Daddy up."

Bronson peered at the dog through half-lidded eyes.

Honey wiggled her way free from Carol's grasp and once again positioned her head so that it partially rested on Bronson's pillow. She resumed with her whining.

Carol's yanked her back.

Honey wiggled her way out, and the dog bolted away from her and back toward Bronson.

"Hush." Carol used her you-better-listen-to-me voice. "He's asleep."

"Not anymore." Bronson sat up and stared at the dog he was still trying to get used to having. "What's wrong, Honey? Do you want a treat? Do you want to go outside?"

Honey yelped, bouncing around on her paws, her curly tail wagging hard enough to resemble a spinning wheel.

Bronson raised his arms in surrender. "Okay. Okay." He swung his legs down and put his shoes on. "You win. I'll take you for a walk." He stood up. As soon as he did, the dog jumped on the bed and made herself comfortable on the same spot Bronson had vacated. She closed her eyes, and Bronson would swear he saw her smile.

"Well, I'll be." Bronson stared at Honey and then turned to Carol who was trying very hard not to laugh. "What kind of dog did we get?"

"There's no *we* to this." Carol threw out her hands, shaking her head. "You found her and brought her here."

Bronson wrapped his arms around his wife. "True, but you've got to admit, when you saw her, you thought she was one heck of a cute dog."

Carol raised her index finger and waved it. "Not

quite true. I saw her and by the look on your face, I knew you wanted her to stay. But still I said, 'No.' Remember?"

He did remember. "'No way,' you said. Yet here we are, new and proud parents to a wonderful dog." Bronson tightened his grip around Carol. "Thank you for lettin' me keep her." He kissed his wife's cheek.

"I didn't have a choice. Within hours, my heart was hers." Carol stared at Honey and remained quiet. A small smile formed on her lips.

Bronson continued, "I knew you would love her. That's why I brought her home."

Carol's smile broadened into a grin. "I've got to admit. She is a cute dog and intelligent as heck. But she's also a dog with a big attitude."

Bronson nibbled his lower lip in deep contemplation. "Do you think I should let her get away with it, or should I make her get down?"

Before Carol could answer, Bronson's phone buzzed. He looked at the caller I.D. A frown wrinkled his forehead as he turned his attention away from Honey. "It's Ellen."

"Ellen? Like Mike's ex?" Carol's voice remained neutral, but the dread behind it seemed ready to explode straight into panic.

"Do we know any other?" Bronson asked.

Carol rubbed her fingers together, a habit she had when she felt unsure. "I'm her best friend. She always calls me, never you. Not unless something went wrong. You don't think something happened to Mike, do you?"

An image of Bronson's ex-partner flashed through his mind. *Mike, his best friend. More than a friend. A brother.* Bronson's hand shook as he slid the phone icon and tapped the speakerphone on so Carol could also hear the conversation. "Ellen? Are you okay? Is Mike okay?" Bronson mentally slapped himself. He shouldn't have jumped in just like that. But he couldn't help it. He had to deny the fears that had been gnawing at him.

The small pause that followed only served to increase his heartbeat.

"Ellen? Speak to me."

"It's Mike." Her voice quivered.

Bronson held his breath. *God, please let him be okay. In his line of work, so many things could go wrong.* He knew because he too had been a police detective for the same department Mike continued to work for. "What about Mike?"

"He called me yesterday—" Ellen choked on her words and failed to finish the thought.

Bronson massaged his eyes with his fingertips. "So he's okay?"

"Yes, well, no. Maybe. I don't know." Her confusion seemed to drive a nail through Bronson's heart.

He drummed his fingers on the bed as he waited for her to continue.

"He…he…"

Bronson held the phone closer to his ear, straining to hear the smallest of sounds. When nothing happened, he said, "Tell me what's goin' on."

"I will. Just stop interrupting." Her voice spiked.

Bronson raised his arm in surrender even though he knew she couldn't see him. "Okay. I'm listenin'." Carol's hand on his shoulder eased the tension stiffening his shoulders, and he released a slow breath.

"Mike told me he found a way to make a lot of extra cash. If he was successful, he could retire in less than a year instead of two. Then we can once again be husband and wife like we were meant to be."

Bronson stared at Carol. Maybe she understood what that meant. Carol's face remained neutral. "That's bad news?"

"No, of course not. If it were strictly up to me, he'd retire now. I don't care about the money. I just want my ex-husband back, but as long as he's on the force, our marriage is doomed, like it was before."

Bronson waited for her to continue.

"He's over-focusing on the money, making sure we have enough to live comfortably for the rest of our lives." Ellen didn't vary her tone. She simply stated a fact that drove a wedge between her and Mike.

Bronson envisioned the tears that streamed down Ellen's cheeks. "He wants the best for you."

"I... I know, but this kind of thinking is making him do things he wouldn't do under normal circumstances."

When Bronson was still a Dallas city police detective, he'd encountered many people who had fallen in this trap. But not Mike. He would never do that. Bronson would be willing to swear to that. "What exactly did he tell you?"

"It's not so much what he said. It's what he didn't say that worries me."

Carol moaned, and Bronson reached for her hand. "Meanin'?"

"Meaning I sensed he's in some kind of trouble." A small pause followed and when Ellen spoke, her voice was barely audible. "When you were going on a major case, you never gave Carol any details."

Bronson raised his head to see if Carol was listening. She shrugged. Bronson continued, "That's right.

I didn't want her to worry." This was more for Carol's benefit than Ellen's.

"That's the same with Mike. He never calls when he's facing a dangerous curve. So why the call now?"

Bronson shrugged, not sure what to say. "What case is he workin'?"

"I don't know. He was tight-lipped, but somehow I got the impression that he's doing something illegal."

Bronson digested Ellen's comments. Mike was a straight arrow. Bronson, on the other hand, was the one who deviated from the rules. Mike was the one who kept him in line. Mike—doing something illegal? No, that didn't sound like him at all. "I wouldn't worry. We both know him. He follows all of the rules to the *T*. He would never think of deviatin' from that straight line of his."

"I'm afraid he has this time." Her voice was firm. Almost authoritative. "Please help him."

Bronson nodded. No ands, ifs, or buts about that. He'd be there for Mike. Bronson could see—could even rationalize—why Mike wouldn't answer Ellen's call. But why hadn't he been answering his calls? The lump in his gut returned. The one that told him something had gone wrong.

He would call Mike right now, and this time, Mike would answer the phone. They would discuss whatever it was that plagued him and then come up with a solution. Bronson was one call away from helping his buddy. "I got this, Ellen. Don't worry. I'm going to have Carol call you from her cell." Bronson's glance bounced to Carol who nodded.

Bronson disconnected and waited until Carol dialed Ellen's number before heading out of the bedroom. As he opened the front door, Honey made a mad dash to go outside with Bronson.

He looked down at her. "Yeah, now you're out of the bed." He smirked. "Come on." He opened the door wider to allow her to go out. He walked several feet away from the camper before retrieving his cell.

Honey followed next to him.

Bronson headed for the Dog Relief area. While he waited, he dialed Mike's number.

The cell buzzed once.

Two times.

No answer.

Three times.

Pick up, Mike. It's me.

Four times.

Pick up.

The phone continued to ring. Bronson stared at it as if the cell had grown teeth and was ready to devour him. *Pick up, Mike. Pick up.*

Even as he urged him to do so, deep down Bronson knew the situation was hopeless. Mike didn't respond yesterday or the day before. Nor the one before that. Why should he respond now? Why? *Are you hurt? What's going on? Talk to me, Mike. Tell me what's goin' on.*

"Speak," Mike's familiar voice said. "When I can, I'll get back to you,"

Bronson waited for the beep. "Call me." He disconnected and stared at nothing. *What's going on? Ellen is right. My gut is right. Something is wrong. Something is terribly wrong.* Bronson felt it in his bones.

TEN

AFTER BRONSON AND Honey wandered around the campground, hoping against hope that Mike would return his call, Bronson gave up and headed to the camper. Carol sat on the couch, deep in conversation with Ellen. Not wanting to disturb her, Bronson went to the bedroom and set the cell down on the bed. He clasped his hands together and tapped them against his chin. He called Mike again. The call went straight to voice mail. Bronson had now left him three messages.

Three unanswered messages.

Why wasn't Mike returning his calls? That wasn't something he would do. He might ignore Ellen's urgent calls begging him to tell her what was going on.

That, Bronson understood. Sometimes, not knowing was heaven sent.

Even under the most strenuous circumstances, Mike would never ignore his calls. Together, they would tear apart the problem and solve it piece by piece. Why was this different?

Honey entered the room and laid her head on Bronson's lap.

"You know, don't you, girl?" He rubbed the area behind her ear. She let out a small whine as she locked her gaze on Bronson's. "I agree with you. Somethin' is wrong. I don't want to scare Ellen, but I need to go to

Mike." He stood up and bent down to retrieve the suitcase from under the bed.

"Going somewhere?"

Carol entered the room so quietly that Bronson hadn't heard her. He shot up to his feet. "I... Honey..."

Carol's gaze bounced from the partially retrieved suitcase to the phone on the bed and back down to the suitcase. She stepped forward and rubbed her husband's arm. "Did Honey roll her ball under the bed again?"

"Uh, yeah." Bronson answered too fast, too soon.

Carol nodded. "I came to tell you that I'm thinking of inviting Ellen for dinner. She hasn't met Honey yet, and that's the reason we're extending the invitation."

"But the real reason is?"

"I'm concerned about her."

Bronson could see that in his wife's eyes.

Carol continued, "She's so worried about Mike. I think the distraction would be good for her."

"Excellent idea."

Carol turned to leave but stopped without turning around. "I'm also thinking you should go to Mike."

Hot diggity dog. He wouldn't have to talk her into letting him go. He turned on his casual tone. "You do?"

She faced him and wrapped her hands around his. "We were going to head up to Canada tomorrow."

He nodded. "I remember."

"As far as I'm concerned, Canada can wait. I think we should turn this camper around and head back home to Dallas."

He planned to go to Dallas, but not with Carol tagging along. "Oh."

"I'm also thinking," Carol continued, "that Ellen will want to come with us."

Oh, good grief. Two tag-alongs. "That might create a problem."

"I know. That's why I'm thinking that Ellen and I should drive the motor home, and you fly to Dallas. By the time we get there, Mike will be safe and sound at home anxiously awaiting our arrival."

That had been Bronson's plan all along, but he had been hesitant to approach Carol. The last thing he wanted to do was worry her. He leaned over and kissed her. "As you wish."

Carol smiled even though both knew it was his wish. She kissed his lips. "Naturally, we'll keep Honey with us. Can you survive without her?"

Bronson bent down to pat her. "It'll be hard, but I can definitely try." He straightened out and wrapped his arms around Carol. "I love you."

"More than the dog?"

"Don't stretch it."

She hit his upper arm playfully, stuck her tongue out, and walked out.

As soon as Carol was out of the room, Bronson opened the closet and pushed the clothes to the side, revealing a special fire-proof safe he had installed when they first bought the camper. He entered the right combination, opened the safe, and stared at his favorite Glock. Too bad he couldn't take it with him. The airlines would not allow that. No big deal, he'd use the one he kept at his house.

Next to the Glock was a small box. From the box, he took out a driver's license with his picture but with the name of Alex Bentley. The passport was also made out to Alex Bentley.

Bronson half-smiled. When he and Mike had finished working that undercover case, Mike had turned in his fake identities. So had Bronson, but Bronson found a way to get them back. When Mike found out what Bronson had done, Mike had scolded him. Bronson had shrugged and told him that it might come in handy one of these days. Looked like now was one of those days.

ELEVEN

THE FLIGHT HOME had been an almost all-day affair, and Bronson wished he could speed up time. He knew he couldn't, so instead, he'd spend the time formulating a plan. Somehow he had to get home. Uber would solve that problem. He checked with the stewardess to make sure it would be okay to use the cell. She assured him it was, and he made the call.

Once home, he'd take the Mazda and head to the Dallas Police Department. If anybody could lead him to Mike, it would be someone in the department. Who knows? With luck, he'd even spot Mike there.

The airplane tires hit the runway, and Bronson's eagerness to get started overwhelmed him. The plane came to a halt, and people started to disembark. *Mike, I'm coming, buddy. Be safe.* Bronson retrieved his carry-on from the plane's overhead storage compartment.

Here we go.

THE DALLAS POLICE precinct looked exactly as Bronson remembered. The same pictures hung on the wall and papers covered every inch of the desks' surfaces. The same smell of leftover pizza permeated the air, and as before, an air freshener had been used in an attempt to hide the other more offensive odors.

"Bronson?"

Bronson froze. He recognized that voice. He turned

to face Chief Kelley, his once upon a time adversary. Kelley was a by-the-books kind of guy. He could not tolerate Bronson's more liberal ethics, and they had often clashed. Bronson looked him straight in the eye. "Mike tells me you're the new Chief of Police."

Kelley straightened up, like a proud peacock. "What can I say? I made it, and you didn't."

What an idiot. "That's okay with me." Bronson raised his hand as though dismissing its importance. "I never wanted it."

"That's the difference between you and me. I have always cared about doing the job correctly." He spoke a bit louder than usual and scanned the area to make sure everyone heard him.

Meaning I didn't? Some things never change. Bronson offered him his hand. "I believe congratulations are due."

The chief looked down at the extended hand and up to Bronson's face. A few seconds elapsed before he accepted Bronson's hand. "Let's go talk in my office."

As they walked past rows of desks, heads went up. Some people Bronson recognized while others were fresh. Bronson nodded a hello at a few of those he had worked with. Mike was nowhere in sight. He increased his pace and caught up with the chief.

Chief Kelley closed the door to his office after Bronson stepped in. "Sit." He pointed to a chair.

Bronson sat down and squirmed. He was at the principal's office instead of a former's co-worker's working space.

"Why are you here?" The chief's tone was as cool as a snake's skin.

"I came to see Mike."

The chief yanked his glasses off and chewed on the eyepiece. "Hoover?"

Bronson grinned. "The one and only."

The chief set the glasses down and swept his hand in a dismissive gesture. "As you can see, you missed him."

Bronson bit his tongue to keep from saying the obvious. "Do you know where I can find him?"

A small smile formed at the edges of the chief's lips. "He and Detectives de la Rosa, Buchanan, and Epp left yesterday for Hobbs."

New Mexico? What was he doing there? Bronson sat up straighter. "I didn't realize he had already left. How's he doing?"

The chief shrugged. "How do you think? His partner is dead, and I'm sure Mike's blaming himself."

Finch dead? How? When? "That's why I'm worried about Mike. I wanted to talk to him."

Chief Kelley leaned back on his chair and stared at Bronson through calculating deep-green eyes. "Are you saying that you haven't talked to Mike? I thought you two were tight."

"We are. That's why I'm here." Bronson frowned. "He says he's fine. I need to see that with my own eyes."

"He looks fine, he acts fine, but underneath? You know how that goes. When your partner is brutally murdered, you do everything possible to turn each rock and dig under it, no matter what danger you bring to yourself."

The news hit Bronson like a shot below his heart. *Finch murdered?* Bronson formed fists but kept them hidden from the chief's view. He put on his poker face and when he spoke, he made sure his voice was devoid of emotion. "I'd like to pay Adela my respects."

"You're too late. She and her son left early yesterday morning. They want to bury Herbert in his beloved state of Michigan."

That made sense. Finch had always raved about what a great state Michigan was. "Is the funeral over?"

"Nope." The chief leaned back on his chair and looked up at the ceiling. "The body is still at the morgue."

"Here in Dallas?"

Chief Kelley flashed him a look that clearly said *How stupid can you get?* "Tell me, Bronson, where else would a body be?"

"If you don't mind, I'd like to see it."

Chief Kelley shot up to his feet, slamming his palm on his desk. "I do mind. You're a nobody. You left the force, and you're not even a reporter. Why would I want to do that?"

Bronson bit his lip as he relaxed his hands and then formed fists once again. "You're perfectly right." He bolted to his feet. "I'll get out of your hair." *Not that there was much of it.*

"You do that."

TWELVE

BRONSON CLOSED THE door behind him and paused long enough to scan the room. Several familiar faces ignored him or stared at him with either curiosity or animosity. One by one, Bronson dismissed them. He needed to talk to someone about Mike, someone who would tell him the truth and keep his mouth shut about the conversation. But who? Maybe—

Well, I'll be. Bronson's face broke into a wide grin when he spotted Paul McKenzie heading toward him. While Bronson was still working for the department, Paul had been a new intern at the lab. Bronson and Mike had taken him under their wings and Paul blossomed. Bronson heard that he was now head of the Forensics Department. Bronson moved toward Paul.

Paul had gained a few pounds since Bronson had last seen him. He no longer had the young-and-eager look Bronson was familiar with. Instead, the more mature adult look gave him an intensity that surprised Bronson.

Paul flashed his old friend a pinched smile. The deep crease lines in his forehead and around the eyes told Bronson something had gone wrong. Did this have to do with Mike? Both he and Paul worshiped the man.

As Bronson increased his pace, his mind spun out of control, like a runaway engine that refused to turn itself off or slow down.

Bronson and Paul stood face-to-face. *Mike?*

Bronson must have uttered the word aloud, as Paul nodded.

"You still love coffee?" Paul spoke loud enough for those around him to hear.

"Can't live without it."

"I know the perfect coffee shop."

"Sounds good to me."

"Good, because even though you've never met them, I've got to tell you about my wife and kids."

"And I'll tell you about Honey." Bronson followed him out.

Bronson ordered a cup of Jamaican Me Crazy. When it arrived, he could smell its rich, fragrant aroma. He could survive by just smelling the fumes. Or maybe not. He needed to taste it. He poured three heaping spoonfuls of sugar and enough milk to drown a cow. He set his cup down next to the manila envelope Paul had brought with him. Bronson sat across from him and noticed that Paul looked as though he was on the verge of throwing up. His sickly green complexion and the constant wetting of his lips told Bronson he wasn't going to like what he was about to hear. "Family okay?"

Paul nodded. "Or maybe not." He sipped his coffee. "Do we consider Mike family?"

"Of course." And that thought caused Bronson to push his coffee away, its enticing aroma no longer appealing to him. He waited for Paul to speak, but he continued to outline the rim of his coffee cup with his index finger.

Paul raised his head and looked at Bronson. "How much do you know?"

"Not much. I just learned Herbert was murdered. Mike and three others are in Hobbs followin' the trail."

Paul drummed the table with his spoon. "It's worse than that and more complicated."

"Tell me about it." Bronson found it hard to swallow, much less speak.

"I was on my way to see the chief when I bumped into you. I got four colored 8 X 12 shots of the crime scene." He opened the envelope, took out the pictures, and slid them over to Bronson.

Bronson took his time studying each picture. The first one had been taken from a distance. The corpse lay on the ground face down in front of what Bronson assumed had been his car. The passenger door remained open and the headlights were still on, clouding the death scene in an eerie aura.

The second picture was a similar shot but taken up close. It showed the victim still face down on the ground, probably the way he had been found. For the third picture, someone, more than likely the medic, had rolled Finch over so that now he faced up. The desert had started to take its toll on the body, drying it out and turning it leathery.

The final picture was a close-up of the chest wound that ended his life. Bronson squinted as he went from picture to picture. "Looks like the perpetrator stood twenty to thirty feet away. I suspect that they knew each other. Why else would Finch step away from the safety of the open door?"

Paul cast him a smile that didn't reach his eyes. "That's the problem I'm facing."

Bronson reached for his coffee and downed a sip.

The smooth, warm liquid did nothing to ease his nerves. "Meanin'?"

The newly acquired creases around Paul's mouth deepened. "I feel it was someone Herbert trusted." He looked down and remained quiet.

"Continue."

Paul retrieved the last of the papers from the envelope. He held on to them as though afraid to show them to Bronson.

"Are those the autopsy reports?" Bronson flicked his attention between the envelope and Paul who nodded but still didn't hand him the report. "What'd they say?"

"Before I answer that, let me start at the beginning." Paul rubbed his forehead and took a deep breath. "A couple of days ago, I received a package addressed to my home address. Inside was the gun with a simple note that read *Is this the gun that killed Finch?* I immediately contacted Mark—"

"Who?"

"Mark. Mark Forest, a good friend of mine. He works for an agency that has its own ballistic expert. I handed him the gun and he fired it into a bottle of water. While I waited, he compared both bullets' striation pattern with the gun I had received. It was a perfect match. I now have the gun that killed Finch."

Bronson leaned forward but remained quiet.

Paul cleared his throat. "I tried tracing the note, trying to find its source so that it'd lead me to the person who sent it. But I met with nothing but a dead end. I haven't been able to find the source and it looks like I never will."

"Tell me about the bullet." Blood as thick as cement pounded inside Bronson's head.

"The bullet...that killed Herbert came from a Glock."

It took Bronson less than a second to make the connection, a connection he wanted to deny. "A common police gun, but not exclusively a police gun." Bronson's lame statement sounded defensive even to his own ears.

"True," Paul said, "except that this bullet came from a gun registered to one of our own."

Bronson felt his chest tighten. "Whose gun is it?"

Paul's skin paled further. "Mike Hoover's."

Bronson closed his eyes and rubbed his lids.

THIRTEEN

Long after Paul had left, Bronson remained sitting in the café, his coffee pushed aside and forgotten. Bronson retrieved his notebook and stared at the blank page as his right hand jiggled the press button of the ballpoint pen over and over again. He took a deep breath and began writing.

Fact: Herbert had apparently been killed by someone he knew and trusted.

Bronson re-read what he had written. Okay, so it wasn't a real fact. More like a theory, but a strong theory. He picked up the pen and continued writing.

Fact: The weapon in question was a Glock.

No denying this.

Fact: The Glock in question was registered to Mike.

As unbelievable as it seemed, Bronson couldn't deny this fact.

Fact: Mike had talked to Ellen about leaving the force early as he planned to come across some unexpected money.

Bronson paused once again. In a court of law, the judge would say it was hearsay. But Bronson knew Ellen, and if she said Mike said that then he did.

Fact: Mike had vanished from the face of Earth, or at least he wasn't returning his or Ellen's calls.

Was he returning anyone's call, other than the chief's? Bronson searched his mind. Who else would he call?

Fact/Theory: Criminals tend to run. Was Mike on the run?

Bronson flipped the page of his notebook to a blank page. He wrote: *Theory: Mike killed Herbert.* Soon as he finished writing this, he dropped the pen as if the words had burned him.

Bronson re-read the three words that tormented him.

Mike...killed...Herbert.

Mike...killed.

Bronson massaged his forehead, fighting the burning pain of a migraine. What was he thinking? Mike was not a killer.

Two words were missing between each of those terrifying words.

Friendship and *trust*.

During good weather, friendship floated smoothly. It was easy to accept and give. As soon as the weather turned, that friendship no longer sailed a smooth path.

Instead, it encountered bumps and holes that could never be filled. What kind of friend was Bronson?

He refused to believe what he had heard. Mike, a killer. No, not Mike. There had to be another reason for his actions. When Bronson had first heard the news, an overwhelming jolt of adrenaline and terror gripped him. Had Mike been attacked and that someone had used his gun to kill Finch? Had the police searched the desert for a second body?

Immediately Paul had calmed Bronson's nerves. The desert had been thoroughly searched. No second body had been found. "Put your fears aside," Paul had said. "Mike is alive."

Bronson searched Paul's face for the smallest indication he was lying. He found none. "How do you know that?"

"The chief told me he had talked to Mike late last night."

Bronson had breathed easier but now the doubts crept in. He wrote down: *Mike, what's going on?*

Mike had always been the straight-arrow detective. The one who would never deviate from the rules. What had driven him to cross that line? What had made him run away? *Mike, what did you do?*

Bronson faltered. Deep down he knew Mike was innocent. He believed in Mike despite the specks of doubt lurking around. If he remained a doubtful friend, then he might as well be called Enemy.

And those two words—*enemy* and *Mike*—could never be used together.

But it was Mike's gun that killed Herbert.

If Bronson could only share one ounce of sympathy for whatever reason drove Mike to do this, Bronson wouldn't feel so alone. So empty. If he could scream without anyone hearing him, he would. He took deep breaths, grasping for control. For a fraction of a second, he hated Mike. How could he turn to darkness so easily? How?

Outside, the clouds drifted allowing the sun's rays to filter in through the window, illuminating the small café and filling it with warmth. The bright sun slapped Bronson in the face, forcing him to see circumstances in a different light. Shame smothered him. He buried his face in his hands.

Mike was his ex-partner, his best friend. His brother. If the shoe were on the other foot, would Mike desert him?

Someone could have stolen Mike's gun then used it to kill Herbert. At this point, Mike wouldn't have been aware that his gun was missing. But now, after so much time had passed, surely Mike would have missed it. If so, why hasn't he reported the weapon as lost or stolen?

One thing for sure, Mike would never be stupid enough to use his gun to kill anyone. He would know that the police would trace the bullet back to his gun.

Another horrifying thought plagued Bronson. Why was Mike hiding?

It didn't make sense. In fact, nothing made sense, but at this point, that's the only premise Bronson had. The gun had been stolen, and Mike was on the run because he was in danger. But that theory quickly evaporated like a puff of smoke. Paul had told him that Mike had talked to Chief Kelley only last night.

That meant that Mike wasn't hiding. He was simply avoiding Bronson.

Bronson swore he'd help Mike any way he could, even if that involved a trip to Hobbs.

He would go there because he had to believe in Mike.

He had to, for friendship's sake—for what is life without the love and support of a true friend?

THE SEARCH

FOURTEEN

MIKE SAW HIS hand reaching for the gun. Raising it. Shooting.

That same hand now reached deep inside, grabbed hold of his insides, and ripped them out.

Mike sat bolt upright in bed as coldness and darkness embraced him. He felt his doubts translate into tensed muscles and a pounding heart.

He jerked the bed covers aside. He had failed to close the night curtains and the moon's light landed on the dresser's mirror located next to the bed. He could hardly recognize the image that stared back at him. His ashen face, the deep anguish in his eyes, the fog of sheer, hopeless misery—all of that would betray him. *Focus, Mike, you've got to focus.* He had to get a grasp on reality. He had a mission to accomplish. Nothing else mattered.

One way or the other, he had to get hold of Cleopatra's statues. But he'd never do it if he didn't gain control of himself. He took a deep breath and headed for a cold shower.

Two figurines. Five million dollars.
Amazing.
Totally amazing.

THE FOUR DETECTIVES assigned to work the Hobbs angle waited outside Chief Schemmel's office for what seemed to be an eternity. The chief was nowhere in sight.

Mike scooted over to the edge of his seat. He looked at his watch. Another minute dragged by.

Gene had busied himself dusting imaginary lint off his pants.

Susan turned the page of a magazine she wasn't reading. She wasn't even looking at the pictures. She simply turned the pages.

Dave sat staring at the floor.

"Any idea how much longer?" Mike asked the deputy sitting at his desk, entering information on the computer.

The deputy's face turned red. "No, sorry. Like I told you before, right before you all came in, Chief Schemmel was called on some kind of an oil emergency. She asked me to tell you that she hasn't forgotten about meeting with you, but that this matter required immediate attention. It shouldn't be that much longer now." The deputy returned to his computer.

"I'd say we get out of here." Gene spoke loud enough for only the three Dallas detectives to hear.

Susan shook her head. "I'd love to, but we promised Chief Kelley that we'd report here first."

"You're right." Mike crossed his arms and slumped down on the chair a bit more. "But I hate wasting time like this."

At that moment, a little past one in the afternoon, Chief Reba Schemmel strolled in. She grabbed two chairs and dragged them into her office. As she did, she signaled for the group to follow her. She placed the two chairs in front of her desk and set her hat down on a bookshelf. "Sorry about that. The oil—the major…" She waved her hand in a dismissive motion. "That's not important." She flopped down on her chair and took a deep swig from her water bottle. "So tell me, what can I do for you?"

Mike sat up straighter. "I think it's the other way around. It's what can we do for you. Chief Kelley said that we should make ourselves available. And by the way, he sends his regards."

Chief Schemmel wiped the sweat off her forehead. "Chief Kelley. Yes, of course. I talked to him earlier this morning. He said he's sending his team because of the murder out in the desert—somebody's partner, right?"

Mike raised his hand as though he were still in school. "Mine."

"I'm sorry." The chief's tone sounded detached, as though she were dictating a letter. She took a deep breath. "I'm really sorry. My mind is still with this oil mess. The major is putting the pressure on me." She frowned. "Your partner's death—that's important too—very important, but I'm afraid we haven't been able to do much digging."

"Hence the reason we're here." Dave's harsh tone made the chief's eyes open wider.

"Yes, of course." She waited for a moment before speaking. "Can you divide yourselves into two groups? Maybe you can dig around. See what you can learn."

"Any particular place we should begin?"

"As a matter of fact, yes. I think we have a smuggling ring operating out of here, and I've heard from the vine that somehow Finch was in the center of it all. With that bit of knowledge, I want you to hit a couple of bars. Sniff around. See if you can pick up anything. Tomorrow, say at nine, we can regroup and work something out. I'll assign some of my men to you. Not many, of course. We have this oil thing. But that doesn't mean I want some drug lords hanging around and ruining our great little city. Report back to me tomorrow and we'll take it from there." She leaned back and crossed her arms. "How does that sound?"

Mike was the first to stand up, followed by his new partner, Gene. "Tomorrow at nine it is." They walked out and Dave and Susan followed.

Dave waited until they reached their cars. "That was nothing but bull. She doesn't care if we find Finch's murderer. All she wants is her precious oil interest protected."

Mike took in a deep breath. "As much as I hate to say it, I agree with you. But us four, we want to destroy that S.O.B. who did this. We'll find him and bring him in. That's why Chief Kelley sent us here."

"That means that we need to come up with some kind of strategy. Where can we go to make plans?" Gene asked.

"I don't know about you guys, but I'm starved." Susan tapped her stomach. "I didn't have much of a breakfast."

Mike snapped his fingers. "Right across the street from our motel, there's a restaurant that the motel clerk recommended. Dave, I was told they serve the perfect steak, and I know how you always love them. Why don't we go there and brainstorm?"

"I'm already salivating," Dave said.

FIFTEEN

Halfway through their meals, Mike closed his eyes and cradled his head in his hands.

Susan's eyebrows furrowed. "Mike?"

Dave glanced away from his steak and up toward Mike. "Are you okay?"

"You don't look too good." Gene set his fork down as though ready to catch Mike in case he fell.

Mike ignored his detective team. Instead, his fingers massaged his forehead.

Susan placed her hand on his shoulder. "What's wrong? Is there anything we can do?"

Mike released his head, and Susan removed her hand from Mike's shoulder.

The seconds stretched as they stared at him, and he at the group. He squinted, and then blinked several times. He opened his mouth to speak, but nothing came out.

"What's wrong?" Gene handed Mike a glass of water. "Would this help?"

Mike cleared his throat and accepted the water. He took a small swig. "Thanks, Gene. It's only the first day we work together, and you're already taking care of your new partner."

Gene's lips quivered as he attempted to smile. "What happened? You gave us a scare."

Mike focused on Gene, then Susan, and finally on Dave. He then looked at the other people in the restaurant. No one seemed to notice him. They continued eating, chatting, or otherwise occupying themselves. "Sorry." He winced and his right hand fumbled toward his forehead. "I suffer from migraines. I have medication back in the motel." He pushed his chair away from the table. "Bad thing about the meds is that they knock me out. Sometimes, I sleep for two, three straight days. In the meantime, I'm not worth much."

"I'll go with you." Gene also moved his chair away from the dining table.

"I appreciate that, but the motel is right across the street. Hopefully, by tonight, I'll be able to somewhat function." Mike took a deep breath. "You can fill me in on today's events. I'm sorry I can't do my share."

"It's probably stress." Susan squeezed Mike's upper arm. "You've been through a lot."

"Our job is always full of stress. I should be used to it." Mike looked down, refusing to meet their eyes.

"Don't worry about us," Dave said. "Finch was your partner. You need time to mourn on your own."

Mike nodded. "Thanks." He unfolded his large frame from the restaurant's chair. "After we finished here, we were supposed to get a feeling for the town. Poke around. See if we could pick up any hints."

Susan nodded. "That's what the Hobbs chief suggested."

"Mind if I don't tag along?" Mike closed his eyes and massaged the bridge of his nose.

"We understand." Dave took a bite of his biscuit. "Go."

Mike nodded. He wobbled and reached for the table to steady himself. "I'll put the Do Not Disturb sign up. Hopefully tomorrow or the next day, I'll join you. In the meantime, if you get any leads, text. It doesn't matter what time."

Dave shrugged. "I'm sure nothing will come up. Yesterday, when I got here early, I snooped around. I didn't get a single whiff. We are on a fool's errand. I'm not even sure why Chief Kelly really sent us here."

Mike reached for his napkin and wiped his mouth. "You came here early, by yourself?"

Dave nodded. "Yeah, just like you."

Mike smiled and realized how lucky he had been not to have run into him. From here on, he'd be more cautious. "I guess you could say we're both eager-beavers." He stood up and ambled toward the motel, just in case the Dallas detectives were watching him. Once he entered the motel and knew they couldn't see him, he sped up.

His first stop was his room where he hung the Do Not Disturb sign on the doorknob. Once inside, he grabbed the rental car keys for the Chevy he had parked on the other side of the motel, away from any inquisitive eyes staring out of the restaurants' windows.

He dashed out. He had bought himself maybe two days of freedom away from his eager new partner and the other two Dallas detectives.

He was free to move, but time was limited, and he still had a lot to do.

SIXTEEN

EARLY TWENTIETH-CENTURY HOBBS consisted of nothing more than a store, a small school, and a cluster of scattered shacks. All of that was destined to change, for in 1928 a giant oilfield discovery brought blooming business to the area. Hobbs was ideally located at the center of the Permian Basin, and the 1930s transformed the town into the fastest growing city in the United States. Today, New Mexico stands as the third leading oil and natural gas-producing state.

The residents of this fast growing community, aware of what the oil industry did for them, decided to band together to protect their oil interest. Almost a century later, they remain protective of their oil interest even if it means turning an eye away from other important matters.

Mike sat on his truck and digested this bit of information. He knew it would come in handy someday. He folded his arms as an idea began to unfold in his mind. As he worked through the intricate details, he smiled. He opened the vehicle's door and slid out. He headed for a real estate company.

That had been a bit over a month ago, and ever since then, he had focused on the smallest of details to ensure his plan would work, and now, all that hard work had panned out. He was ready to test his plan.

Mike leaned against the abandoned, non-working

Jack Stand and yawned. He had leased the land around him so he felt confident that no one uninvited would come along. He glanced at his watch. The digital read 2:33. He wiped his brow. Even at night, the desert was warm. Or maybe the warmth came from within him.

Twenty-six more minutes until showtime, and he was set to go.

The first to arrive was a white pick-up with Pedro at the steering wheel and someone else in the passenger seat. Two more occupied the back seat. A brown sedan, carrying four men, followed closely. When Pedro stepped out, the other men did too. They hung close to the car while Pedro approached Mike. "Do you know what you are? You're a crazy *gringo*. There's a reason we don't do night drops. In case you haven't noticed, it's too dark."

Mike took a step toward Pedro. "And good morning to you too."

Pedro barked out some words in Spanish Mike didn't recognize, but from his tone of voice, Mike knew exactly what Pedro said. Not that it mattered. Mike smiled and leaned casually against the Jack Stand.

Pedro's hand swept the area. "Why did you choose this location for the drop-off? The place is nothing but one oil well after another. How's the pilot supposed to know which oil well is the right one?" He pointed to the sky. "And even if they somehow know which one it is, we won't be able to see where all the goods are dropped. And to make matters worse, you even chose a moonless night. It's too dark."

At that moment, Mike's watch beeped. He looked down at it: 2:50. "Now it starts."

Pedro squinted, staring at Mike through small slits in his face. "What starts?"

Mike placed his hand on the Jack Stand nearest to him. "This oil pump is rigged. Its top has a solar-powered infrared light system that's visible only to the pilot if he's wearing night goggles." He picked up the rumbling of a Piper Cub. Mike looked up and soon spotted the plane. "Watch what happens."

As the plane neared, a small landing strip near them lit up. "Best if we steer away from the strip. The Piper is going to land."

"You think the plane is going to land?" Pedro hit his head with the palm of his hand. "*Stupido*. The plane makes a fly-by and drops off the goods."

Mike shrugged. "Looks like the rules have changed."

"I don't like changes." Pedro crossed his arms. "My men don't like changes either. If it's not broken, it doesn't need to be fixed."

Mike took a step forward, invading Pedro's private space. "Do you or don't you want your merchandise?"

Pedro remained quiet, but his jaw jutted forward in an angle of contempt.

"Just as I thought." Mike backed off.

The Piper Cub landed and the pilot turned off the engine and stepped out. He removed the special goggles. In a loud clear voice, he said, "In five minutes I'm taking off. If you haven't finished transferring your goods from my plane to your vehicle, that's not my problem." He stepped aside.

Pedro signaled for the men to start unloading and both he and Mike kept a close eye on them.

Mike's attention shifted to the pilot as he approached them.

"Which of you is Mike Hoover?" the pilot asked.

Neither answered.

The pilot looked directly at Mike. "You look like a *gringo*. You've got to be Mike Hoover."

"And what if I am?"

"My boss was very impressed with this set up. He has a shipment he needs to move and you're the man for it. You need to come with me."

Pedro stepped forward. "Your boss works with me. Not him." He pointed to Mike. "I'm the one he wants."

With the speed of a jaguar, a gun appeared in the pilot's hand. He cocked it and pressed its barrel against Pedro's chest. He inched forward so that the men unloading the plane had no idea what was going on. "I don't think so. He specifically asked for Mike, and I never disappoint my boss." Without moving his eyes away from Pedro, he asked Mike, "Are you coming, or do I need to kill him?"

Mike took a deep breath. "That all depends on Pedro."

"How so?" the pilot asked.

"I was promised Cleopatra's two god figurines. If I can take them with me, I'll go with you. If I can't take them, then I'll have to join you at a later time. If you need to kill him, do so. It makes no difference to me. I'll get the statues either way."

Pedro glared at Mike with a fierceness that could ignite a fire.

Mike looked at his watch. "Time is ticking. If I were you, I'd be telling those men to find the statues and give them to me."

Pedro's lips quivered but he refused to bark any orders.

"Now!" Mike pointed with his index finger to emphasize his demand.

Pedro glanced at the gun shoved against his chest. He turned his head and yelled out, "Jose, Raul. Come!"

The two men set down the boxes they carried out of the airplane and headed toward Pedro. As soon as they saw the gun pointed at their boss, they froze.

"Tell them what you want them to do," Mike said and slightly nodded at the pilot. He shoved the barrel of the gun deeper into Pedro's chest.

Pedro gasped. "The two Lapis Lazuli statues. Cleopatra's gods. You know which ones I mean?"

Both Jose and Raul nodded.

"Bring them to me." Pedro spoke through tight lips.

"Sí, señor." They waited for further instructions.

"Are you deaf? Get them now!"

They bolted toward the boxes that had already been placed on the truck's bed. They ripped them open and began their search.

Less than three minutes later, Jose ran back to Pedro, carrying the box that contained the two exposed eight-inch figurines. "Are these them?"

Mike looked at the treasure, and his heart skipped a beat. "That's them." *I'm looking at five million dollars.*

The pilot lowered the gun but kept it visible.

The atmosphere charged with tension as Pedro glared at Mike. "Give them to him." He pointed at Mike and anger burned in his eyes.

Jose did as told.

Mike rewrapped them in their original boxes. "I'm out of here."

The pilot moved the gun from Pedro to Mike. "Of course you're out of here. You're coming with me, remember?"

"I was hoping you'd forgotten."

SEVENTEEN

DARKNESS STILL ENVELOPED the room when Dave's phone buzzed. Dave stretched his arm and fumbled for the cell. He had thought that by coming to Hobbs and away from Dallas' constant craziness, he could at least sleep in late. "Detective Dave de la Rosa." His eyes remained half-closed.

"Dave? This is Chief Rudy Kelley."

Dave's eyes snapped open. The chief had identified himself by using his full name. That meant this was an official call. What had gone wrong?

The motel's alarm clock read 4:40. Since the chief was calling him at such an ungodly hour that meant trouble. Suddenly wide awake, Dave sat ramrod straight in bed. "Chief, what's going on?"

THE FIRST PERSON Dave contacted was his partner, Susan. "Get dressed and grab your gun. Meet me in my room. ASAP." He disconnected, dialed Gene's number, and gave him the same instructions.

Within five minutes, they arrived.

"What's going on?" Gene's hair stood up at the side of his head.

"Chief Kelley called."

Susan and Gene exchanged looks.

"Bad news?" Gene ran his fingers through his hair in an attempt to plaster it down.

Dave cleared his throat. "They think they know who killed Finch."

Susan and Gene remained still.

Dave continued, "Of course, they're not certain yet, but evidence strongly points to...Mike."

Gene's face remained impassive, but his eyebrows knit slightly in puzzlement. "That's...not possible."

Susan stared at both of them, swayed on her feet, and grabbed hold of the chair's back. She looked down and shook her head. "Mike? I've known him for years. That can't be." She released her grasp on the chair. "Tell us exactly what the chief said. Why does he think Mike is guilty?"

"The bullet that killed Finch came from Mike's gun."

"Something doesn't add up. Why would Mike want to kill Finch? Maybe he's been framed." Gene's eyes searched the room as though the answer lay hidden within the walls. "I know I've only worked with him for a couple of days, but he's got this reputation. He's a good man."

"Maybe so, but whether or not we like it, we need to do our job. Chief Kelley said to arrest him and take him back to Dallas. Those are direct orders." Even though Dave's face was flushed with confusion, his eyes remained as hard as crystal. "I thought maybe both of you would like to come with me when I arrest him."

"Yeah, sure." Gene ruffled his hair, but this time not because of the way it looked.

"One more thing." Dave reached for the doorknob. "The chief wants me to stay for a while and explain things to Chief Schemmel. Maybe say, 'Thank you' for hosting us. I'm not sure what Chief Kelley wants me to do here. Either way, both of you are to take Mike back. Can I count on you to do that?"

Both Gene and Susan nodded and looked away.

"I know," Dave said. "It stinks."

Without uttering a word, they headed toward Mike's room. Dave took a deep breath and knocked. All three planted themselves beside the door, waiting for Mike to open.

Mike didn't come to the door.

Dave knocked a bit louder. "Mike, open up. It's us. We want to know how you're feeling." Dave stared at the Do Not Disturb sign hanging from the doorknob. He knocked again.

Still no answer.

Susan twisted the doorknob. As expected, it was locked. She pointed to herself then down the hallway toward the reception desk.

Dave nodded and dismissed her with a wave of his hand.

Susan made no noise as she left the group.

"Hey, Mike. Open up," Dave said. "You're worrying us."

The door remained closed.

Minutes later, Susan returned with a youthful-looking clerk following close to her. He carried a set of keys in his trembling hands.

Dave withdrew his weapon and placed it against his thigh. He nodded to the clerk. The youth opened the door and almost fell in his attempt to quickly step aside.

Dave burst into the room and flipped on the light.

Susan and Gene followed close behind.

The bed had not been slept on. Dave pointed to the closed bathroom door.

Gene stepped to the side and opened the door. He waited for a few seconds.

Nothing happened.
With his gun pointed forward, he stepped into the bathroom.
It too was empty.

EIGHTEEN

EARLY THE NEXT DAY, Bronson pulled off the main highway and retrieved his cell. "Hey Google, what motels are there in Hobbs?" From where he was parked, he could see the Hobbs, New Mexico city limits sign.

Google informed him that he had a choice of about fifteen motels.

"Google, are any of those Choice Motels?" Bronson knew that whenever possible, Mike would book a Choice Motel so he could earn points for a free night. Bronson hoped that hadn't changed.

Google informed him that Hobbs had two choice motels.

Hot-diggity-dog! His search had just been drastically reduced. He jotted down the addresses and headed for the nearest Choice motel.

Ten minutes later, Bronson stood in front of the reception desk. The youthful clerk at the Sleep Inn had a small mustache, which he probably grew in an attempt to hide his youthful looks. "Hello. What can I do for you?" He didn't bother to look up from his paperwork.

Bronson read the clerk's name tag. "Top of the mornin', Felipe."

Felipe glanced up but didn't say anything.

Bronson retrieved a folded piece of paper from his wallet. "I need to get this information to my friend.

Would you mind puttin' it in his mailbox or handin' it to him when you see him?"

"Your friend, he's a registered guest here?"

"Yep."

Felipe reached for the note. "What is your friend's name?"

"Mike Hoover."

Felipe's hand froze halfway to the note then quickly withdrew it as if he had been burned. "Uh…uh…"

"It's okay, Felipe. I got this," a voice behind Bronson said.

Bronson turned and vaguely recognized the face. His mind searched for the correct name. "Detective De La Rosa."

Dave offered him his hand. "Call me Dave."

Bronson accepted the handshake and noticed the fancy ring on his hand. "Call me…Bronson. Everyone does, even though my first name is Harry."

"I knew that." Dave smiled. "You're Mike's ex-partner."

Bronson nodded.

"We need to talk. If I recollect correctly, you love coffee. Right across the street, there's a restaurant. They serve the best coffee in all of Hobbs, or so I'm told. How about it?"

"You don't have to ask twice."

THEY CHOSE A window seat and waited for the waitress. When she arrived, they each ordered coffee. Dave took his black, Bronson's as white as a virgin sheet. When the waitress served them the coffee, Bronson smothered his with sugar.

Dave shook his head. "How you manage to survive drinking your coffee like that is beyond me."

"But somehow, I've managed." He stirred his coffee. "Do you know why I'm here?"

"I can only imagine." When Bronson didn't say anything, Dave added, "Mike."

Bronson nodded. "What can you tell me?"

"Before we talk about Mike, let me lead you down the road we've traveled." Dave told him about talking to the Hobbs' chief-of-police and how she suspects Finch was involved with a drug drop-off ring, and how she wanted the four Texas detectives to sniff around the city for leads. "But as it turned out, only the three of us did the digging."

"Why's that?"

Dave mentioned Mike's migraine. As he did, Dave's eyes narrowed as though studying Bronson. "He said he suffers a lot from migraines."

Bronson maintained a poker face. "Lots of migraines are due to stress."

Dave shrugged and continued with his narrative. He told Bronson about the call from Chief Kelley, and how they had gone to arrest Mike only to find an empty room. "Susan and Gene were supposed to escort Mike back to Dallas, but obviously they went empty handed."

"But you're still here," Bronson said.

"I am. Someone has to stay behind to fill in Chief Schemmel. Hopefully, I can do that tomorrow, and then I'll be on my way home. Unless she tells me to stay here and help her unravel this mystery."

"Do you plan to look for Mike?"

"I'm sure the chief will assign several people to that task. Maybe both of the chiefs will. I can answer that question better tomorrow."

Bronson took a sip of coffee and set the cup down. "Doesn't look good for Mike, does it?"

Dave shook his head. "No, it doesn't. I've known Mike for a long time. It's hard to believe he's gone rogue."

"Has he now?"

Dave's eyes widened. "I know he was your partner, and you two are tight. Naturally, you want to believe in him. But the evidence speaks for itself."

"Tell me, Detective De La Rosa, what that evidence says about a seasoned detective who would use his own gun to kill his partner." He signaled for the waitress to refill his cup. "Tell me that he wouldn't know the bullet could be traced back to his gun."

Dave leaned forward. "What are you saying? That the gun was stolen and that Mike's been framed?"

"Exactly."

"If he's innocent, then why didn't he report the weapon missing, and why is he on the run?"

"That's somethin' he'll have to explain when we meet up with him."

Dave expelled some air through his mouth. "What exactly are you trying to say?"

"I'm thinkin' I should talk to those drug dealers."

Dave waved his hand. "Hold on. No offense, but you're not in the force anymore, and you're not a detective either. You can't go meddling somewhere you don't belong. I can arrest you for obstructing an ongoing investigation."

"You could do that, but you won't."

Dave smirked. "Why wouldn't I?"

"Because deep down you believe that somethin' bigger is goin' on. Mike is the key to this puzzle. You are desperate to find out what's happenin', but your hands are tied. Me, on the other hand, I'm just a friend tryin' to connect with his buddy."

The clock ticked away while Bronson waited for an answer. Dave took a deep breath. "Okay. We'll treat this like you're my informer. Go talk to them, but do nothing more. You report back to me immediately."

"Sounds like a plan."

"Maybe not a very good one." Dave's forehead wrinkled as it often did when he focused on an uncomfortable task. "If they Google you, won't they find out you were once one of Dallas' finest?"

"I'm one step ahead of them."

Dave set his coffee cup down and stared at Bronson. "What does that mean?"

"I didn't register under my name, you know, just in case."

Dave nodded, but his frown spoke of disapproval. "So you had this entire thing all planned out."

Bronson remained quiet.

"What name did you give them?"

"Alex Bentley."

"All right, Mr. Bentley, I want you to remember that you're just my informer. Nothing else. Is that clear?"

"As clear as a clean lake."

Dave frowned and ignored his comment. "There's something else you need to know."

Bronson looked up at Dave.

"The consensus is that all of this involves drugs. It doesn't."

Bronson remained silent.

"After Susan and Gene left, I had a free afternoon. I went to Pete's Happy Place to have a nice, relaxed drink. I babied a Gin Tonic and kept my ears open."

Bronson remained quiet, waiting for the rest of the story.

The waitress approached, refilled Bronson's cup, and handed them the bill. After she left, Dave looked straight into Bronson's eyes. "I found two men there. Both of them were a little intoxicated. No, make that a lot intoxicated. They were either drunk enough or stupid enough to discuss things that shouldn't be mentioned except in private. After they left, I asked the bartender who they were. He told me he only knew their first names: Raul and Jose." Dave paused to make sure Bronson was following.

Bronson's silence continued as he stared at him.

Dave continued, "They were talking about some Egyptian treasure, and how that was going to make them rich. I got the impression they were smugglers, but I kept my cool. I let them talk. They lowered their voices, and I couldn't make out much of what was said. But I did pick up something about a 'dead policeman.'"

"Finch?"

"My guess."

Bronson retrieved his notebook and pen from his pocket. "What was the name of the bar?"

"Pete's Happy Place."

Bronson wrote that down. "That's an unusual name for a bar."

Dave half-smiled and nodded. "What are you planning to do?" Dave watched him record the information.

"I'm goin' to talk to this Raul and Jose. See what information they can give me and then report back to you."

"Do you plan to go after the smugglers?"

Bronson shrugged. "If as a result of my meddlin' we bring down a smugglin' ring, more power to us—or really to you since you're the one who will be doin' the real work. But as for me, that's not my purpose. I simply want to know if they can lead me to Mike."

Dave reached for the bill. "If they don't?"

"I'll dig somewhere else. Isn't that what informants do?" Bronson took out his wallet and pushed two one-dollar bills toward Dave.

He accepted the money. "Chief Schemmel warned me that these men are very dangerous."

Bronson wrote down in his notebook: *jerks*. "I've had my share of bringin' down tough men. This should be no different although I'm not goin' after them. As I said, it's Mike I want."

"If you find him, will you talk him into turning himself in?"

"It's the right thing to do." Bronson stood up. "Apparently, I'm goin' to face a tough gang that will probably not want anythin' to do with me. Will you back me up, as your informer?"

"Always."

NINETEEN

As far as bars went, Pete's Happy Place wasn't exactly a happy place. It was dingy and poorly lit. The bartender, a college-age student, busied himself mixing drinks for the three men who sat at the far end of the bar. Behind him, the large mirror failed to fully reflect the bar's images. Its caked-on crust offered poor visibility. Bronson headed for the isolated end of the bar, flopped down on the stool, and placed both open hands in front of him on top of the counter.

"What can I get cha?" The bartender wiped the area in front of Bronson.

Bronson scooted his right hand to reveal a fifty-dollar bill. He leaned forward and spoke so softly that only the bartender could hear. "It's yours for some information."

The youthful man took a step backward but didn't remove his eye from the bill. "I don't want any trouble, mister."

"I'm not here to cause any problems. All I want is some information."

"What kind of information?"

"I'm lookin' for two men, Raul and Jose. Can you point me to them?"

The bartender's eyes widened long enough to show a flash of fear. He looked away from Bronson. "Don't know anybody by those names." He busied himself wiping the counter. "As I said, I don't want any trouble."

Bronson covered the bill with a slight movement of his hand and drew it toward him.

"Wait." The bartender wet his lips. "I meant to say I do know them, but they're not here. But they normally show up around this time."

"What else can you tell me about them?"

"They are part of a gang known as *Los Muertos*— The Dead. Rumor has it that they got that name because of all the people they supposedly killed." The bartender stroked his goatee. "Look, you seem like a nice enough guy. If I were you, I'd stay away from them."

"Thank you for your concern. What else can you tell me?"

The bartender shrugged. "Not much. I take my own advice and stay away from them, except to serve them their drinks."

"Since they're not here, where can I find them?"

"You're in luck. They just walked in."

Bronson's glance shifted to the mirror. He could barely make out the two images of the men as they headed toward a table to his right. "Get me a coffee, would you, please?"

The bartender glared at him.

"Okay, make it a Coke. Better yet, diet Coke, but make it look like alcohol." Bronson removed his hand and the bartender grabbed the bill with a speed of an animal who didn't quite trust the person feeding it.

When the drink arrived, Bronson took a sip, headed toward the men, and stood looking down at them. "*Hola.* Mind if I join you?"

Raul's hand slid under the table. Maybe he was reaching for a gun.

Bronson remained still, his hands in plain view.

Coming from behind him, he heard the clinking of glasses and the murmur of voices between the bartender and three other men at the bar. More scattered voices came from the dark recesses of the bar.

Bronson smiled and looked at his drink as he spoke. "Raul, I have somethin' to offer you."

The man sitting to his left swallowed a short breath. Good. Now Bronson knew which one was Raul. Bronson focused on the other man. "So, Jose—" He looked at his companion. "Raul, can I join you?"

"Who are you?" Raul kept his right hand hidden under the table.

"All in good time. Right now, all I want to do is to sit down and talk. I'll even buy both of you a drink of your choice. What'd you say?"

Raul and Jose exchanged looks. "You talk. We listen," Jose said. "We don't like what you say, you're a dead man."

"No need for that. All I'm askin' for is your time, nothin' else. So, can I sit?"

Raul nodded. "What about our drinks?"

Bronson signaled for the bartender. He then reached for the chair and sat down so that he was equidistant to each.

TWENTY

BRONSON WAITED UNTIL Raul and Jose ordered their drinks before he began to speak. "You can call me Alex, but my name is not important. It's what I have to say that is of interest to you." He sipped his Coke, which with a bright red plastic stir stick sticking out, looked like an alcoholic beverage. "Ever heard of El Dorado?"

The bartender arrived with the hoods' drinks and set them on the table. Bronson handed him a twenty-dollar bill. "Keep the change." Carol was going to kill him for giving away all of their hard-earned money, but he had no choice. She'd have to understand.

The bartender nodded and left.

Raul's hand reappeared from under the table. He gulped down almost half of his White Russian and wiped his mouth with the back of his hand. "You were saying?"

"El Dorado."

Raul downed the rest of his drink. "El Dorado? You're talking about the mythical city that was made of gold?"

Bronson held in the gasp. He hadn't expected him to be so knowledgeable. It might make his charade a bit more impossible to accept. "Yes, that's the one I'm talkin' about."

"What possible interest would I have on that? It doesn't exist."

"I beg to differ." Bronson lowered his voice. "True, it's a legend, but legends are often based on loose facts."

Both men kept their eyes glued to their drinks, but Bronson could tell they were listening. He waited a few breathless moments before he continued, "I will start at the beginnin' so that when you repeat the story to your boss, he will know where I come from. Fair enough?"

Both nodded.

"The story goes that in Columbia a king so rich existed that each day he covered himself in gold from head to toe. Each evening, he would wash it off in a sacred lake." Bronson paused and sipped his drink. "Now legend has it that when the ruler died, the people of Muisca carried a right of passage ceremony.

"On the day of the ceremony, the highest four priests adorned themselves with feathers, gold crowns, and gold body ornaments. The new leader—the designated 'golden one' would stand naked, except for a coverin' of gold dust. The ceremony began when the Golden One made an offerin' to the gods. He would throw gold objects, emeralds, and other precious objects into the sacred lake. At the edge of the lake, a gold raft held four fires and when the priests extinguished them, the people who had gathered to watch the ceremony cheered their new leader."

"Good story, but what does it have to do with us?" Raul asked.

Bronson drank his Coke and wished it were coffee. "In 1969, three villagers found a gold raft located in a small cave in the hills south of Bogota. The carvings on it showed a man covered in gold and going out into the sacred lake to offer it gems and gold. That discovery led to the belief that El Dorado does indeed exist, at least it does in the deep waters of Lake Guatavita."

Jose rubbed his chin. "What year was this? 1969, you said? That's a long time ago."

Bronson nodded. "I'm not finished with the story." He looked around, making sure no one was listening. "They tried to drain the lake but all they managed to do was to lower the water level enough to find hundreds of pieces of gold along the lake's edge. These finds are worth millions of dollars." Bronson left out one small detail. The attempted draining of the lake happened in 1545. "These were good finds, but the real treasures found in the deeper water remained beyond anyone's reach." He took another sip of his so-called alcohol drink. "Until now." He set the glass down with a loud thump. "Modern technology, you know."

Jose and Raul looked around to see if the unexpected noise had attracted anyone's attention. No one seemed to notice.

"This modern technology. What do you mean by that?" Raul asked.

"It means that my friend and I have access to this new knowledge which we quickly put to use. The result—you can well imagine what that is. And that led us to a small problem. We're very anxious to get all that gold and jewels out of Columbia and into the hands of U. S. collectors. Are you willin' to help us?"

Jose licked his lips, and Raul looked around as though the answer could be found hidden somewhere in the bar's walls.

"I repeat. Will you help us?" Bronson spoke a bit louder.

Jose shrugged. "It's not up to us. We'll have to talk to Pedro."

Bronson leaned back. "Is he like your head honcho?"

"Sí."

Raul formed a fist and hit Jose's upper arm. *"Cállate, tonto."*

Immediately Jose hushed.

"It's okay. You go talk to Pedro, and I'll wait for an answer. Just make sure you tell him we're in a hurry. There are a lot of people who'd jump at the chance to help us. I'll wait only until tomorrow mornin'. Make sure Pedro knows that."

"Where can we find you?"

"Here." Bronson stood up. "I'll be here." He walked away.

TWENTY-ONE

"*ESTÚPIDOS!*" PEDRO BANGED his fist on top of his desk. "Did it ever occur to you that he may be a cop? You didn't get a full name other than Alex. Who is he? What proof did he have? Did he show you a sample of the gold or jewels? Did he even have any pictures?"

Jose squirmed in his chair. "No, but he sounded like he knew his stuff."

"*He knew his stuff?* That's it? Did it ever occur to you that he might be a cop?" Pedro pounded Jose's forehead with his index finger. "Think!"

Jose's eyes widened. He shifted his sight toward Raul as though asking for help.

"Can I speak?" Raul asked.

Pedro started to say something but changed his mind. He nodded.

"Let's for a moment assume that Alex is telling the truth. If so, we'll be rich, and you'll be powerful. Everyone would know that you're the one who brought in the big money."

Pedro rubbed his chin. "But what if he turns out to be a cop?"

"I'll guarantee that he'll meet with a deadly accident, and his body will never be found. That's a promise."

Pedro nibbled his lower lip, digesting every word. He remained quiet for a minute, then said, "I like the way you think. What do you suggest we do?"

"You're the boss." Raul shrugged. "But if it was up to me, the first thing I'd do is eliminate the possibility of him being a cop."

"You're right." Pedro's face lit up. "I think I know how we can find out."

Bronson texted Dave. Made contact.

Seconds later, Bronson's phone pinged. Meet me at the men's room in the motel.

By the time Bronson walked in, Dave was already there. Dave nodded a hello. "It's secure." He moved his index finger in a small circular way. "Give me the details."

Bronson liked that. Dave was a man of few words who immediately got down to business. Bronson told him about setting up the meeting.

Dave's jaw dropped. "You're crazy, you know that?"

"I've been called worse."

"You do realize that you're going to be in a heck of a pickle if they demand to see some kind of proof. They'll be wanting to see some gold or jewels. Or some kind of track record. You've got nothing. What do you plan to do about that?"

"I've wracked my brain tryin' to come up with a solution. Unfortunately, nothin' has come to mind. Havin' no choice, I'm movin' on."

"That's a really good strategy." The sarcasm in Dave's voice was thick enough to cut with a knife. "Let's—"

The door opened and Dave and Bronson began to wash their hands. A boy, around four or five, ran in, giggled, and hid behind the trash can. Seconds later, the door opened again and a bewildered looking father stepped in. He reached for his son. "Don't ever do that again." His tone frightened his son. The father took a deep breath and in a calmer voice said, "You can get lost. Someone can grab you. I'm just trying to protect you. Do you hear me?"

The little boy's lip quivered and his eyes watered. "I'm just playing, Daddy."

Dad wrapped his arms around his son. "I know, son. Just don't do it again." He picked him up in his arms. "Come on, let's go." He looked up at Bronson and Dave. "Sorry."

"No harm," Bronson said. "I had two little girls who did the same thing. It's all part of being a parent."

The man flashed him a thankful smile and left.

As soon as the door closed, Dave turned to Bronson. "What are you planning to do?"

"Hopefully, Raul and Jose took the bait and talked to Pedro, then hopefully again, Pedro will say 'Yes' and send for me. Once I'm in, I'll find out what they know about Mike's whereabouts."

Dave took a deep breath. "But before you can do any of that, you'll have to prove to them that you are who you claim to be."

"I can stall them. I'll tell them that I'll have proof in a couple of days. That will buy me some time to dig around and see if they know anythin' about Mike."

"That's a risky plan."

Bronson spread out his hands. "What can I say? Desperate times call for desperate plans."

Dave looked down and shook his head. "It's your call. I can't stop you. It looks like you've made up your mind."

"I have."

"In that case, I'll do whatever I can from my end, which will be hard as we shouldn't be seen together. Most of those gang members recognize me as a detective."

"We can meet discreetly," Bronson said.

"We could. Let's set up some kind of a communication system."

Bronson looked around the room. "Bathroom looks good to me."

Dave smiled. "If you get in a bind, text me 88, and I'll come find you."

"88?"

"Eight is an easy number to reach on the phone. Two consecutive numbers will tell me it's not a butt call, and you really need help. Of course, being my informant, you'll always let me know ahead of time where you are and what you're up to."

"I wouldn't have it any other way." Bronson nodded. "Do you want me to text you 88 right now to see if it works?"

Dave flashed him an irritated look.

TWENTY-TWO

PETE'S HAPPY PLACE welcomed customers as early as ten in the morning. Bronson glanced down at his cell. The bar would open in eight more minutes. Good. He'd use the extra time to find the ideal place from which to watch the entire area.

Seeing that the parking lot was deserted, he parked his car across the street and strolled toward the bar, keeping a constant eye on its windows and door. The place looked deserted. No one seemed to be lurking around the place. Bronson breathed easier.

"Excuse me, sir," a voice behind Bronson said.

Bronson froze. Where had he come from? His thoughts strayed toward his Glock.

Slow down. The man sounded polite. In fact, too polite. Bronson's hand inched its way toward the Glock. He turned to face a 6'5 middle-aged man with a lot of muscle and no fat.

Bronson braced himself.

"I'm looking for 5th Avenue." The giant held a map in his hand. "It's supposed to be somewhere around here, but I can't seem to find it. Can you help me?"

"Sorry, no. I'm not from—" Before he could finish the sentence, he felt the shove of a gun barrel on the small of his back. Bronson froze and silently scolded himself. He should've seen that coming. It'd been the perfect setup.

A black sedan screeched to a halt by Bronson.

"Get in," the giant said.

Bronson stood still.

The person behind Bronson shoved the gun deeper into Bronson's back.

Bronson threw his arms up in the air. "All right. All right. I'll get in."

"Good idea. Keep those hands up high in the air." The giant moved toward Bronson and frisked him. Seconds later, he held Bronson's Glock in his hands. "If you're just an ordinary guy, why do you carry this?"

"I'm a treasure hunter, and I often encounter men who are not as nice as you. I keep it for protection. Wouldn't you?"

The giant shoved Bronson into the back seat. Had he not ducked, he would have bumped his head on the car door. Once he was in, the giant scooted next to him. He kept the Glock pointed at Bronson.

Bronson mentally slapped himself on his forehead. He should've been more careful. He should've told Dave where he was going. Bronson had underestimated the enemy, and now he was going to pay for his carelessness. "So where are we goin' this fine mornin'?"

The giant stared at him with eyes that burned with fierceness. "Are you always this cheerful?"

"No, not always." Bronson sat up straighter, focusing on the buildings and any landmarks he could later use to lead him to the gang's den. "In fact, many people claim I can be a royal pain."

"I can see that." The giant switched his view from Bronson to outside the window.

For a fraction of a second, Bronson considered overtaking him. But maybe, if they were going to take him to see Pedro, he just might learn something. It'd be best to wait. Other opportunities would present themselves. He hoped.

He too stared out the window, memorizing each detail.

TWENTY-THREE

BRONSON WATCHED WITH interest as the black sedan pulled into Hobb's Auto Shop garage. From the outside, it looked like a legitimate business. Mechanics in dirty overalls worked on the cars that had been mechanically raised. People in the reception area waited for their vehicles, while a line of trucks and sedans waited their turn to be served.

Bronson attempted to glance past that, but as far as he could see, the shop held its secrets deep inside.

"Get out." The giant waved the gun.

Bronson's attention returned to the inside of the car.

The giant glared at Bronson.

Bronson opened the door and stepped out. He noted that five cars were inside with mechanics working on them. None of the men paid attention to him. As far as they were concerned, he was just another customer.

"That way." The giant pointed to the closed door with the sign Office: Employees Only. "Go inside." Bronson opened the door. Jose half sat and half stood by the desk. He nodded at Bronson.

Bronson nodded back. "I thought I was supposed to meet with Pedro." Bronson made it a point of looking around the crowded office. "Where is he?"

"Are you blind? Don't you see that he's not here?" Jose forced a laugh as insincere as a shark's grin. "He will come. In the meantime, you wait."

Bronson nodded and reached for a chair.

Jose took a step forward, blocking Bronson. "That's not where you're waiting." He pointed to a closed door. "That's where you'll be."

The giant opened the closet door to reveal a three-by-three empty room. "What are you waiting for? Go on in."

"How long will I have to wait for Pedro to show up?" Bronson studied the door's locking mechanism as he inched his way toward the closet. The normal one would pose no problem to unlock. Maybe all it would take was a strong shove. The one that worried him was the deadbolt.

"As long as needed." The giant pushed Bronson in. "There's a string hanging from the ceiling. Pull it. That will turn on the light. I'm afraid that's the only accommodation you will have in there."

Bronson took a cleansing breath to calm his inner voice. He reached for the string and pulled. A twenty-five-watt bare light bulb cast a dull yellow glow on the tiny room. Bronson stood still, listening. He heard the click as the door was locked, followed by the snap of the deadbolt. As if that wasn't enough, something was being dragged. A file cabinet or maybe the desk. The sound stopped when the item reached the front of the closet door.

Even if Bronson could break the locks, he'd still have to push whatever had been shoved in front of the door. All of this for him to wait for Pedro to show up. Uh uh, he didn't think so.

Another thing bothered Bronson. He had been frisked and his gun had been taken away, but they had let him keep the cell. Something didn't add up.

Bronson punched in 88 and pushed the send button.

Nothing. He didn't have service in this tiny room. He raised the phone as high as possible. He put the cell down by the floor. Still no service. He tried placing it by the door. Same results, no signal. With a grunt, Bronson returned the cell to his pant pocket.

He ran his open hands against the wall. It felt as smooth as a baby's bottom. He did the same to the floor. No splinters. Nothing he could use. For the first time in his life, he was one-hundred percent helpless. He slumped down on the floor and rested his head on his bent knees.

TWENTY-FOUR

A NOISE WOKE him up.

For a moment, Bronson felt disoriented. Where was he? He nodded. He remembered. The closet cell.

Shortly after he had been locked up, Bronson had plastered his ear to the door, listening—hoping—someone would free him. One by one the sound of footsteps retreating left him feeling desperate and cold. Then the place fell as silent as a tomb. Until now.

He looked at his watch. Three hours had crept away, and now, a bit past eleven o'clock someone had returned.

Pedro? Why was he coming this late at night?

He reached for the dangling cord and turned off the light, drowning the room in complete darkness.

Then instinct drove him to bolt toward the side of the door. As soon as the unlucky bastard entered, Bronson would knock the breath out of him and hold him hostage. He rubbed the bridge of his nose. What would that accomplish? The entire purpose of this operation was to find Mike. He had waited this long for something to happen. He could wait a little longer.

Bronson plastered his back against the rear back wall and waited for the door to open. He could hear the shoving of the heavy object that blocked the door. Two clinking noises told him the door had been unlocked.

Bronson took a deep breath and waited.

"Alex? It is me, Raul." He opened the door but didn't enter the cell. "Alex?"

Bronson remembered him but chose to remain quiet.

"I thought you might be hungry. I brought you a sandwich and chips. I'm going to let you out, but you better behave yourself. I thought it would be nicer to eat dinner out here rather than in that crappy cell."

Bronson remained quiet, listening for a trap.

"Do you need to use the bathroom?" Raul waited for a response. When none came, he added. "If you don't want to come out, that's fine with me. It's late. I'm going home." He started to close the door.

"No, wait," Bronson said. "I'm comin' out." He stepped into the brightly lit office and waited for his eyes to adjust to the light.

Raul stood a few feet away, holding a bag and no weapon.

"Is that for me?" Bronson pointed to the paper bag.

"*Sí*, but it isn't much. Sorry." He handed Bronson the bag.

"Don't fret. I'm starvin'. Anythin' will do." He opened the bag. He saw a store-bought wrapped sandwich and potato chips. He dropped the bag on the desk. "I wouldn't mind using the facilities first."

Raul nodded. "This way." He led Bronson out of the office and down a corridor. "There." He pointed to the men's room. "I'll wait here."

Bronson gave him a thumbs up.

First thing Bronson noticed was the window. It was big enough to escape, but it was one solid piece with no opening mechanism. That meant that he would have to break the glass. He looked around, absorbing each detail. Nothing there to help him. He'd have to use his shoe.

As he glanced around, he retrieved the cell from his pocket. His fingers quickly hit the keys: 88. Hobbs Auto Shop. Office. Closet. He pushed the send button.

He memorized each detail of the bathroom, just in case he would need it later. He used the facilities and walked out.

Raul stood straighter when Bronson approached. "I was beginning to worry. You took a long time."

"Sorry about that. You know what it's like. I haven't had the chance to go since early this mornin'." He looked at the office. "Another thing I hadn't done is eat. I'm starvin'. Is my dinner still there?" He pointed toward the office.

Raul nodded and followed Bronson into the office.

Bronson unwrapped the sandwich and separated the two slices of bread. Mayo, American cheese, lettuce, and one thin slice of ham. No matter. To Bronson, this looked like a gourmet meal. The only thing lacking was the coffee. Bronson took a big bite and his stomach rumbled in delight. This was the best ever. "Any idea when Pedro is comin'? I don't like bein' there." He pointed to the closet.

"I don't blame you. I imagine it's not a good place to be. Sorry about the inconvenience." Raul shook his head and looked down. "Maybe you and I can work some kind of a deal. I can help you bring in the merchandise."

"It'll take more than one man to do this successfully. Do you have any men?" Bronson tore open the bag of chips and offered Raul one.

Raul shook his head. "I can get some men."

"How many?"

"Five or six."

"With experience?"

"They work for Pedro, but they follow me. If I tell them what to do, they'll obey."

"That sounds good, but I need at least one good man with a lot of experience. Not that you're not a good man for the job. It's just the experience I'm lookin' for. Do you have any of that?"

Raul frowned and shook his head. "I'm a good learner."

"I'm sure you are. But we still need that experience." Bronson finished his sandwich and wrinkled the wrapper. He arranged his features to make Raul think he was in deep thought. "There's one name that comes to mind. He's real good at settin' up things like these. Maybe you know him?"

"Maybe."

"His name is Hoover. Mike Hoover."

Raul's eyes widened and then returned to normal so fast that Bronson wasn't sure if he saw a reaction.

"I know that name."

Bronson leaned forward and lowered his voice even though the two of them were the only ones in the room. "Can you arrange a meeting with him? Then the three of us can make arrangements. You can also bring any men you want."

"What about Pedro?"

"We'll forget about him." Bronson placed his index finger on his lip. "My lips are sealed."

"I'll see what I can do. I'm not sure I know exactly where Mike is but I know how to reach him." He stood up and pointed to the closet. "Let's get you back before anyone becomes suspicious."

"I don't particularly want to get back in there."

Raul's eyes darkened as he squinted.

Bronson shrugged. "But I understand that I have no

choice. We want this meeting to be a secret, and if I'm out, naturally, Pedro will grow suspicious." He stood up and headed toward the closet and paused. "You will set up a meeting between Mike and me, right?"

Raul nodded. "I'll do my best."

Hot diggity dog!

TWENTY-FIVE

BRONSON LOOKED AT his watch. 10:52 A.M. There had been no bathroom breaks, no breakfast, and worse, no coffee. Rethinking his situation, maybe that wasn't the worst part. There had also been no Raul. Bronson had hoped that Raul would spring him out before Pedro returned.

Raul wanted those treasures all to himself. Bronson could see it in his eyes. Maybe Bronson should have talked his way to freedom last night. Together, they would look for Mike. Together, they would bring those treasures to the U. S. and sell them to the highest bidder. That's what's Bronson should have said. His one chance and he had blown it.

Slow down, Bronson. Slow down. At least we've established that Mike is somehow connected with this gang. If Raul couldn't do it, maybe Pedro will lead me to Mike. Or maybe not. He would soon find out.

Bronson leaned against the wall and slid down. An image of Carol came to his mind. What was he thinking?

His mind drifted and his eyelids felt heavy. He must have dozed off for a now-familiar noise yanked him out of the world of dreams. He perked his head up and listened. Someone on the other side of the door was dragging the desk away so that it wouldn't block the entrance anymore. Bronson bolted to his feet.

Raul or Pedro?

It didn't matter. He wanted out and he wanted Mike. No matter the cost. He waited—and heard—the two locks being unfastened. Bronson braced himself. The door swung open, temporarily blinding him.

"It's time to come out."

Bronson recognized the giant's voice. That meant that Pedro had been the one to come to the rescue. If he could call that a rescue.

Bronson straightened himself and stepped out. His sight landed on the chair behind the desk. He could tell someone sat there, but since the chair faced the small window and away from Bronson's view, all he could tell was that its occupant was a large man.

"Pedro?" Bronson took a step forward. "My name is Al—"

The giant raised his hand, stopping Bronson from continuing. "Sit and be quiet."

Bronson did as told.

The chair on the other side of the desk slowly began to swivel so that its occupant would soon face Bronson. He couldn't immediately make out the man's features. All he could tell was that this was a big man, larger than most Mexican-Americans. He had heard Pedro was not very tall. This was not good news.

The chair continued to swivel until Bronson came face-to-face with the occupant.

Mike Hoover.

For a fraction of a second, they remained quiet, staring at each other.

The giant glanced from one man to the other, finally focusing on Mike. "Do you recognize this man?"

Bronson held his breath.

Mike nodded. "I do."

TWENTY-SIX

Chief Rudy Kelley stormed into the police station and past the detectives' desks. As he dashed past Detective Susan Epp's cubicle, she looked up. "Chief, you're upset. What's wrong? How can I help?"

He grumbled and ignored the look that passed between Susan and Gene. Without answering, Kelley bolted toward his office.

He closed the Venetian blinds that covered the windows separating his office from the rest of the Dallas Police Department. He flopped down on his chair, closed his eyes, and rubbed his temples. Everything had gone wrong today. At moments like this, he wished he could quit but then, how could he pay for his wife's mounting medical bills?

Slowly he opened his eyes. That's when he saw it. A large vanilla envelope on top of his desk. The block letters read, FOR CHIEF RUDY KELLEY'S EYES ONLY. "What the—?" He reached for it and opened it. He withdrew its content, and his eyes widened in horror.

The eight-by-ten glossy showed the chief and Patsy embracing. His hand squeezed her butt. That had to have been taken at least six months ago. Before he found out about his wife's cancer. He slammed the picture down and looked at the envelope. It contained no other markings. Who had placed it on his desk? He looked up and even though the blinds were closed he knew where each detective sat. He "looked" from desk to desk, wondering.

No one stood out as the culprit because deep down, he knew its origin.

His phone beeped. He recognized the number and a chill ran down his spine. *No, not today. Not ever again.* He knew he had no choice but to pick up. "Kelley here."

"Meet me at the normal place," the voice over the phone said. "4:30. Not a second late." The line went dead.

The chief glanced at his watch. He had thirty-three minutes to get there. If he hurried, he could make it. He grabbed the picture and stuffed it back into the envelope.

He stormed out, his shoes whispering his urgency.

THROUGH HIS REARVIEW MIRROR, Kelley spotted the black sedan approaching. He didn't have to look at the license plate to know this was the government car he was expecting. After all, here under the bridge, drivers seldom came. That's what made this place ideal. It was isolated.

Chief Kelley got out and stood by the hood of his car. He watched the sedan pull in beside him. Its driver turned off the engine and a distinguished-looking man in his early 40's stepped out. He stood by the open door. "Chief."

Kelley acknowledged the nod. "Why did you send me this?" He waved the manila envelope with the picture still inside. "I thought we had a deal."

"Soon, you will know why the picture. But first things first. Hand me your phone."

Sweat formed on Kelley's upper lip. "Why?"

"I don't want you using it and ruining everything. I'll take it and drop it off at work or your house."

The chief took deep breaths in an effort to maintain

control. "You have no business near my family." He heard the venom in his tone.

The government employee extended his hand. "Hand me the phone."

Kelley frowned and gave it to him.

The man placed it in his pocket. "Are you carrying?"

The chief frowned. "Why does that matter?"

"Answer the question."

"Of course, I am." The chief straightened himself so he could look taller. "Again, why does that matter?"

"I'm a man of few words so listen carefully. As soon as I leave, I want you to put your gun on your forehead and pull the trigger."

Kelley gasped and took a step backward. "You're... crazy." His mouth felt as it had been stuffed with cotton and he had trouble speaking. "Why, why would I...do that?"

"Why wouldn't you?" The man straightened his necktie. "I'm going to paint two pictures for you. One, you shoot yourself and your wife will have the best medical treatment. Her funeral will be an elegant Dallas event, and your daughter and the grandkids will also be well provided for." He offered the chief a warm smile. "On the other hand, you don't pull the trigger, and the story is out about you and Patsy. Sure, the scandal will ruin Patsy, but imagine what it'll do to your poor dying wife and your daughter and grandkids, forever in poverty's home." He shook his head. "Then imagine how they'll feel when all the other news is released. The bribes, the times you framed innocent people so the guilty could continue to line your pockets. How about all those times you looked the other way? Oh, so many ugly truths will be revealed."

In spite of his efforts to maintain composure, Kelley's hands violently shook. "I... I ne-never did anything you d-didn't order me to do." He paused, trying to regain his breath. "T-that information will come out. You will be ruined."

The man shook his head. "You still don't get it. I got lawyers that will discredit everything you say. Money speaks." He stared at the chief as though he were a displeased parent. "You should know that by now."

"I-I can kill you now."

The man swept his hand around the area. "There is a high-powered rifle aimed at you as we speak. You so much as touch your gun before I leave, you're shot dead on the spot. Then the pictures and history will be revealed. Your choice." He stepped into the driver's seat and started the engine. "Choose well." He put the engine on drive. "Goodbye, Chief Kelley. Working with you was, well, interesting."

He drove off.

TWENTY-SEVEN

THE GIANT CLOSED the gap between him and Mike. He leaned forward and pointed at Bronson. "Tell me what you know about this man."

Mike leaned back on the seat and rested his arms on the chair's armrest. "Actually, not much. We're just acquaintances."

"I can't accept that." The giant stepped away from Mike and pulled up the chair beside Bronson. He sat down. "You both share the same interests. Surely you know something about him. Begin by telling me his name."

Bronson formed a fist—the symbol of the letter *a* in sign language. He crossed his arms and tapped his fist on his upper arm.

Mike's glance shifted from Bronson to the giant. "His name is..."

Bronson held his breath.

Mike looked directly at Bronson. "Alex. Alex Bentley."

The giant visibly relaxed. "That's what he told us. So I can assume he's legit."

Bronson shifted in his seat and huffed. "Look, I don't know what all of this is about. I asked to see Pedro so he can help me get those treasures out of Columbia and into the hands of U. S. collectors. So why am I meeting with Mike? Is he Pedro?"

Mike half laughed. "No, I'm not Pedro, but that's a

good question." Mike turned his attention away from Bronson and toward the giant. "Why did you bring me here to meet Alex?"

"Because you're the one who will need to decide whether or not you want us to work with him. If you say 'yes,' we're all behind you. But if you say no, I can make him disappear." The giant snapped his fingers. "Just like that, quickly and easily. Permanently or not, your choice."

Mike's eyes narrowed. "Who am I to make that decision?"

"Word coming from the top says you're the new replacement." The giant waited a few moments for his news to sink in. "From here on, you will be the one organizing all the drops—and you will be very well compensated. Congratulations on your promotion."

Mike's facial expressions didn't change, but his body tensed a bit. "Who am I replacing? Pedro?"

The giant shook his head. "Higher up."

Mike's forehead kneaded. "Who?"

"El Patron."

Mike ran his fingers through his hair. "Does he know?"

"I'm sure he suspects. For a while, there's been talk about replacing him. I'm sure he's heard the rumors, but right now, he doesn't know that they're no longer rumors, and he certainly doesn't know it's you."

Mike nodded and stared at the giant. "What's going to happen to *El Patron*?"

"You're the boss, now." The giant's smile matched his nickname. "You tell me."

Mike intertwined his fingers, placed them behind his head, and leaned back. "Let's leave that up to him."

"How's that?" The giant's eyes narrowed.

"Set up a meeting between us. I will offer him a job. He could possibly be a good asset. Maybe he can even train me on the fine details."

"Chances are he will refuse the lower position. He's a very ambitious man. What then?"

Mike spread his hands out. "Then we have no choice. We can't have any loose ends."

The giant nodded. "I get you. Loud and clear."

"Good. Then set up a meeting. Somewhere discreet—just in case this goes south." Mike turned his attention to Bronson. "Now tell me why you're here."

Before Bronson could answer, the giant said, "He found El Dorado."

Mike's eyes widened as he switched his glance from the giant to Bronson and back to the giant. "El Dorado?"

"Yeah. I too found it hard to believe," the giant said. "But here he is, and he needs us to help him bring the treasures from Columbia."

Mike nodded. "In that case, Alex and I have a business deal to discuss."

"I've been kept prisoner for almost twenty-four hours." Bronson forced his tone to sound indignant. "I am starved for a good meal. Right across from my motel is a good restaurant."

A smile slowly spread across Mike's face. "I know the place. It's too open. I have a better suggestion." He stood up. "Follow me."

As they stepped out of the office, a black-and-white cruiser came to a stop. Its doors snapped open and a uniformed policeman stepped out of the driver's seat. From the other side, Detective Dave de la Rosa made a mad dash toward the auto shop.

"I'll take care of this," the giant said. "You two go."

Mike led Bronson to the side and used the backdoor to escape.

TWENTY-EIGHT

As Mike and Bronson ran out of the building, Mike pointed to a green Chevy rental. He and Bronson dashed in, and Mike pulled away without attracting any attention. Once on the road, Mike pounded his hand on the steering wheel. "What the hell are you doing here?" He spoke through clenched teeth.

"Yeah? Well, it's good to see you, too. *Buddy*."

Mike huffed and remained quiet for a while. With each deep breath he took, he seemed to relax. When he spoke, the anger in his tone had subsided. "Actually, Bronson, it is good to see you, too." He paused, as though considering what to say next. "It really is. There were so many times I wanted to talk to you, but this is not the time. The bottom line is you have no business here." As he spoke, his breathing increased in pace. The light changed to red and Mike slammed on the brakes. "None." He drummed his fingers against the steering wheel. "None whatsoever." The green light blinked on, and Mike peeled off.

Bronson stared outside the passenger window. Mike was speeding and one building blended in with the other. This Mike, Bronson did not know or for that matter, care to know. "You're in trouble, Mike. I came to help."

"Help?" Mike flashed him a look filled with anger. "All you've managed to do is make a mess of things."

"I made a mess of things? How about you?"

Mike slowed down as he pulled in behind Rosa's Bar and Grill. "This is it. I use the back door and sit in the back room away from everybody."

"This is what your life has come to." Bronson's tone came out icy even to his own ears, but he didn't care. "Runnin' away. Hidin'."

"It's all part of the job."

"And exactly what's that job?" Bronson's voice rang with bitterness. "The one where you are in charge of all of *Los Muertes*?"

Mike stopped and turned to stare at Bronson. "*Los Muertos*. Get it right."

Bronson faltered and stared back at Mike.

Both laughed at the same time and with that, the anger, the bitterness, and the doubt flew away. "Mike."

"Bronson."

Both began speaking at the same time. "I wasn't sure—"

"I'm really touched—"

Both stopped talking. "Let's go in and order," Mike said. "Then we can talk."

Bronson nodded but remained still. "I was worried. I'm glad you're okay."

"Sorry for giving you more gray hairs." He smiled. *"Buddy."*

They embraced, awkwardly and briefly. "Let's eat." Bronson headed toward the door. Mike followed him in.

As soon as they stepped in, a waitress with long black hair greeted them.

"Lupe." Mike greeted her back.

"The usual?"

He nodded.

She led them to the table closest to the door. "What would you like to drink?"

"Coffee," Bronson answered. "With lots of cream and sugar."

Mike smiled. "It's good to know some things don't change. I'll take some sweet tea."

Lupe handed Bronson a menu and left. A few minutes later, she returned, took their orders, and headed toward the kitchen.

"I'm listenin'." Bronson stirred his coffee.

"My goal is to penetrate this organization and bring down its leaders. I suspect *El Patron* may only be the go-between the top of the organization and the working thugs. If I can become *El Patron*, which it seems I have, I will have access to the men on top. I have no idea how high it goes, but I'm willing to follow the leads all the way."

"And for that, you're willin' to do anythin'."

Mike sipped his tea. "Basically, yes."

"Even murder."

Mike's mouth slowly dropped open. "What are you talking about?"

Bronson stared him straight in the eyes. "I know about Finch."

Mike leaned back in his chair as though he felt a great burden being released. "Oh, that. Yeah, sure. I pulled the trigger, but it was all part of the plan."

I pulled the trigger...

The statement hit Bronson like a straight shot just below the heart. "Explain."

Mike rubbed his nose bridge. "Oh hell, why not? You're already involved." He leaned forward and whispered, "I'm going to swear you to secrecy. Only three people know about this—well, four with you now."

Bronson nodded and leaned in.

Mike continued, "The three in the know are Chief Kelley, Herbert Finch, and me. That's it. No one else knows. This is strictly hush hush."

"What exactly do the three of you know?"

"You probably already guessed, but a very powerful smuggling organization is taking over the U. S. They'll smuggle anything, including humans. They have become so powerful that they're branching out to other illegal matters. They need to be stopped, but simple police procedures won't hack it. This goes way up high. We don't know who the real ring leader is, but with me here, we will find out. We figured that the only way to destroy them is for me to infiltrate them and destroy them from within. The chief came up with the plan and asked Herbert and me if we'd do it. Naturally, we said yes—and that's even before the chief offered a huge bonus increase."

"So you're workin' undercover."

The smile faded even before it formed. "Of course. Did you ever think otherwise?"

Bronson, unable to look at his ex-partner in the eye, looked down.

"You did." Mike leaned back and expelled some air. "My God, you did!" He raked his fingers through his hair. "I can't believe this."

"What am I supposed to think? You just told me, you pulled the trigger. How can you kill an innocent man, even under the pretense of being undercover."

Mike's eyes widened. "Oh, I see. You don't know." He half-laughed. "Of course you wouldn't know."

Bronson remained quiet but continued to glare at him.

The waitress arrived with their orders, enchiladas for Mike and tacos for Bronson. "Looks good," Bronson said.

"It is." Mike picked up his fork and the waitress left. He waited until he was sure she couldn't hear him. "Herbert is not dead. He's in Michigan, hiding until this is all over and enjoying a much-needed vacation with his wife and son. He had to *die*—" Mike put finger quotes around the word *die*. "—so that the plan would work."

A rush of relief rushed through Bronson's veins.

Finch, not dead.

Then doubts crept in.

Bronson's eyebrows knit slightly in puzzlement. He had seen the autopsy reports. The pictures of the corpse. If not Finch, who was that corpse? It looked a lot like Finch. If Finch wasn't dead, then Paul had to be in on the secret. But Mike said only three people knew, and Paul wasn't one of them. Besides, Paul wouldn't lie. He wanted to help Mike, even if he thought he was guilty. "Paul showed me the murder scene pictures. If that wasn't Finch's body, then it was somebody that looked very much like him."

Mike's face took on the look of an animal corralled in an unfamiliar pen. "What are you talking about?"

"I saw the autopsy pictures. I read the reports. Paul showed them to me."

For a few long seconds, Mike remained still. He wet his lips. "Are you saying Herbert is dead? You're wrong. Herbert is alive, I tell you."

"You said that you pulled the trigger. How is that keepin' him alive?"

"I shot him with a blank."

Bronson steeped his fingers against his lower lip. "Are you sure it was a blank?"

Mike's face grew white. The familiar doubts slithered in. *There's something wrong. The gun. The bullets.* "The chief himself handed me the gun, ready to use. So yeah, I'm sure they were blanks, and no, I didn't check the gun. Why would I?"

Because it's proper police procedure. Bronson leaned forward, looking at Mike steadily, absorbing every detail, and listening to every word he said. "Why didn't you check to make sure the gun was loaded with blanks?"

"I… I didn't have to." Mike's face turned even whiter than before, making it look milky and as translucent as a clouded glass. "Why would I? I knew it was a blank." Mike's throat tightened and his eyes glistened. "I was thinking of what had to be done. I was on automatic when I reached for the Glock." He held his head in his hands, a look of utter defeat enveloped him. "Herbert's alive. He's got to be."

Bronson squeezed Mike's upper arm. "Let me walk you through that night. Maybe we can find somethin' that doesn't click."

Mike shook his head. "I'm telling you. He's alive." Mike's face brightened, and he sat up straighter. "I know how to prove it." He fumbled for his cell. "Herbert gave me a phone number. He said to call him only if something had gone drastically wrong. He said no matter what he was doing or what time it was, he'd answer the phone. No matter what."

From memory, Mike punched in the numbers. The phone rang once.

Twice.

Three times.

"Pick up, Herbert. You said you would."

Four times.

Five.

"Answer the phone."

Six times.

Seven.

The call went to voice mail.

Mike disconnected, his face asking the obvious question. Why hadn't Finch answered? Why?... Why? An agitated look gripped Mike's face, and he expelled his breath in an audible hiss. "He...didn't...answer."

Bronson patted Mike's hand. "I'm goin' to call Paul. I'm sure he can set up a phone meeting between Chief Kelley and you and me. We'll find out if the chief loaded the weapon himself or if he had somebody do it. And if so, who?"

Mike nodded but didn't look up.

Bronson found Paul in his contact list, called, and put the phone on speaker.

Paul answered on the second ring. "Bronson, is that you?" His voice lacked the normal enthusiasm Bronson was accustomed to hearing.

"Sure is. You sound—"

"I guess you're calling about the chief."

"What do you mean?"

"I thought you heard, and that's why you're calling."

"Heard what?"

"The chief—he killed himself."

TWENTY-NINE

BRONSON HAD DEVOURED one taco and was making his way through the second one before calling Paul. After their conversation, the tacos lost their appeal. Bronson scooted his plate away. Beside him, Mike pushed his food around the plate with his fork.

"I know this is not how you wanted this to end, but it's over." Bronson wiped his mouth with the napkin and set it down. "The best thing to do is to turn yourself in."

Mike took a deep breath and remained quiet.

"I'll be by your side."

"That won't help." Mike set his fork down.

"When they hear your side of the story—"

Mike raised his hand and waved it. "Hear me out first."

Bronson nodded.

"I'm about to find out who *El Patron* is. That's huge, and not only that, I'm in a position to bring down the organization. But there are some problems with that."

"You think?"

"When *El Patron* finds out I've replaced him, he is going to be furious. True, I don't know this man, or even who he is. I can't tell you how he'll react. But based on what I've heard, he's not going to be a happy camper. He'll send some of his thugs to kill me, or he'll do it himself. Either way, I've got to constantly watch my back."

"I've got it covered."

"I know you do, and I appreciate that. But that doesn't change things. I'm in constant danger, and I don't want to expose you to that."

"That's another reason you should turn yourself in. You'll be protected."

"In jail? I don't think so." Mike paused for a second and looked around, as though considering his options. "Not jail. Herbert isn't dead. If...he is—God, I pray not—he won't be able to testify that I'm working undercover. The only other person who knew decided to conveniently kill himself."

"What are you sayin'? You don't think it was a suicide?"

"I know it wasn't. Somehow, his death is connected to this."

"My gut tells me the same thing."

"We have always listened to your gut."

Bronson nodded.

"I feel that the only chance I have of surviving this is to destroy this gang and bring down those powerful leaders. Maybe that will prove I'm working undercover. Will you help me?"

"On one condition."

"Name it."

Bronson took a deep breath while he considered how to phrase what he had to say. "I have a strong feelin' that at one time or the other, we're goin' to need help. We need someone on the inside that we can rely on."

"And who do you suggest?"

"Detective Dave de la Rosa."

"I know him," Mike said.

"I figured you did. Do you trust him?"

Mike nodded. "He's a hard working detective."

"That's more the reason to bring him in." Bronson told Mike how Dave had hired him to be an informer. "He already knows you're here somewhere."

"I know. He's been hunting me down. On top of everything, I've had to stay one step ahead of him."

"He told me he wants me to bring you in. If we explain to him what's goin' on, he'll help us, but we'll need to explain everythin' to him."

"You really think he'll go for it?"

Bronson shrugged. "I have no guarantees. But if he's as smart as I think he is, he'll see the benefits of lettin' you continue workin' this case. I'll talk to him alone, and I won't tell him where you are. When, and if, you feel comfortable, then the three of us can meet and brainstorm. What do you say?"

"He could provide police backup when we need it." Mike thrust his hand in the thumb-up position. "I can also see him helping out in other ways. But he's going to have to believe in me."

"That's a given."

"In that case—"

Lupe came rushing toward their table. "Get out." She mumbled the word *now*. "Three men just pulled in."

Mike and Bronson bolted to their feet.

The front door slammed open and two men stepped in.

THIRTY

Something didn't add up.

Lupe had distinctly said three men had pulled in.

Only two men entered the restaurant through the front door.

The third must have worked his way to the back of the restaurant.

Bronson opened his mouth to warn Mike, but by then, Mike had already thrown the backdoor open and dashed out. As he ran, he pushed the car clicker button, unlocking the car doors. "Let's get the—"

Bronson ran toward Mike, spread his arms out, and threw his weight on him, both landing on the ground.

Mike, still on the ground, attempted to push Bronson off him. "What the—"

From somewhere above them, a bullet whizzed by.

Bronson rolled off Mike and at the same time retrieved his gun. He aimed for the gray sedan that had stopped in front of the restaurant's back parking lot.

Mike too had his gun out and joined Bronson in the shooting marathon, but the car sped away, its tires squealing as it made a sharp right turn. "Were you able…to recognize…the driver?" Bronson spoke between breaths. An action that would have been so simple a few years back now took the breath out of him.

Mike shook his head. "I couldn't…get a good look… at him." He too was out of breath. He pocketed his gun, took a deep breath, and bounced to his feet. "Let's get out of here before the police come."

Bronson nodded and stood, his knee joints popping with the effort. He dusted himself as he scrambled to the car.

"What was all that about?" Bronson asked once Mike had pulled away from the parking lot and blended with the traffic.

"I may be wrong, but I believe that might have been one of *El Patron*'s men sending me a message." He maneuvered a left, turning away from the main street. Soon, they were bouncing along the potholes of Hobb's back streets. "Do you think he's long gone?"

Bronson looked behind him to see if anyone was following. All looked well. "If we're lucky, he's long gone. Where are we goin'?"

Mike shrugged. "Head for the hills? That may be the only place I'll be safe."

For a second, Bronson smiled, but then the grin fell off his face as if it had been made of sand. "That's a wise decision, but you can't hide in the hills forever. You're up to somethin'. Tell me what it is."

"You know me too well." Mike's focus stayed on the rearview mirror longer than normal.

Bronson glanced at the side mirror. A gray sedan crept toward them. "It's him, isn't it?"

The car sped up.

"I think so." Mike executed a fast left, then a right, another right, a left, a right.

Both Bronson and Mike checked their mirrors. The sedan was nowhere in sight.

"I think I lost it, again." He headed three blocks in a straight line, and then just to be sure, he turned right.

Bronson looked at the side mirror. "I don't see the car." He turned so he could see better. "I think your outstanding drivin' skills out maneuvered it."

"I agree with you, buddy. We lost him, but for how long?"

Bronson pouted. "You're thinkin' someone planted a bug on your car."

"Yep. But it wouldn't be wise to stop now to check. If there's a shootout, I want it to be out of town. No use putting innocent lives at risk."

"Totally agree." Bronson adjusted his seat belt so it was tighter. "Now what?"

"I have an idea." Mike stepped on the gas and the car sped down the highway, heading away from town.

THIRTY-ONE

Fifteen minutes later, Mike turned off the main highway and followed the dirt road. "What's up?" Bronson kept a constant eye on the rear view mirror. So far, no one followed them.

Mike made a left and continued down a not too well maintained road. "See that small hill over there?" Mike pointed to his right.

"Yeah?"

"I'm going to park the car on the other side. You can help me cover the car with mesquite branches and anything else we can find." He slowed down and brought the car to a stop. "Unless *El Patron*'s thug is very observant, he won't spot the vehicle until it's too late."

Bronson's sight followed the road as it snaked down the hill and away from them. "I see what you're doin'. We each hide behind opposite sides of the dirt road. Once the car gets close enough, we shoot the tires."

"You got it, buddy. You read me like a book."

Both slid out of the car. They searched and found several large branches and began their task. "I want that driver alive." Mike cut another branch and placed it on top of the car.

"Can't get any answers from a corpse."

Satisfied that the car blended in with the desert scenery as much as possible, they returned to the road. About fifty feet away from the car, each stepped off opposite sides of the road. "He'll come, real soon." Mike disappeared from Bronson's view.

Almost directly in front of Mike's hideaway, Bronson found a dent on the road. That would serve as the perfect hiding place. He lay on his stomach and waited.

Five minutes went by and still, they waited.

Ten minutes.

"Maybe I was wrong." Mike spoke loud enough for Bronson to hear but still remained hidden.

"Learn to trust your gut." Bronson wished something would happen very soon. He looked down the road and half-smiled. A cloud of dirt rose and seemed to grow bigger as the vehicle approached. "There's a car comin'." He repositioned himself so that he could have easier access to the advancing car.

Two long minutes dragged by before the car crested the hill.

Gotcha. Just keep headin' this way. We're ready for you. Bronson steadied his hand as he pointed the gun to the car's right front tire.

But instead of continuing down the road, the car came to an abrupt halt. The passenger's and back doors opened. Three men stepped out. The driver remained in the car.

Four men total, not one.

Too late, Bronson realized he and Mike should have discussed this possibility.

The three men held their guns in front of them as they headed up the road. Behind them, the driver turned off the engine. The three advanced steadily, their focus on the road ahead. As they neared Mike's and Bronson's hidden location, they seemed to grow bigger, more threatening. They were now within earshot.

"Be careful," the one in the middle said. "The car is right over that hill. That means Mike is somewhere around there. Keep your eyes open. We need to take him alive."

At least that's somethin'. Bronson drew a deep breath and wished he could talk to Mike.

"Beto!" Mike called out to the man closest to him but whispered loud enough for all three to hear.

They froze and turned toward the sound of the voice. Beto nodded toward a bush, the one Mike used to hide behind. Smirks formed on their faces. The man in the middle signaled Beto. *Go down toward Mike. We'll remain on the road, guns ready*, he said using his hands to speak for him.

Beto nodded. He descended the road's shoulder and headed toward the bush.

Mike sprung up and grabbed him. Before the other two could react, Bronson lunged forward, clasping his hands together. He brought them down on the back of the man's neck closest to him, driving him to the ground.

From behind, Bronson grabbed the other man's shoulder and spun him like a top. Bronson opened his hand and threw a right. The heel of Bronson's hand landed under the man's nose.

He yelped, dropping the gun.

Bronson punched him on the belly. The man folded up and Bronson brought his knee up to impact with his face. He fell on top of the other man.

Bronson ducked when he saw the car speeding toward them, the driver shooting at him even as he steered following a wavy pattern.

Mike reached for the gun, aimed for the tire, and released several rounds.

A large *whoosh* sound exploded as the air escaped from the tires. The driver lost control and the sedan careened for several seconds before flipping over.

By now Bronson had retrieved his gun and pointed it at the three men who looked like quarterbacks who had been sacked and dazed. Mike stood next to Bronson, his gun also aimed at the men.

"You, Beto," Mike said. "Go check on the driver and don't even think of doing anything stupid. I've got the gun, and so does he." He pointed to Bronson.

Beto attempted to get up and for a few seconds, it seemed his body didn't know whether to straighten up or fall back down.

"Go!"

Beto half-stood and half-crawled toward the wrecked car. He took a peek through the window. *"¡Dios mío!"* He crossed himself. He half-turned so that his voice would travel toward Mike. *"Estan muerto!* He's…dead."

Mike shrugged. "That's too bad."

Bronson froze and fought the urge to punch Mike. How could he be so callous? Mike's lack of action went against all police procedures. This was the Mike Bronson feared he had become. Bronson took a deep breath. He had to let it go. Surely, Mike would explain later and everything would be fine.

"Get back over here," Mike told Beto.

Beto joined the other two men who sat on the dirt road.

"This is how this is going to go." Mike glared at the men, daring them to contradict him. "First, you tell me who sent you."

The men looked down.

"You." Mike pointed to the man who had been in

the middle as they walked toward them. "Your name is Antonio?"

Antonio nodded.

Mike cocked the gun and pointed it at him. Bronson felt sure Mike wouldn't hesitate to shoot. He forced himself to remain still, doing his darnest to push all doubts away.

"If you value your life, answer my question." Mike shoved the gun closer to the trembling man.

Antonio slowly raised his eyes and met Mike's angry glare. "Who do you think sent us?"

Mike spoke without hesitation. *"El Patron."*

Antonio straightened himself up as though pushing all fear away. "Give the man a point for being smart." Antonio flashed him the thumbs-up position.

Mike remained quiet for the moment, as though considering his options. "You do know that you no longer work for him."

The men did not move, but their eyes remained on Mike.

"You now work for me. Me, the new *El Patron*."

"We had heard that rumor, but we didn't know it was true." Antonio pointed to himself and his two *compadres*. "We were just following orders. We were told that's what *El Patron* wanted. We didn't know you had taken over."

"You'll find I'm a forgiving man, but from here on your loyalty is mine. Is that clear?"

All three nodded, but none maintained eye contact.

"Good," Mike continued. "From now on, I expect you to be faithful only to me. In return, I will spare you, and I'll even consider giving you a bigger share of the take."

This time, all three looked up. Antonios's lips quivered. He swallowed hard. "Does this mean we're free to go?"

"In a minute." Mike pointed to Bronson. "First, I want you to meet my right-hand man, Alex Bentley."

Bronson waved.

"I expect you to listen to him as you would me. Is that clear?"

They nodded.

"Beto, tell me what the plan was. You capture me and then what?"

"Soon as we apprehend you, we were supposed to contact *El Patron*. He would then tell us what to do with you. That's all I know."

Mike pointed to the other two men. "Do either of you know anything else?"

Antonio nodded. "When we contact *El Patron*, he was supposed to tell us where to take you. He wanted a meeting with you."

Mike nodded. "Good. I want to keep that meeting. In a while, I want you to do just that. Call him and tell him you got me. Then agree to deliver me to him. All will go as planned, except that when I meet *El Patron*, the three of you will be there to protect me. Can I count on that?"

Antonio was the first to nod, then Beto, and finally the third man.

Mike offered Antonio his hand. Antonio accepted it and Mike helped him up. He did the same with Beto.

Mike headed for the third man. "I haven't had the pleasure of meeting you." Mike helped him up.

"I'm Ignacio Contreras."

"Ignacio, welcome to my team."

Ignacio flashed him a shy smile. "We'll be good to you."

Mike's grin stemmed from ear-to-ear. "That's what I want to hear." He pointed to the wreck. "First thing I want you to do is to get rid of the body and the car—the usual way. Then set up that meeting. Contact me with the details as soon as you know them. Then we'll meet and you can deliver me just as you promised." He took out a piece of paper and wrote down his cell number. He handed it to Antonio. "Is that clear?"

"Sí, Señor," all three said in unison.

"Good. Get in the car. Alex will drive us back to Hobbs, and we'll drop you off at the edge of the city. You're on your own from there."

Bronson flashed Mike The Look. Mike knew he hated to drive.

Mike smiled and tossed him the keys.

THIRTY-TWO

HALF AN HOUR LATER, Bronson watched Antonio, Beto, and Ignacio walk away from the car and toward the city. "Do you really trust those men?"

"The only one I trust is you, buddy."

Mike's words registered in Bronson's brain, but somehow they seemed automatic as though Mike was playing the game Bronson wanted him to. Bronson chewed the inside of his cheek, remembering Mike's recent disregard of human life. He let some time pass. "Then let me help you."

Deep crease lines formed in Mike's forehead and around his eyes. "What are you suggesting?" His sudden cool and distant tone could have given birth to an iceberg.

"It's time to brin' Dave in."

Mike stared at Bronson with unblinking eyes. "This great Detective Dave de la Rosa, what's he to you?" The anger in his words filled the atmosphere with sparks of tension. "Why do you keep throwing him at me?" Mike's jaw stiffened. "What's in it for you, Bronson?"

Bronson, not buddy.

Bronson took in deep breaths, trying to keep himself under control, yet he could feel the anger—the resentment—building up within him. "This has got to end sometime." His voice came out robotic. "Just sayin'."

"Just saying what?" Mike's animal-like eyes glared at him. "That what I'm doing is wrong? That I should turn myself in? Is that what you're trying to say?"

"It's the best possible scenario." An image of Mike destroying all he had built flashed before Bronson's eyes. He rubbed his eyes, willing the image to fade. He forced his words to come out smooth, but strong. "I'll stand by you. Just don't block me out. Talk to me."

Mike's eyes examined Bronson with the unmistakable gaze of an opponent who weighed a betrayer's promise. A few seconds passed and gradually, Mike's rigid body went slack. "I'm...sorry. I'm under a lot of stress, and I blow up easily. I shouldn't have taken it out on you. Let's talk about Dave. What are your plans?"

For the moment, Bronson remained quiet. He wanted to acknowledge the apology, but Mike had not given him a chance to do so. Instead, he had switched the topic. Two could play that game. "I'm thinkin' you should set up your meetin' with *El Patron*, just like you want. When you have all of the details, tell me where and when this meetin' will be held. Dave and I will be there to cover your back, and even protect you from those three goons, which I'm sure are not as loyal to you as they claim to be. Once you have established who *El Patron* is, Dave will arrest him."

Mike looked out the passenger window and remained quiet.

Mike was holding something back, and Bronson knew it. "That's what you want? Arrest *El Patron* and destroy the gang." Bronson held his breath while he waited for an answer.

"It's...not that simple." Mike spoke so softly that Bronson had trouble hearing him.

"Explain."

Mike flashed him a smile as fake as a three-dollar bill. "You know, you're right. Soon as I have the details about that meeting, I'll call you. You go meet with Dave and prepare him for what's about to happen."

Mike's relaxed expression was gone, and the newly acquired creases around his eyes had deepened—a detail that made Bronson's stomach churn. "After the arrest, what do you plan to do?"

Mike threw his hands up in a form of surrender. "Give myself up, of course. Isn't that what you want?"

Bronson's gaze analyzed him like a teacher monitoring a student who was ready to cheat. "What do you want?"

Mike took in a deep breath and collapsed onto the back of the passenger's seat. "For this mess to be over."

Bronson nodded. "*El Patron* will be arrested, you will turn yourself in, and your name will be cleared. Is this how you see this endin'?"

Mike looked slightly to the right and away from Bronson. "That's exactly how I see it." He continued to stare out the window.

Liar! What are you not telling me? Bronson's hands formed fists. That was the first time Mike had lied to him.

THIRTY-THREE

EL PATRON LEANED back on his chair while Antonio related the evening's events. When Antonio finished, *El Patron* sat back and stared at the ceiling. His fingers formed a steeple, and he tapped his chin with them. He set his hands down. "Let me see if I got this right." He pointed at Beto. "You agreed to work for Mike instead of me. You even swore to be faithful to him."

Beto shrugged. "I only said what he wanted to hear."

El Patron leaned forward and tapped his chest. "And now you're saying what I want to hear."

Beto's eyes widened in fear. "No. No! I only said that to him, not to you. For you, I speak from my heart."

El Patron stood up and hovered over Beto. "You're saying that you're faithful to me?"

"*Sí, sí.* You are the boss. You will always be the boss. I'll do whatever you say." Beto's Adam's apple bopped as he swallowed hard. "Anything. Anything you want."

El Patron retrieved a switchblade from his pocket. He snapped it open. "You'll do anything I tell you to do?"

Beto eagerly nodded.

El Patron jabbed the blade toward Beto. "Then cut."

"*Que?*" Beto looked down at the blade and up to *El Patron*'s eyes, and then back at the blade. The vein in his temples bulged.

"Cut."

"Cut what?"

El Patron waited a few seconds. "Your arm. Cut deep. I want to see blood pour out."

Air fled Beto's lungs in harsh gasps. Sweat soaked his shirt.

"You cut, or I cut." *El Patron* held on to the knife and pressed its blade against Beto's cheek. "You choose."

Antonio's phone beeped and he looked down. "It's from Mike. What do you want me to tell him?"

El Patron snapped the switchblade shut, straightened up, and looked at Beto. "Thank your lucky stars." He turned his attention to Antonio. "Tell him I'm not available to talk. I want him to sweat. Tell him—" He thought for a moment. "Tell him I'll call him whenever I can."

Antonio nodded. "Hey, Mike."—"Yeah, of course. Beto told us you're willing to meet. The thing is *El Patron*, well, you know how busy he is. But he does want to talk to you. He told me to tell you that he will call back as soon as he can." He disconnected and returned his cell to his pants pocket.

"I need to think." *El Patron* pointed to Beto and Ignacio. "You two go. I'll call you when and if I need you."

Beto sprung to his feet and headed toward the door. Ignacio followed close behind.

"Me, too?" Antonio remained sitting.

"No, you stay."

Antonio nodded and waited until his two co-workers had closed the door behind them. "Mind if I ask you a question?"

"Ask away." *El Patron* walked around the desk and sat down. "How do you want to handle Mike?"

"As always, through the chain-of-command. We'll let Pedro bring him in."

Antonio's forehead wrinkled. "Here?"

"No." *El Patron* cast him a look that told him he was being an idiot. "Too many things can go wrong if we do it here. Tell Pedro to set up the meeting in the desert. The body will be easier to dispose of there."

Antonio took in a deep breath. "The body. That means you plan to—"

"—kill him. Of course. What other option is there?"

Antonio didn't speak for a long moment. He shrugged. "I can't think of an alternative."

El Patron leaned toward Antonio. "You have something against killing Mike?"

Slowly, Antonio shook his head. "It's just that first you killed Finch, then—"

"Technically, it was Mike who killed Finch. He's the one who fired the shot."

"But after the chief loaded Mike's gun, you're the one who switched the blank for the live ammo."

"Mike is a trained detective. He should have made sure that his gun had a blank."

Antonio nodded. "I can't disagree there. But what I'm saying is that maybe we're attracting too much attention. For years, we've had this nice quiet operation. I don't want to see it jeopardized."

"Make no mistake. Mike is a dangerous animal. That's why we must get rid of him. I'll kill him and tell the police I shot him in self-defense. He pulled out a gun on me while refusing arrest. I will be cleared of all charges. I'll be the hero. After all, Mike is the number one enemy right now and everyone is on the lookout for him."

"That will work—except for one minor detail."

"What's that?"

"Mike's right-hand man, Alex Bentley. Do you think he will transfer his loyalty to you?"

El Patron puffed. "Hardly. But you leave Bronson to me."

Antonio's eyebrows knit slightly in puzzlement. "Who?"

"There's no Alex Bentley. His real name is Harry Bronson. He was Mike's first partner and still remains his best friend."

Antonio gasped. "He's a policeman, too?"

"A detective. Actually, an ex-detective. He's retired, and he should have stayed retired. He had no business butting in."

Antonio ran his fingers through his hair. "That really complicates matters. What are we going to do about... about—"

"Bronson."

"Bronson," Antonio finished the sentence.

El Patron leaned back and smiled. "I've been thinking. I'll meet with Bronson and tell him we are both going to be there when Mike meets *El Patron*, but before that happens, some of my men will capture us and hold us prisoners. They will take me to a separate room to interrogate me, but of course, I'll manage to escape so that I, as *El Patron*, will be able to keep my meeting with Mike."

Antonio nodded. "I can see the possibilities." He frowned. "But you still haven't answered my question. What are we going to do about Bronson?"

"By the time Bronson manages to escape and heads toward the designated place, Mike will be dead. Bronson will find me, a very grieving detective, mourning over having to kill Mike." *El Patron*'s smile broadened into a grin. "I can't wait to see Mike's reaction. All of this time he has been wanting to meet *El Patron* and all of the time, I've been right in front of his nose."

Antonio curled a smile. "And the great Detective Dave de la Rosa strikes again."

Dave threw his head back and laughed a sound between a bark and a snort.

THIRTY-FOUR

"I HEARD SOME very disturbing things so I decided to follow up." Dave looked at the cell to make sure he wasn't on speakerphone. "I'm here at the Hobbs Police Station. Give me half an hour and then we can meet. I'm sure you'll want to hear what I have to say." Dave leaned back on the wooden chair located in the Hobbs Auto Shop office. He put his feet up on the desk and smiled when he told Bronson the lie.

"Half-an-hour it is," Bronson said. "Where do we meet?"

"How about Green Meadow Park? There's a bench facing the lake. I'll be there. Do you need the address?"

"I can find it."

Dave disconnected and looked at Antonio who sat across from him. "And that's how that's done."

"You don't think Bronson suspects anything?"

Dave smirked. "He doesn't have a clue, and do you know why he doesn't?"

Antonio shook his head.

"Because he allowed his feelings to interfere with logic. He is so desperate to help his friend that he can't see what's in front of his face. Take that as a lesson. Always put the job before your feelings."

Antonio nodded then nodded again. "That's why you reached the top."

Dave bolted upright. "Make no mistake about that.

I haven't yet peaked. Stick with me, and we'll both get there."

Antonio grinned from ear to ear.

BRONSON SAT QUIETLY staring at the lake. He sipped his coffee and set the cup down on the park bench. *Mike, what have you done?* His fingers drummed on his lap. *How can I help you when you refuse to be helped?* He reached for his coffee but didn't drink any.

A few yards in front of him, a bird dove and scooped a mouthful of something, maybe water. He flew to a nearby branch and chirped. For a long time, Bronson watched the bird as it graced one limb then another and another.

He moved swiftly and with no apparent purpose to its actions, but all the time, Bronson knew the bird alerted to any possible dangers.

Possible dangers.

Should he alert?

"You're here early."

Startled, Bronson looked up to see Dave staring down at him.

"You beat me to it." In his hands, Dave held two cups of coffee.

Bronson pointed to the cup on the bench. "That one is empty. Thanks for the refill." He reached for the one Dave held. He set the other one down and almost spilled its full content.

"I ordered it the way you like it: full of sugar and cream."

"Perfect. Thanks."

Dave sat beside him and pointed to the lake. "Beautiful, isn't it?"

Bronson nodded. "Very peaceful."

"It is, and it's the opposite of you."

Bronson's sight pivoted from the lake to Dave's face.

"I can see it in your eyes," Dave said. "You're worried. Truthfully, so am I. Mike is no longer the Mike we both know and respect."

Bronson looked away.

Dave ran his fingers through his hair and frowned. "Don't tell me. Mike refuses to turn himself in."

Bronson gulped down some of the coffee. "He said he would."

"But?"

"But I can't seem to read him as I have before. All I know is that he wants to bring *El Patron* in. He said he'd turn himself in after that."

"But you're not sure he will."

"Exactly."

Dave tapped Bronson's arm in a brotherly way. "Maybe he thinks he's got bigger fish to fry."

"What does that mean?"

"That's part of the story I want to tell you, but please, don't ask me for my source." He looked around as though making sure they were alone. "You know how that goes."

"I do."

Dave leaned closer to Bronson and whispered, "Right after Finch was murdered, Mike set up the delivery of what I believe was a very lucrative drop off Egyptian artifacts. Mike's share was two Egyptian god figurines that belonged to Cleopatra. They're worth $5 million, and he said he had a buyer."

Bronson's body sagged as though the words wore him down. His grip on the coffee cup tightened and the hot, brown liquid overflowed. Bronson set the cup down but didn't bother to clean his hand.

Dave continued, "Soon as several huge boxes filled with Egyptian artifacts were dropped off, Mike demanded that the statues be given to him immediately. Once in his hands, he boarded the contraband plane and disappeared for a couple of days. Rumor has it, he sold the statues to a private collector. I don't know what else happened back there, but by the time Mike returned, he was ready to be head of *Los Muertos*. That means he plans to replace *El Patron*, and that's why he is so eager to hand him to the police." Dave shrugged. "Who knows? Maybe Mike even figured a way to frame *El Patron* for Finch's death." He remained silent for a moment. "Look, I know this isn't what you want to hear, but I know that Mike has no plans to turn himself in. Soon he will become the new *El Patron*, and who knows what he plans to do after that."

Bronson bent down and picked up his cup. He took a swig and set it back down by his feet. "I see a huge hole in that theory."

Dave moved his index finger back-and-forth, indicating *no*. "Not a theory but facts. Facts that I can prove. But we can get back to that later. Let's talk about that hole first."

"Let's."

A cool lake breeze blew and for the moment, Dave remained quiet. When he spoke, his tone was soft. "Mike hands *El Patron* to us, he turns himself in, and Mike is acquitted." He looked at Bronson. "So far, so good?"

Bronson nodded.

Dave paused for a brief moment. "This is where we part ways. The way I see it, once we have *El Patron* under custody, he'll squeal in an effort to avoid jail time. That means he'll reveal Mike's involvement in Finch's death. No way is Mike going to allow that to happen."

"But Mike is innocent, and we'll be able to prove it. He—"

Dave waved his hand, silencing Bronson. "Okay, let's look at this from a different perspective. Mike tells us where he's meeting *El Patron*, but by the time we get there, *El Patron* is dead. And Mike? He disappears and takes his business elsewhere." Dave lowered his head and rubbed his eyes. "Can you see this happening?"

Bronson bit his lower lip. "As I was sayin'. I know Mike. He wouldn't do somethin' like that."

"So you're still defending him."

"Let's just say this doesn't sound like Mike. So humor me. Let's for a minute go with the theory that Mike is innocent."

Dave shrugged. "An unbelievable theory, but I'll hear you out."

"*El Patron* is settin' a trap."

Dave's eyebrows arched. "How so?"

"Mike is goin' to the desert believin' that Antonio, Beto, and Ignacio, along with a handful of other men, are goin' to stand by him. Instead, their loyalties remain with *El Patron*. Before he has a chance to hand *El Patron* to us, they'll kill Mike."

"What do you propose we do to prevent that?"

"We notify the local authorities. We arrive in large numbers. This way, we not only apprehend *El Patron*, but we'll also arrest several of the gang members. With luck, we'll destroy *Los Muertos*."

"That would be ideal, but it's a no-go."

Bronson remained quiet, waiting for Dave to explain.

"Remember I told you I was at the police station?" Bronson nodded.

"I had the same plan you outlined. But when I got there, I saw a mass movement to apprehend 'that cop killer.' What I saw, I didn't like. The hate. The anger." Dave shook himself. "They want to bring him in alive or dead, and dead seems to be the preferred method. If you treasure Mike's life, I'd advise you not to get the local police involved." He opened his hands and waived them, telling Bronson it was up to him. "I'll go with you to protect Mike, but this is your call. What do you want to do?"

Bronson took in a deep breath. "I feel we're gropin' like blind men in a maze. I suggest we get there early so that when Mike and *El Patron* and his men arrive, we're ready for them."

"That's not a bad idea." Dave nodded. "Do you know where this meeting is taking place?"

"I talked to Mike right before I called you. He told me they're meetin' in the desert. He gave me specific directions, but since I'm not from here, I was hopin' you'd get us there faster."

"Tell me what you know."

"Someone named Pedro took care of the details. Mike and Pedro are to—"

"Alex Bentley." The loud, firm voice came from behind Bronson.

Bronson recognized Antonio from the meeting after the car chase. What was he doing here? He forced a smile. "It's Antonio, if I remember right."

Antonio nodded. "That's my name. Too bad you can't say the same."

Bronson shrugged. "I'm not sure I could convince people I was an Antonio."

"Very funny, Mr. Bronson." He spread the word out so it sounded like *Brr-oon-son*. "Or should I say Detective Bronson?"

Inside, Bronson screamed. On the outside, he put on his poker face. "Bronson is fine."

Antonio continued, "Speaking of funny, I find it very amusing that you're keeping company with another detective. Tell me, what plans have you two come up to destroy us?"

"Thing is—" As he spoke, Bronson's hand reached for his gun. "—we're more action than planners."

"Freeze right there," Antonio said. "Both of you. Look to your right."

A man, leaning on a tree, held an open book. As Bronson and Dave glanced his way, he moved the book down just far enough to reveal the gun pointed at them.

"Now look to your left."

Bronson and Dave did. This man held the gun behind an open newspaper.

"There are three more men, not including me. If you want to live, I would advise you to head slowly toward the red sedan. Get in and keep your hands where we can see them. That's Beto standing by the car. He will relieve you of your weapons."

Bronson headed for the car, Dave followed close by.

At his side, Bronson's hands formed tight fists.

THIRTY-FIVE

As soon as the sedan turned onto Main and 5th Avenue, Bronson knew where they were being taken. The auto shop. He and Dave would be thrown into that makeshift cell he had previously occupied. He searched his mind, recalling each detail. Small. Empty. Nothing in there that could help them.

He looked down. On the floor, he spotted a wadded piece of paper. Next to it was a paper clip and a penny. He scooted over, placing his left foot on top of the clip. He dragged it as close to the edge of the seat as possible.

He raised his right hand and formed talons with his fingers. He scratched his head with slow, jerky movements. All eyes reverted to his right hand.

He inched his left hand forward and felt around until his hand located the paperclip. He pocked it.

He should have also picked up the penny. Who knows? Maybe that would have been the lucky penny.

"Hands on your lap where we can see them," Antonio said.

Bronson brought down his right hand and placed both hands on his lap. "As you wish."

Beto turned into the shop's parking lot, but instead of parking in the front, he drove around to the back. He turned off the engine when they reached the back door.

"Out," Antonio said. "And no funny business from

either of you. Do I need to remind you that I'm the one carrying the gun?"

"No, no need to do that. We remember." Bronson scooted out and stood next to the car. He scanned the area, searching and processing information.

Beto pushed him. "Inside."

Bronson regained his balance and moved toward the building. Dave followed close to him. As soon as they stepped inside, Bronson noticed that the door to their cell was ajar, an open mouth ready to devour its victims.

Beto pushed them inside the cell and slammed the door shut. Bronson managed to pull the light string hanging from the ceiling just before the darkness swallowed them. The bulb bathed them more in shadows than light.

Dave looked around. "Not exactly a Holiday Inn."

"Not even a Motel 6."

"What do you suggest we do?"

Bronson stood still, like a bird ready to take flight.

Dave stiffened. "What's wrong? What do you hear?"

"It's not what I hear. It's what I don't hear."

Dave frowned. "Huh?"

"Last time I was here, they pushed the desk against the door. If I managed to open the door, I still couldn't get out."

"Did you?"

"Did I what? Manage to get out?" Bronson shook his head. "Look around. There's nothing we can use to open that door. Unless you see somethin' I don't."

Dave ignored the question. "Is that why you think they didn't push the desk against the door this time?"

Just as Bronson opened his mouth to speak, the doorknob turned. Antonio stood holding the door open. "*El*

Patron is here. He wants to talk to you both, but one at a time. Who wants to go first?"

Bronson and Dave exchanged looks.

"Bronson it is!" Antonio said.

Bronson stepped forward but at the last moment, Antonio extended his right arm, preventing him from going any further. "I'm thinking that the one who has the most information is Detective De La Rosa. So we'll start with him." He moved to the side, allowing Dave to step out.

Antonio locked the door behind Dave, leaving Bronson in semi-darkness.

Antonio reached for the deadbolt.

Dave stopped him.

Antonio tilted his head as though asking *why not lock it?*

As an answer, Dave shook his head.

Antonio pointed to the desk and then to the door that held Bronson prisoner.

Again, Dave shook his head, grabbed the car keys, and headed out. Antonio and Beto followed him out. They stood in the garage part of the building. Dave ignored Antonio and Beto and instead focused on the three mechanics who worked on the cars.

"Sure you don't want me to lock the deadbolt or shove the desk against the door?" Antonio asked once they were outside.

"No need. It'll take Bronson a while to escape, but by then, we'll be long gone." He smiled a shark's grin. "Besides, I have a better idea." He pointed to the mechanic who worked on the car closest to them. "Go get Rick."

Seconds later, Rick stood in front of Dave.

"Your sole job is to stand guard," Dave told him.

"There's a man in the cell. His name is Bronson. No matter what he tells you or demands or whatever, you're not to answer. Let him think no one is around. Is that clear?"

Rick nodded.

Dave continued, "When he breaks out and he's in full view, shoot to kill. Tell the police he locked you in the closet while robbing the office, but you retrieved the gun and shot him in self-defense."

Rick licked his lips.

"The key to this working is the shoot to kill part."

Rick smiled. "I know that."

Dave nodded an approval. "Go to your station. Remember, when Bronson steps out of his cell, wait until he completely steps out. Then shoot."

"To kill." Rick checked his gun. "Question, if he doesn't break out, then what?"

Dave grinned. "Figure it out."

Rick's smile widened. "I open the door for him, wait for him to come out, and then shoot to kill." He headed inside the office space.

Dave turned to Antonio and Beto. "Now let's go meet Mike. He has a big surprise coming."

Beto followed but Antonio hesitated. He stared at Rick.

"What's wrong?" Dave asked.

"I have a feeling Rick is going to blow this for us. Let me stay and take care of Bronson. Soon as Bronson is dead, I'll join you."

Dave placed an arm around Antonio. "You worry too much. Let it go. Rick knows how to do his job. You come with me." He applied some pressure to Antonio's shoulder. "Now."

Antonio nodded and left with Beto and Dave.

THIRTY-SIX

BRONSON WAITED IN the semidarkness. He pressed his ear against the door. No sound came. He knocked. "Is anyone out there?" He stood perfectly still, listening. "I have to use the restroom." He used his fists to pound on the door. "Hello?"

Still, no answer.

He bent down to look at the doorknob and squinted. He could barely see. If only he could flash a light on the keyhole. He sighed. No need to waste time wishing for the impossible. He allowed his finger to be his eyes.

He took out his credit card and slipped it between the door and frame. He leaned close and listened as he gently slid the card in a north-south direction. By now he should hear the telltale clicking sound as the latch pulled back.

But he didn't.

He returned his credit card back to his wallet.

He retrieved the paperclip from his pocket. He straightened it out and used his shoe to make a shift spear. He eased the metal spike into the keyhole. He jimmied it around hoping it would catch. He pushed lightly feeling for a pop that would tell him the lock had been disengaged. He never heard it.

He sighed and pocketed the paperclip. He'd never know if it would come in handy.

He removed his shoe and retrieved his key ring. He

felt the edges of the keys, trying to feel which one would work best as a bumper key. He settled on the third key. He inserted it one notch short of full insertion. Using his shoe, he bumped the key inward to push it deeper into the keyway.

The key transmitted the force to the driver pins which then jumped from the key pins, moving the key above the cylinder. Bronson applied a light rotational force to the key during this process. The cylinder turned, instantly opening the lock.

Bronson formed a fist and pulled it down. *Yeees!*

He remained in the room while he put his shoe back on, all the time listening for the slightest noise. None came.

That was the problem. Someone should have come in now and then. One of the mechanics should have entered to hang or retrieve a key. Someone should check on unanswered calls. Someone, something—anything.

If *El Patron* was questioning Dave, where were they?

The silence filled Bronson with dread. Why hadn't they moved the desk in front of the door? Why hadn't they locked the deadbolt? The answer came to him with a realization that drenched him with apprehension. They wanted him to escape. Why?

Bronson removed the shoe he had already put on and then removed the other one. He held them close to him. He reached for the rope and pulled it, immediately drenching him in darkness. He braced himself, plastered his back against the wall, and pushed the door open.

He held his breath, waiting for something to happen.

He waited a second. Two seconds.

Nothing happened.

He counted to three.

Still nothing.

He took a deep breath. In one swift movement, he threw the shoe toward the right-hand side of the room, then threw himself down on the floor and rolled out of his prison. For a fraction of a second, he saw a head dodge down behind the desk. Whoever he was, Bronson was sure, he was armed.

Like a soldier, Bronson belly-crawled out of the room.

A shot rang out and bounced inches away from him.

Bronson sprang forward and cleared the door leading out of the office. He moved to his left and straightened up.

His would-be assassin dashed out of the room, his attention focused on the open space that led outdoors.

But instead of running, Bronson stood his ground. He waited, his back to the wall, for the shooter to come out. Soon as he stepped out, Bronson extended his arm, hitting him on the throat.

The man's eyes widened as he dropped the gun and tumbled forward. Bronson raised his knee, impacting with the attacker's head. The snapping sound told Bronson he had broken the stranger's nose. With a loud *humph*, the would-be assassin landed on the floor like a half-full sack of sand.

Bronson retrieved the .38 Special and shoved it between his jeans and belt. He looked around. One of the mechanics continued to work. The other one stared at Bronson.

Bronson pointed to the gun.

The employee immediately turned his attention to the car he was working on.

Bronson picked up his assailant by the scruff of his

shirt and dragged him back into the office and the cell. He bent down to make sure he was all right. He had been knocked out, but he'd survive. Bronson locked the door and dragged the desk to cover the door. He locked the deadbolt, and then retrieved his shoes, put them on, and stepped out. "I need a car." He used his loud, commanding tone.

Both of the mechanics ignored him. Bronson took out the gun and waved it above his head.

The mechanic who had previously been watching him pointed to a gray sedan. "Company car. Keys hanging in the office. Second ones, first row."

Bronson retrieved the keys and as he ran past the mechanic, he said, "Much obliged."

"Whatever." The employee returned his attention to the car's engine.

Bronson dashed toward the gray sedan, gunned the engine, and sped away.

THIRTY-SEVEN

EVERY INSTINCT TOLD Bronson to head toward the police department. That was the correct thing to do. They would help Mike. He had always trusted his gut. Why not on this?

Bronson bit his lip.

Maybe Dave had lied. Something was off about him and the more Bronson thought about it, the more likely it seemed that Dave wasn't the model detective he seemed to be.

Bronson turned the car around, heading toward the police department. He slammed on the brakes and pounded his hands on the steering wheel. What if Dave had been telling the truth? What if the police hated Mike for killing one of their own? Mike would be on the defensive, and the police might interpret that as an act of aggression. There would be no time for explanations.

Bronson had to get to Mike. He was running out of time—if he wasn't too late by now.

He made a u-turn and headed out of town, following as well as he could the directions Mike had given him. Ten miles later, Bronson saw the dirt road that led him to the designated place.

It took a span of a few seconds for Bronson to absorb the scene. Beto, lay on the ground, either dead or almost there. Blood gushed out of him, saturating the dry, cracked dirt with rich, red pools of blood.

Dave—*El Patron or a detective trying to bring a suspect in?*—and Mike, both disarmed, fought each other like raging animals.

Ignacio, who had apparently been knocked down, struggled to stand, all the time, his hand raising the gun, pointing it at Mike. Ignacio was still wobbly and couldn't aim.

Even before Bronson came to a complete stop, he rolled down the window and stuck the .38 Special out, pointing it toward Ignacio's direction.

Ignacio's eyes opened wide at the unexpected intrusion. He moved his aim from Mike to Bronson. Both shot at the same time.

Ignacio fell to the ground, hitting his head on a rock and knocking himself out.

For a fraction of a second, Dave turned his attention toward the new commotion.

That was all Mike needed. He formed a fist and swung it hard toward Dave's mid-drift. Dave doubled down.

Mike clasped his hands together and brought them down hard on Dave's back.

Dave fell face first and did not get up.

Out of breath, Mike sank to the ground and watched his ex-partner throw the driver's door open and bolt out.

"Bronson."

"Mike."

"You got good timing."

"So I've been told."

Mike pointed to Dave. "Meet *El Patron*."

Bronson nodded. "I suspected as much."

Mike stared at Dave's inert body, then at Ignacio's. "Of course." He took a couple of breaths. "How long have you known?"

"Not until now for sure." Bronson walked toward Mike and stood by him. "But I've had my suspicions before this."

Mike nodded. "We need to secure these guys before they regain consciousness."

Bronson was one step ahead of him. He checked on Beto. "Too late for this one."

Mike closed and opened his eyes. "The other two are alive for sure. Do you have your handcuffs?"

Bronson always kept a pair in his glove compartment. But this time he had driven the company car. "Not hardly."

"Our belts?"

Bronson eyed the car. "Let me check the trunk first. We may get lucky."

It took him two tries to find the correct key. "Bingo! There's enough rope here to tie the entire desert." He took out some rope and tossed it to Mike.

"It's about time Mother Luck worked with us." Mike secured Dave. "You better get out of here, buddy."

Bronson took care of Ignacio. He checked on his wound. Blood oozed out at a slow, steady clip. That meant that no major artery was involved. Using Ignacio's belt, Bronson created a temporary tourniquet. Ignacio would survive, but he would need medical attention. "Why do you want me to leave? What are your plans?"

"My plan is to not get you involved. We've broken a couple of rules."

"Yeah? You think so?"

Mike ignored him. "After you're gone, I'll call the police and give them a modified version that doesn't include you."

"Are you goin' to wait here for them?"

Mike half-smiled. "Is that your discreet way of asking me if I plan to turn myself in?"

Bronson had no time to answer. From behind them, a male voice said, "Keep your hands where I can see them."

Both Mike's and Bronson's heads pivoted toward the source of the voice. Antonio stood with his gun pointed at them.

Mike and Bronson exchanged looks. So much for Mother Luck.

THIRTY-EIGHT

"First, throw the weapons toward my direction and no funny moves. Nice and easy."

Both Bronson and Mike did as told. Still pointing the gun at them, Antonio retrieved the guns one at a time, flipped the cylinders open, and dumped the bullets. He set the two .38 Specials down. "Mike, I know you had a Glock. Where is it?"

"Somewhere out there." Mike pointed toward his right. "It got lost during the fight."

"Bronson," Antonio said.

How long had he known his real name? First Dave and now Antonio. They surely had been played.

Antonio continued, "I'm sure you took Beto's and Ignacio's guns. Yet you only gave me one gun. Where's the other one?"

Bronson threw his arms up in the air. "Looks like you got me." He reached into his pants pocket and using two fingers retrieved the .38 Special. He threw it toward Antonio. As Bronson did, Beto's gun stuck in the small of his back jabbed him, but Bronson didn't complain. Antonio didn't know that gun existed, and Bronson wasn't about to give it up.

As before, Antonio dumped the bullets. "Now, let's talk."

The heat beat down on Bronson draining him of any energy he had left. The worst thing about the desert, it provided no shade from the relentless heat. "It's such a beautiful day out here in the open desert, Mike and I would love to sit and chat with you. You go first."

"Fair enough, but first I have a question for you, Mike. Are you undercover? Were you sent here to expose *El Patron*, or as you now can prove, Detective Dave De La Rosa?"

Mike looked away.

Antonio continued, "Or are you a dirty cop and here only for your own financial gain?" The disgust in his voice rang high and clear. "Did you actually plan to replace *El Patron* and take over the business?"

Mike looked down.

Answer, Mike, answer. I need to hear the truth come out of your mouth. Bronson formed a fist and covered his mouth. He knew Mike was innocent. *He knew it.* But still he felt the doubts creep in.

"I'm waiting for an answer," Antonio said.

Mike smirked. "Do you really expect me to answer that? If I were an undercover cop—" He stressed the word *undercover*. "Do you really think I'd admit it? You're the genius one here. Figure it out yourself."

"I need an answer, but before you say anything incriminating," Antonio said, "I must warn you that you're under arrest."

For a brief second, the confusion Bronson felt mirrored in Mike's eyes. Bronson switched his attention to Antonio's face. It bothered him that he couldn't read Antonio. He had the perfect poker face. "Under arrest?"

Antonio ignored Bronson. "You have the right to remain silent. You have the right to have an attorney present. Anything that you say, can and will be used against you in a court of—"

Mike sprung to his feet. "Enough of the Miranda Rights. Who are you?"

"As a police officer, you know I have to read you your rights before arresting you. Now let me start over." He did and when he finished, he said, "My name is Antonio Eduardo Corbalan. Make that Special Agent Antonio Corbalan."

"FBI." Mike said it more as a statement than a question.

"Prove it," Bronson said.

"I'm not stupid enough to carry the badge and I.D. with me. I keep them hidden in the car." Antonio pointed with his head toward his right. "I can go get them if you want proof."

"We want proof," Bronson said.

Antonio put the gun away. "Mike, no funny business?"

Mike shook his head. "Wouldn't think of it. Besides, Bronson over here would make sure I'm still around when you return."

Bronson detected an edge of sadness in Mike's voice. A sadness that bordered on betrayal. Yet Bronson couldn't deny it. He had ignored many rules in his career. At times, he had looked the other way. But this, he couldn't let go.

"Bronson, you're in charge." Antonio walked away.

Bronson looked at Mike, but Mike wouldn't look at him. Instead, he lowered his head, closed his eyes, and shook his head. He opened his eyes and sat back down, giving Bronson his back.

"Mike."

Mike ignored him.

Antonio returned. He shoved his badge and I.D. forward. "Now will you talk to me?"

Mike took a deep breath and began his narrative.

MIKE HOOVER

THIRTY-NINE

Seven Months Ago

THE KNOCK ON the door came at exactly 1:16 A.M., Sunday morning.

Like an animal sensing danger, Mike bolted out of bed and stood still listening. He still held the book he was reading in his hands. He set it down and reached for the Glock in the nightstand drawer. Silent footsteps led him to the living room. He felt his way through the darkness, not daring to turn on any lights.

The knock came again.

He crept toward the side window and barely moved the curtain.

Two men stood side by side behind a woman he couldn't quite see. Although he saw no weapons, Mike got the impression the men were armed.

Knock. Knock.

"Mike, open up. I know you're in there. It's me… Naunet."

Mike almost dropped the gun. *Naunet!*—a name from his past he thought he'd never hear again. An Egyptian goddess stood on the other side of the door—his door.

"Mike?" She pronounced it *Mee-ke*, just as she had back then when they were a twosome. Mike smiled at the memory.

What was she doing here? He held the gun behind

his back. With his free hand, he opened the door. The two men stepped aside to reveal the beautiful woman he had worshiped during his college years. Even though thirty years had passed, the shine in her deep-brown eyes still swallowed him whole.

"Naunet."

She lowered her head and her long, brown curls hid her features. She flickered her head, moving her hair away from her face as she raised her head to meet his. "I didn't know if you'd still remember me."

"Last time I saw you, I told you I would never forget you." Mike's voice came out sounding rough, and suddenly he was very much aware that he wore only pajama bottoms. He cleared his throat. "I kept my word."

"May I come in?"

Mike felt the blood rush to his face. "Yes, of course. Sorry." He opened the door wider. She stepped in and the two men stationed themselves by the door.

Mike looked at them, then back at Naunet.

"They will wait outside. They know I'm safe with you," she said. "Close the door so we can talk."

Mike closed the door and slid the gun into a drawer in the stand located next to the front door.

"You haven't changed." Her smile was warm and genuine. Yet, underneath that surface, Mike detected a sense of grief so strong, it was palpable.

He wanted to reach out and hold her. Comfort her. He thought of Ellen, his ex-wife and the love of his life, and took a step back. He remained standing by the door staring at the woman who in his younger years had been his everything. Then the guilt set in.

A longing for Ellen flashed before his eyes. He idolized Ellen, yet...

Yet, here stood this woman whom he had so much wanted to marry in his youth. This goddess. This Naunet. His forbidden love. He wanted to embrace her and hold her tight. *Ellen, forgive me.* Guilt consumed him. He swallowed hard.

She sat on the couch and patted the space next to her. "Come. Sit. We have a lot to talk about."

Mike chose to sit on the recliner facing her. "What brings you here?"

"I wish I could say unfulfilled memories and dreams." If possible, her eyes darkened as she placed her open palm to her chest. "But just like in college, I will always tell you the truth."

"And that is?"

"Remember back then when we were so much in love, and I couldn't marry you because of my family situation?"

Mike nodded. "Why are you bringing up the past? It's over."

"I know that, but please, allow me to finish. I need to start at the beginning in order to tell you my entire story. Can I do that?"

Mike sat up straighter. He was amazed at how much the past could still hurt. He nodded.

"What do you remember?"

Mike didn't have to think of the answer. It came automatically. "I remember that you broke my heart because you had to marry some rich dude your parents had promised you to."

"It broke my heart, too. But you have to have known that I had no choice. I had to marry him to bring peace to my family. If I went against my parents' wishes, I would have never been able to go back to them or back to my land."

"And I told you Egypt was a long way from here, and you could do whatever you wanted to because you were in the United States." Mike bore his eyes into hers. "You chose him over me."

"I regretted it, and I still do. And so many times I've thought about you. But he is my husband, and I've learned to love him." She folded her hands and placed them on her lap. "And you? Are you married?"

Mike shrugged. "Divorced, actually."

Her beautiful eyes clouded with sadness. "Oh, Mike—"

Mike waved his hand to hush her. "It's okay. Ellen and I still love each other with a passion that will never end. It's just that she couldn't stand being married to a policeman—always wondering if I'd come home. She hated the long hours, the missed anniversaries and the holidays. She wanted me to be a full-time husband and father, but my career wouldn't allow me that luxury. Being a cop is all I know. But soon I'll retire, and we're going to remarry. She's a wonderful woman. You'd like her."

"I'm sure she is, and I'm sure I would like her." She took in a deep breath, and Mike wondered what she was thinking. After a long pause, she asked, "Did you tell her about me?"

Mike shook his head. "No one knows."

Naunet nodded. "It's best that way."

"So why are you—and your bodyguards—is that what they are?"

She looked away, and Mike took that to mean yes.

"Why are you here?"

"Because I need you."

Mike stiffened.

Naunet smiled. "Relax. It's not like that." She sighed. "But wouldn't it be nice, if we could, just once—" She let the image fade away from her eyes. She sat up straighter. "I'm not here to take you away from Ellen, and I don't plan to interfere in any way."

Mike leaned forward, still enthralled by her great beauty. "What can I do for you?"

She smiled—that same smile that had so captivated his heart. "We are all business, are we? Some things don't change." Back in their college years, when they discussed their future, Mike adopted a formal tone which Naunet called his business voice.

"Naunet."

She took a deep breath. "Mohamed and I married, just like we were supposed to. It hasn't been a bad marriage, even though he could never fill your shoes. He gave me only one child, a little girl I absolutely adore." Her eyes filled with tears, and she sucked in her lips in an attempt to keep from crying. "She's…dying, Mike." She covered her eyes with her hand.

The next thing Mike knew, he was sitting beside her, his arms wrapped around her.

"We live in Houston, now. The cancer center there is supposed to be the best in the world. But a little over a month ago, they told me there was nothing else they could do. I took her to our Houston home…to die." A sob stemming from deep inside her erupted and the tears gushed out.

Mike kissed her forehead and held her closer.

For a long minute, Naunet rested her head on his shoulder. "Last week, I asked her if there was anything she wanted. She said, 'Yes.' I was delighted. There was something, after all, I could do for my child. I would give her anything."

Her tears fell on his bare chest. He wanted to kiss them away. He wanted to— He forced his mind back to Naunet's sadness. "What did she ask for?"

"She has always been fascinated by anything Egyptian, maybe because of our heritage. She told me she wished she could fly home to Egypt and see the two statues she has always been drawn to ever since she was a little girl."

"What statues are those?" Mike asked.

"Cleopatra had two figurines made out of Lapis Lazuli, the most treasured gemstone of Ancient Egypt. They always considered that precious gem to be of godly importance. Both statues are of the ancient gods, Osiris and Isis."

"But those statues are in Egypt and you're here in America. And your daughter is too weak to make the long flight." Mike thought for a moment, and then added, "But with your money, your influence, and your power, why can't you arrange to have those statues flown over here?"

"That is precisely what I tried to do. When I made the call, I learned that a couple of months ago our precious museum had been robbed. Most of the Egyptian artifacts were stolen, including the two figurines."

"So you want me to find them."

Naunet raised her hand. "Let me finish. As you pointed out, a woman in my position can find things out that others can't. In three months, all of those artifacts that belong in my country for our residents to see and enjoy will arrive to your country. The drop-off will be in Hobbs, New Mexico. From there, they will be sold to private collectors all over the world. Someone named

El Patron is making all of the arrangements. I want you to infiltrate his organization and retrieve our treasures."

Mike massaged his temples. "Wow. I'm not sure I can—"

She reached for his hand and held it tight. "Please, Mike, for old memory's sake."

"I—I don't know."

"There's more."

Mike waited. She still held on to his hand and Mike sensed a spark of electricity stemming from this simple touch. He slipped his hand away.

"If you can arrange to replace *El Patron* or get close to him, you will have access to all the locations the artifacts will be sent. You are a great detective and working undercover, I know you can do this. Imagine what this will do for your career."

Mike ran his fingers through his hair as he considered the possibilities. "I know if I could bust that ring, it would mean a great deal, a promotion even. The problem is I don't have any jurisdiction in New Mexico."

"Leave that to me. I can arrange that. I know departments cooperate with each other. I can make a few calls if you want me to. But there's one thing more. The final thing, you could say. The favor, if you must call it that."

There was more? Mike remained quiet.

"You've got three months to make your move and become *El Patron*'s confidant. As such, you will demand payment for your services. You will ask for the two figurines, which, by the way, are worth five million dollars, and that is little compared to what the other artifacts will bring."

Mike whistled, not sure if he was shocked at the price of the loot or the demand she was making.

Naunet continued, "On the day of the drop-off, the pilot will demand that you go with him. You will bring me the statues which I will place in my daughter's—" Naunet choked and Mike held her. She waited a moment and continued, "Hands. When she passes on, I will personally make sure the statues make their way back to the museum in Egypt where they belong." She looked deep into Mike's eyes. "Will you do this for me? Because of the nature of this situation, you're the only one I can trust. Please. Please, help me."

There was a time when Mike wouldn't have denied her anything. The years had come and gone, but the desire to do her will had never left him. Still, there were so many factors involved.

She looked at him through those sorrowful huge brown eyes, and he knew there was no way he could not do this. "Let me see what—if anything—I can arrange."

"Thank you." She bit her lip.

Mike frowned. "What else is there?"

"Because of my situation, because of who I am, no one can ever know this conversation took place. That's why I came in the middle of the night. You can understand that, can't you?"

"I understand."

Naunet leaned forward and kissed Mike on the cheek and all the anguish and regret he'd ever felt came rushing back.

"You will always be in my heart." As silently as she had walked in, she walked out.

Mike gently closed the door behind her. He leaned against the door. He shut his eyes and tightened them as much as he could to prevent the tears from rolling down.

FORTY

Current Time

THROUGHOUT THE ENTIRE NARRATIVE, Bronson sat with his knees drawn up and his arms around them. He didn't look at Mike. Instead, he kept his focus on the ground. Often, Mike glanced at him and wondered what was going through Bronson's thoughts.

His *buddy* had betrayed him by not completely believing in him, and now probably Bronson felt the guilt. Good. Let him soak in that guilt.

"Mike!"

Startled, Mike turned his attention to Antonio. "I'm sorry what did you say?"

Antonio rolled his eyes. "I asked you if this mystical Egyptian goddess would be willing to testify on your behalf?"

"You heard the story. I'd rather not get her involved."

The Special Agent folded his arms, shifted positions, and studied Mike through small slits in his eyes. "You obviously agreed to do her the favor, for here you are. But I need to know the rest of the story. What happened after she left?"

"The next day, I approached Chief Kelley and told him that one of my sources had informed me about the huge shipment that was due to arrive in Hobbs and would later work its way to Dallas. I added that bit of detail to make him agree to let me go. To my surprise, the chief didn't question me about my source but he did ask if it was reliable."

Mike nodded several times. "Very reliable. Without a single doubt."

Chief Kelley tapped his fingers on his desk as though considering what to do. "And you want the case?"

As much as he wanted to be shot in the head. He nodded.

"It's yours, then."

The simple statement startled Mike. He thought he would have to beg and plead. Mike got the feeling the chief knew about this shipment before he mentioned it, but seeing that would be almost impossible, he dismissed the idea.

"Will Herbert be willing to work with you on this case?"

"I haven't discussed it with him, but I don't see why not. We always take the cases assigned to us."

The Chief leaned back on his chair. "Let's bring Herbert in."

Once Herbert had joined them at the Chief's office, Chief Kelley turned to Mike and said, "Fill in your partner on the case's details."

Mike did.

When he finished, both Mike and Herbert turned to look at the chief.

The chief leaned forward. "Here's how I see this thing going. Herbert makes arrangements to meet *El Patron*. His story is that *Los Muertos* need his service. After all, he can provide inside police knowledge enabling the gang to move undetected. He would also provide police protection. In return, he wants to be a member of the group. He's tired of the small police check, and this is his opportunity to make his dreams come true. Naturally, *El Patron* is going to be suspicious. So Herbert moves in, giving them a few bits of controlled information. Eventually, *El Patron* will learn to trust him but will probably hold on to a bit of doubt."

"What about me?" Mike asked.

Chief Kelley waved his hand. "That's where you come in. You will erase all doubt from his mind."

Herbert and Mike exchanged glances. "How so?" Mike asked.

"Let me finish," the chief said. "On the day they set up their drop off, you will show up early. They will be expecting Herbert. You will tell them that Herbert plans to double-cross them. To prove it, when he arrives, you murder your partner in cold blood right in front of their eyes."

Mike's eyes widened. He turned to look at Herbert who was staring at him. His eyes were as huge as Mike's.

"Relax." The chief smiled. "It will be a complete Hollywood setup." He pointed to Mike. "You will shoot him using blanks." He pointed to Herbert. "You will take lessons on how to fall realistically and release the bag of fake blood at the precise moment."

"THAT'S HOW I know Herbert is alive. I shot him, yeah, but I used a blank." As Mike spoke he stared at Bronson. "Just as I always said, he's with his Mrs. and his son, enjoying a well-deserved vacation."

"Except that he's not," Antonio said.

Mike cocked his head. "Oh?"

"Detective Dave De La Rosa—or *El Patron*—

whichever way you want to think of him—knew ahead of time what was going to happen."

"That's impossible. Chief Kelley said only us three would know about the plan. 'The less who know, the less chance of something going wrong,' he told me. I agreed."

The FBI agent nodded. "That's as good an excuse as any, but we have reason to believe Chief Rudy Kelley was in on it from the very beginning. That's why he always covered up for De La Rosa."

"The chief crooked?" Mike frowned. "No, that's not possible."

"And yet it is. How else can you account for the fact that De La Rosa knew what was going to happen?"

"What makes you think he knew?" Bronson asked.

"Because he's the one who switched the blanks for real bullets. He told me so himself. That means that you, Mike, really did kill your partner."

Mike staggered a few feet backward and a little grunt escaped him. It was the sound of a man who had lost everything. He dropped his shoulders, his face, ashen and frozen.

Bronson went to him and placed his hands on Mike's shoulders.

A stone-like expression of dread filled Mike's face. He stared at Bronson through vacant eyes. He shrugged Bronson off and ran deeper into the desert.

FORTY-ONE

Bronson followed Mike but did not approach him. He gave him time to digest the information. Once Mike had slowed down, Bronson advanced toward him. "Mike."

Mike's eyes had filled with tears of anguish and anger. "Go away, Bronson. I don't need you." His voice came out rough.

Bronson inched toward Mike. "It was an accident."

"A needless accident. Just before the shooting, I remember staring at the gun as though something wasn't quite right. Then that night, the doubts crept in. I recalled the sound the bullets make when being discharged. It is completely different than those created by fake bullets. I dismissed the doubt as nerves. I should have checked the gun, made sure it was loaded with blanks. God, why didn't I check the gun?"

"Under the circumstances—"

"No matter how you cut it, I killed him." He rubbed his forehead. "Oh my God. How's Adela doing? I should be with her." He attempted a smile that wilted before it bloomed. "She probably hates me."

Bronson wrapped his arms around Mike. For a fraction of a second, Mike leaned in toward Bronson, receiving comfort from the stabbing pain. Seconds later, he pulled away. "Go away, Bronson. You didn't have faith in me, and now I know why. You knew I murdered my partner, and for that, you'll never be able to forgive me."

"I—"

"Go away."

Bronson stared at Mike and knew Mike could see the pain in his eyes.

"Just walk away," Mike said. "Nothing matters anymore." He raked his fingers through his hair. "Nothing." He walked away from Bronson, deeper into the desert.

Bronson headed back toward Antonio.

"He really didn't know, did he?"

Bronson looked up, toward the source of the voice. "No, he didn't."

"Did you?" the Special Agent asked.

Bronson shook his head. "I knew Herbert was dead, but I didn't know the details."

Antonio pointed to a large creosote bush that provided much-needed shade. "Sit over there and wait for us. I'll go get Mike."

Bronson looked toward the direction he had left Mike and then back down at the bush. He nodded and headed toward the bush. He watched as the FBI agent approached Mike. From the look on his face, it looked like he was ordering Mike more than offering a comforting shoulder.

Whatever he said, it worked. Mike and Antonio headed back and Bronson joined them.

"I know I have no reason to ask," Mike told Antonio, "but now, more than ever, I would like to see this thing through. When I flew to meet Naunet to hand her the statues and to meet her daughter, I found out that *El Patron* isn't the one in charge."

"No, he isn't," Antonio said. "This runs a lot deeper. Some higher-ups are involved, but we don't know who.

We just know that this is going to get real ugly real soon. I was hired to infiltrate the gang, but you, Mike, have been doing a better job at doing that."

Mike raised his head and swallowed hard. "I'd like the chance to find the bastard who ordered all of this. After that, I will turn myself in. Right now, all I want is the chance to give Herbert a good reason for giving up his life."

Antonio shrugged. "I can see where you're coming from. If I were in your shoes, I'd want the same thing. But this is beyond me. Mike, you're under arrest, and I have to take you in."

Mike nodded. "What's going to happen, not to me, but to the gang here?"

"I'm pretty sure you took care of that. The Hobbs police will come swarming in. Those who can will get away. But basically, it's over for them. Thanks to you."

"That's not how I imagined this would end."

"You did good and that will speak well at your hearing."

Mike shrugged. "For whatever good that will do. The damage has been done. Herbert is still dead."

"I'll do whatever I can to help you prove your innocence." He paused for a moment. "I don't think there's any reason to use handcuffs. Just don't do anything stupid."

"I'm through with that." Mike folded his arms and lowered his head. He was the picture of a defeated man and Bronson's heart went out to him.

"As for you, Bronson," Antonio said.

Bronson looked up.

"Consider yourself really lucky. Get out of here. You were never here. We will cover for you. In return, you go back home and do not set one foot anywhere near this case. And not one word as to what transpired here today. Understood?"

Bronson nodded but remained still.

"Go," Antonio said. "Now."

Bronson's eyes snapped shut, and his features tightened like a fist. Through clenched teeth, he hissed. "Mike."

Mike turned, giving him his back.

"We need to clear the air between us," Bronson said. "Please, buddy."

Mike walked away.

Bronson lowered his head and headed for the car. Loneliness and sorrow, like the twin sisters of depression, engulfed him.

HARRY BRONSON

FORTY-TWO

It had been eight long days since Bronson had seen Mike. He scanned the newspapers every day to see if there was a mention about Mike's arrest or anything relating to the case. He watched all of the local news. So far, nothing.

Even though he knew better, Bronson gave in to temptation. He called Mike. When the call went to voice mail, he texted him.

He sat in the front swing of his porch, his right hand gripping the cell as he waited for an answer.

His unseeing eyes stared at the street. Cars zoomed by. Neighbors strolled. Children played in their yards. Above him, birds chirped. Someone was barbecuing steaks. Bronson's mind didn't register any of these. Instead, his numbed senses were gripped by a fear such as he'd never known before. His left hand clenched in futility and despair.

A few days ago, he had stared directly at Ellen and told her Mike was okay. He was working undercover and didn't know for how much longer. But in the end, he would be okay.

God, he hoped that was true. He hated lying, especially to Ellen. He wondered if Ellen had seen through the lie.

Bronson stood up. He looked at his phone. No new messages. Had he really been expecting any? He headed indoors and flopped down on the recliner.

What if Mike—

Bronson shook the thought away, took in a deep breath, and slowly let it out. He picked up a magazine. It remained unopened in his lap. He focused on his breathing. That was the key. If he could control his breathing, he could control his thoughts. His doubts. His fears. Was that too much to ask of a single breath? Maybe, but who cares?

Honey jumped up beside him. He patted her, and she rested her head on his lap.

The two remained sitting for what seemed an eternity. During this time, Bronson's breathing had not yet returned to normal, and his mind had not quieted down.

Mike.

Breathe in.

Always Mike.

Breathe out.

He needed to get out of the darkness that Mike had taken him into and step into the light.

Breathe.

Breathe.

Breathe.

"You broke the dog."

Bronson looked up to see Carol staring at him. He opened his mouth to speak, but at first, nothing came out. "W-What?"

"The dog." Carol pointed to Honey. "You drained all of her energy out."

Bronson looked down. Honey had brought him a pull toy so they could play tug of war. She had brought him two balls so they could play catch. She had brought him the worn-out towel so Bronson could hide her toys. She had brought two teddy bears. She had brought the empty water bottle stuffed inside of an old sock so Bronson could take it away from her. When had she done all of that? "I—I—" Bronson cleared his throat. "I didn't break the dog. I can fix it. She likes to play catch, so we'll do that."

"I thought you weren't going to play that anymore because she never brings the ball back and you hate having to go retrieve it."

"I solved that problem. I started giving her a treat each time she brings the ball back. She caught on real fast." Bronson bolted to his feet. "We'll play catch, but I don't want her to get used to the idea that she'll get a treat each time she brings the ball back. So, I'll give her one every other time."

Carol smiled. "Good for you. I like seeing you filled with energy. You've been moping around the house for the last few days. Is it Mike?"

"He'll be fine." He lied and he knew Carol knew he was lying.

She took a step forward. "Honey."

The dog wagged her tail.

Carol rolled her eyes. "The other Honey." Naming a dog Honey had been a horrible mistake. Carol wrapped her arms around her husband. "Seriously, you've got to let this go. He will be fine. He always has and always will. Let it go."

Well, yeah. She was right. He had to let it go. He kissed Carol on the lips. "Thanks for the pep talk."

Honey stood on two legs and attempted to join in the embrace. Both Carol and Bronson laughed. "Yeah, girl, we love you, too." Bronson broke the three way hug and picked up the ball and treats. "Honey and I will be in the backyard."

Carol nodded, a frown on her face.

Out in the yard, Bronson threw the ball. Honey's curly tail wagged and she caught the ball in mid-air. She watched Bronson.

He showed her the treat.

She handed him the ball and ate her treat.

Bronson repeated the process but this time, he didn't give her a treat. Honey looked at him as though she was analyzing him. Still, she handed him the ball.

Five minutes later, Bronson joined Carol in the kitchen. Honey followed close behind.

"How did the lessons go?" Carol asked.

Bronson shrugged. "They didn't."

"What happened?"

"Like before, she figured out the pattern. She knew she'd get the treat only every other time. So she wouldn't give me the ball unless I gave her the treat first."

"And you gave in."

Bronson lowered his head. "I gave in."

Carol laughed. "Who is training who?"

"What can I say?" Bronson shrugged. "She's a smart dog." His phone buzzed, and he looked at the message. A breath of air escaped his mouth.

"Harry?" Carol reached out for her husband.

Despite his efforts, Bronson found himself back in the dark place.

Breathe.

Carol's forehead wrinkled. "Honey, what's wrong?"

The dog wagged her tail and jumped up on Carol. She ignored her.

Carol squeezed her husband's arm. "Is everything okay?"

"Mike texted me." He walked away.

FORTY-THREE

The single word text read Come.
Where? Bronson texted back.

Meet me in Round Rock, at the rock itself.

Bronson was familiar with the place. When?

Tomorrow @ 3.

Will be there. You ok?

A breathless moment passed before Mike texted back. Bring Alex.
Bronson bolted toward the bedroom and began to pack.
Early the next day, he and Honey were on the road, heading from Dallas to Round Rock.

Bronson glanced at his watch. He had already reached the Round Rock city limits sign, and it wasn't even 2:30. Maybe he should stop at McDonald's and get himself a cup of Ice French Vanilla Coffee and a plain hamburger for Honey.

He saw the approaching McDonald's sign. The thought of coffee turned his stomach. He couldn't drink anything now. Not until he settled things with Mike.

Amazing. There would be no coffee for him and no hamburger for Honey. "Sorry, girl."

Honey whined and buried her head in her paws.

Bronson turned on Chisholm Trail Street and soon found himself in the middle of Brushy Creek. He parked the car and spotted a three-foot-tall rock wall fence under the shade of some trees. The wall was thick enough to provide a nice sitting place.

If he sat there to wait for Mike, he had a clear view of the large round rock located in the middle of the creek, the same rock that gave the city its name. He glanced down at the rock. Wagon wheel ruts were embedded in the exposed rock. Hundreds of wagon trains had crossed the river there because, at one time, this had been the lowest part of the creek.

Bronson sat on the fence, and Honey rested by him as though keeping watch.

Bronson retrieved his cell. Maybe Mike had texted him.

He hadn't.

Bronson returned the phone to his pocket and saw Mike approach. He stopped in front of him.

"Bronson."

"Mike."

Honey stood up and studied Mike.

"What's with the dog?"

Bronson swallowed a smile. Prior to all of this mess beginning, Bronson had told Mike he had found a new Honey. Mike had assumed Bronson was planning to replace Carol. Bronson fed that belief and never explained that Honey was a dog. "I want you to meet Honey, our new dog."

Honey wagged her tail and approached Mike.

Mike squatted and patted her. "A dog?" His eyes widened. "Honey? Really, Bronson?"

Bronson shrugged. "What can I say?"

Mike took in a deep breath. "A dog. That's good. It's one less thing I have to worry about." He smiled. "A dog. I should have known."

Honey licked Mike's face.

Mike stood up. "You actually brought the dog to work this case?"

Bronson briefly told him how he had met Honey and how she had saved his life several times. He was sure, although he had no way of proving it, that she was a trained police dog.

"We'll see how she works out." Mike sat down beside Bronson. They sat in silence, staring at the creek.

"Talk to me," Bronson said. He reached out and patted Honey.

"Apparently Antonio pulled some strings, and I remained on the case, on the condition that when this is over, I turn myself in."

"I'm glad to hear that, about you stayin' undercover. I know that's what you wanted." Bronson retrieved a Milk Bone from his pocket and gave it to Honey. "So how's the case goin'?"

"During these past few days, I've made some real progress. I am now *El Patron*."

"Congratulations."

Mike shrugged. "It's no biggie. Now that we've moved our headquarters from Hobbs to Austin, I'm actually low-man on the totem pole. There's nothing left in Hobbs. The police made a clean swipe."

"So where does that leave you?"

"I've got to prove myself all over again, and that's where you come in."

Bronson cocked his head. "Oh?"

"I told them about Alex Bentley. They're eager to meet the man who will bring them the El Dorado treasure."

"I can tell them the story, but I can't produce a single artifact that will back me up."

Mike stretched out his legs. "Antonio has taken care of that. The first thing he did was give you your own website."

"My own website?" Bronson cocked his head. "I have a website? I love bein' famous."

"Don't get your head all swollen. The website is not exactly yours. It's Alex Bentley's."

"And there goes my claim to fame."

"Yep, we cops are at the bottom of the totem pole. But this Alex Bentley, he is quite the adventurer. You should check out all of the pictures of you and the vast number of treasures you've recovered."

"What can I say? All in a day's work." Bronson puffed up like a peacock. "Gotta love that Alex. Quite the guy. Hope all the pictures of me are complimentary."

"Only you can be the judge of that."

"Yep." Bronson stared at the peaceful creek and tried to imagine what this place looked like when all those wagons made their journey through here. "I've got to memorize that website. Just in case."

"Not a bad idea."

"I hate homework." Bronson saw a car pull into the parking lot. The driver remained in the car.

Mike shrugged. "Sometimes you can't live without homework."

"What else have you got?" Bronson kept his eyes glued on the car.

Mike followed Bronson's line of sight. "We have, on loan, a gold medallion."

Bronson let out a whistle. "How did Antonio manage that?"

"He apparently has very good connections."

"You think?" The car door opened and a man stepped out. Bronson immediately recognized him. "What arrangements did you make with Antonio?"

"I told him we were meeting. He said he'd be here." Mike pointed to the man heading toward them from the parking lot. "In fact, there he is now."

Bronson stood and offered him his hand. "Special Agent Corbalan. I didn't think I'd see you again."

The agent accepted Bronson's hand. "You can drop the special agent crap. Call me Antonio."

"Antonio, call me Bronson."

Antonio ignored Bronson's comment and instead said, "I have something to say, and I want you to listen carefully because I'm only going to say this once."

"I'm listenin'." Bronson sat back down and Antonio sat next to him.

"I don't know how much Mike has filled you in, so I'll just hit the highlights. In order to infiltrate and eliminate these powerful figureheads, we had to revive Alex Bentley. The men here in Austin have never seen you, so I considered several of my colleagues for the job. Many were eager to do it, but Mike said it was you or nobody."

Bronson glanced at Mike. He cocked his eyebrows.

Antonio continued. "We argued long and hard until I finally agreed. Getting you approved for the job took some doing. But in the end, I won. Of course, it helps that the mayor owes me favors, and we've developed a deep friendship. The mayor pulled some strings, and here you are."

"I appreciate all of the trouble you went through to approve me."

"Don't thank me. Thank your ex-partner. I was dead set against it, and I still am. I'm telling you this because I know you're—what should I say?—an individual thinker. You like to do things your way. Not this time. Everything you do goes through me first. Is that understood?"

"Yes, sir." Bronson considered saluting him but decided against it.

"Good. I'm glad we see eye-to-eye on this." He stood up. "As of this moment, consider yourself a special member of the FBI. As such, you will uphold the high standards we maintain."

An FBI agent. Cool. "Does this mean I'll be getting an FBI badge?"

Antonio's eyes narrowed and he shook his head. "Don't push it." He looked at Mike. "I'm holding you personally responsible for this man's actions."

"We'll do well by you."

"You better." He turned and walked away.

"He's a very pleasant man," Bronson said once Antonio was out of hearing range.

"He'll grow on you."

"So you requested me." A statement, not a question.

Mike shrugged. "What can I say? I'm already a doomed man."

"Don't worry. We'll get this worked out, and you'll come out smellin' like roses."

"Ellen and Carol can smell like roses. I don't particularly want to."

Bronson smiled. "So what's the plan?"

"We're supposed to find out who's the brain in the organization and bring them all down. Then, as a reward, I get to turn myself in. After that, who knows?"

Bronson frowned. "I'll be there for you, buddy."

"Yeah. Sure thing." Mike looked away from Bronson.

Honey returned to her spot beside Bronson. She sat down and laid her head on his lap. Bronson rubbed the area behind her ear. "I guess I should go memorize that website."

Mike stood up. "I guess you should. We have a meeting, tonight, at seven. I'll pick you up at 6:30."

"I don't know where I'm stayin'."

"I do. You're staying at the Four Seasons Hotel. Courtesy of Uncle Sam. Nothing but the best for Alex." Mike retrieved the car keys from his pocket.

Bronson's eyes widened at the mention of the hotel. "And you? Where are you stayin'?"

Mike shrugged. "I'm sure Austin has a lot of Choice Motels."

"I'm sure they do, but you're welcome to stay with me." Honey nudged Bronson. "With us. Think about it. We never get the royalty treatment. Might as well take advantage of it."

Honey walked over to Mike, sat in front of him, and raised her paw.

Mike stared at the dog. "Am I supposed to shake her hand?"

Honey lowered her paw.

"I guess not." He switched his attention to Bronson. "As for your invitation, sure. Why not?"

Bronson smiled. "But just remember that I'm FBI now, and you're still just a cop."

Mike rolled his eyes.

FORTY-FOUR

Bronson and Mike ordered an early dinner delivered to their hotel room. Much to Bronson's surprise and delight working once again with Mike felt like old times. The strain had vanished. It was two friends—two brothers—enjoying their man time together.

A bit past six, they were ready and headed for their meeting. On the way, Mike drilled Bronson with questions he assumed the group would ask. Bronson answered everything like a champ. "You're ready for this. How do you feel?" Mike asked.

"Like a high school kid who over-prepared for a test."

Mike smiled and eased off the gas. "That's always good." He slowed down. "This is it." Mike turned into a long, driveway that snaked through rows of trees. To Bronson, it seemed they would never reach the house.

Minutes later, Bronson stared at the biggest mansion he'd ever seen. It loomed before him, stretching somewhere between 100 to 150 feet and stood three stories high. Lights gracefully streamed from various angles and directions, competing with the full moon for attention. "Quite the house," Bronson said.

"If you think this is breathtaking, wait until you see the inside." Mike smirked. "Whoever said crime doesn't pay doesn't know what he's talking about." He pointed to the dog. "What are you going to do about Honey?"

"I'll let her out and tell her to stay. She'll be here when we return." Bronson patted Honey's head.

Mike frowned. "Are you sure? We can leave her inside the car with the windows partially rolled down."

"That won't be necessary. She'd prefer to stay outside."

"In that case, do your thing, and don't forget to grab your backpack."

Bronson reached into the backseat and retrieved the bag. He carried it instead of placing it on his back. He looked at Honey, spread his right hand, and slightly moved it up and down. "Stay." Bronson walked away. The dog whined but obeyed the command. "Back soon," Bronson said and turned to Mike. "Ready."

"In that case, let's ring that doorbell, and let's get this thing started."

A petite woman in her early twenties opened the door. The smile she flashed resembled that of a homecoming queen's. "Mr. Hoover. It's so nice to see you again." She stepped aside to allow them to enter. "You must be Mr. Bentley." Her one-hundred-kilowatt smile spread from ear to ear.

Bronson smiled back and stepped into the foyer covered with black-and-white tiles. The chandelier overhead sprouted thousands of crystal drops that illuminated the shiny floor giving it a mirror-like effect. "I am."

"Andrew—um, Mr. Beauregard and company are eager to meet you." She led them down an elegant hallway that displayed art pieces that put the best art museum to shame. "We are meeting in the sitting room."

She opened a pair of light brown oak doors revealing a large room with high ceilings. A maid stood just inside the wide doorway. Two men sat on a luxurious couch. Another man sat on an upholstered couch which faced the other one. He bolted to his feet, stepped between matching antique Georgian tables, and offered a welcoming grin. "Mike, thanks for coming."

Through his years in the police force, Bronson had learned that stereotypes belonged only in novels and on the screen. Traditionally, the man standing before him should have been a middle-aged cowboy displaying well-formed muscles. Instead, he was greeted by a youth who couldn't be more than what? Sixteen—seventeen?

The young leader focused his attention on Bronson. Who knows? Maybe Bronson didn't match his expectations either. Maybe he had been expecting Indiana Jones.

"You must be Alex Bentley. I am Andrew Beauregard." He offered Bronson his hand.

Bronson accepted the firm handshake. Nothing about this boy/man spoke of weakness. Bronson moved his age up to the early twenties.

"Can I get you anything to drink?" Bronson noticed the boy/man held a half-drunk Mojito.

"Coffee, please. With lots of sugar and milk."

Andrew's eyebrows shot up. "Coffee? Really? A man like you, I would have thought your preference would be hard liquor." He set his drink down.

"You pegged me right, but I make it a point never to drink while I'm workin'."

Andrew clasped his hands together and shook them. "Very good, Mr. Bentley. I like that. Coffee it is." He turned to Mike. "What about you, Mike?"

"I'll follow his example, except make mine lemonade or tea."

Andrew looked at the middle-aged woman who stood by the door. "You heard them, and bring me some tea, too."

"Yes, sir." She bowed her head and let herself out.

Andrew pointed to the couch. "Please make yourselves comfortable."

Bronson set the backpack by his feet and sat down. Mike sat next to him.

As soon as they settled, Andrew began speaking. "Let's begin with introductions." He pointed to the young woman. "You met Linda, my fiancé. She's not only beautiful, she's also gifted. She's my accountant, and as such, I invited her to the meeting."

She glided over to Andrew, and he wrapped his arm around her.

Next, he pointed to a slightly overweight middle-aged man sitting on the right-hand side of the couch. "That is Eric Stapleton, my second-hand man. I never make any decisions without his approval."

"Good to know," Bronson said and nodded a hello.

"Next to him is Larry Web."

Finally, Bronson thought. A man who fits the description of a true Texan from his cowboy hat right down to his pointed boots. And, oh yeah, the huge buckle.

Andrew continued, "He's in charge of making all of the arrangements, so I thought he should be included in the conversation."

Bronson and Larry exchanged hellos.

"There's one more," Andrew said. "But Nick is a flake. I don't know if he'll show up although he knows he's supposed to." He sat down and Linda sat next to him, leaving enough space between them to let everyone in the room know this was a business meeting, but still close enough to claim him as hers.

Once everyone settled in, Andrew said, "With that, I'll turn the floor over to Mr. Bentley. Tell us exactly what you have and what you expect from us."

A knock on the door interrupted them.

"That must be Nick." Andrew raised his voice. "Enter."

It wasn't Nick. It was a maid—a different one this time—bringing in the drinks and a tray filled with cookies and what looked to be scones. From a silver kettle, she poured two cups of tea and offered one to Andrew then to Mike. "Is the tea all right, sir? Do you want milk or sugar?"

Mike sipped his and made a pleasing face. "This is perfectly fine."

Andrew waved her off.

She handed Bronson his coffee. "You, sir? Is it all right?"

Bronson sipped the coffee. "It's more than all right. I'll probably want seconds later on."

"Yes, sir." She took a small bow. "As you wish." She backed out of the room and didn't give them her back until it was time to open the door.

When the door closed, Andrew began speaking, "I've been to your website. It's very impressive. What else can you tell me?"

Bronson set his cup down. "Not much. I'm a man of few words."

Eric leaned forward, rubbed his belly as though it ached, and smiled. "Action. You're strictly a man of action."

"You could say that."

Andrew reached for a cookie, broke it in half, and

ate it. "In that case, let's cut to the core. You claim you found the El Dorado treasure—a treasure that has eluded thousands of treasure seekers. Why were you so lucky?"

Bronson opened his hands and spread out his arms. "Simple. I took my time studying the legends, then the facts. They led to a completely different area that others ignored."

"But you knew where to look." A statement, not a question.

"Exactly."

"Care to expand on that?" Andrew sipped his tea but did not remove his sight from Bronson.

"The fools continue to search for a city so rich that its streets are paved with gold. They search the mines. They search the caves for signs of the buried treasure."

Eric leaned forward and smirked. "And where did you search?"

"I searched the lake. Specifically, Lake Guatavita." He told them about the Muisca people who lived in Central Colombia from AD 800 to modern-day. Bronson spoke of their king and how he offered the lake gold, emeralds, and other precious objects. He told them about the three villagers finding a gold raft in a small cave in the hills just to the south of Bogota thus authenticating the story. "It took me three long years to work the area until one day I was successful."

Eric clapped. "Bravo, Mr. Bentley. That was a fascinating story." He reached for his Bloody Mary and took a large gulp. "But I see a huge hole in your story." His eyes narrowed and pierced Bronson's face.

FORTY-FIVE

Bronson took his time sipping his coffee. He was a man in no hurry. He had nothing to worry about. "And what hole are you talkin' about?"

"Surely the Columbians knew you were digging around, searching for their treasure. They certainly don't plan to let you keep it. So how can you sit here and tell us otherwise?"

Bronson raised his cup in a salute. "Ah, very good question. Of course the Columbian government knows that I've recovered their treasure, and they are at this very moment digging it up and gettin' it ready to display in their museums." He lowered his cup. "And that's precisely why we have to move fast on this."

Andrew leaned forward. "That didn't answer the question. How can you get the treasure out without the Columbian's approval?"

"What none of you understand is the vast number of gold, silver, and precious stones that I've unearthed. With the help of a few trusted men, we dug and hid the best of the treasures. Even as we speak, my men are continuing to do that. After that initial find, we did our civic duty and notified the authorities."

Andrew nodded. "And the hidden ones, those are the ones you want us to help you bring here?"

"Exactly."

"Another thing that bothers me." Eric picked up his

Bloody Mary and took a sip. "Why has this not been on the news? This is huge. It should be the headline news in every major channel. Yet, not a peep."

Bronson leaned forward. "You apparently don't understand how Columbia works. The government, the people, let's just say each wants their own take. So the archeologists are keepin' the level at low sight. They work, they dig, they get their displays ready for their museums. They are workin' as fast as they can before word leaks out." Bronson reached for his coffee and slowly drained it. "I'm in the same boat. I want to get everythin' out before the area is inundated with TV cameras and reporters, and worse, government officials."

Andrew and Eric exchanged looks.

Eric rubbed his forehead as though digesting all the information into neat compartments. "These treasures that you have, how much are they worth?" He shrugged. "A million? Maybe two?"

"Try. More. Like. Five-hundred. Million." Bronson leaned back and the room filled with silence.

Eric grabbed his Bloody Mary and emptied the glass. "Can you prove any of this?"

Bronson shot to his feet. "I can, but if you're so filled with doubt, perhaps Andrew is not the man I'm lookin' for. Thank you for your time." He grabbed his backpack and began to walk out.

Andrew bolted out of the couch. "Mr. Bentley, please wait."

Bronson stopped but did not turn around.

"You've got to understand that we need to be careful. We have to thoroughly research everything before we give our approval. Eric here was just doing that. No offense."

Bronson turned. "Fair enough." He sat back down. "My coffee cup is empty."

Andrew pressed the intercom button. "We need more coffee. ASAP."

"Right away, sir," came the voice over the intercom.

Larry stroked the brim of his cowboy hat. "Could you tell us what plans you have? How can we help you get the goods over here?"

"I'm assumin' you have connections." Bronson leaned back and relaxed.

"What kind of connections are you looking for?" Larry asked.

"Whatever it takes. That's not my department. I need you to arrange for an airplane to land in Bogota. We will load the plane and fly it back here."

"That will take some time to arrange." Larry reached for a scone and bit into it.

"That's not good enough." Bronson hoped his firm tone left no doubts in everyone's minds. He was a man in a hurry.

"What I meant to say," Larry quickly corrected himself, "is that I'm sure it will be done." Larry pointed at Andrew. "Our host, as you know, is very well connected. His best friend is Thomas Morris, our senator's only son."

Andrew cleared his throat and Larry hushed.

Eric immediately picked up the void. "Before we make any arrangements, can I ask what kind of merchandise we're talking about?"

Bronson bent down, picked up the backpack, and opened it. He carefully unwrapped the gold medallion that Antonio had loaned him. He handed it to Andrew.

Andrew whistled as he admired its beauty. "I would

like to keep this so I can authenticate its origin. Can I do that?"

"I rather not," Bronson said. "You've got to understand. It's very valuable, and I'm not lettin' it out of my sight. However, whenever you're ready to authenticate it, let me know where and when and I'll be there."

A knock at the door interrupted them. Bronson assumed it was the maid bringing his second cup of coffee. Instead, a lanky cowboy in his early twenties with a big Adam's apple stepped in. The big, bushy Texas mustache straight out of a nineteenth-century painting made him look somewhat comical. "Sorry I'm late. What did I miss?" His mustache bopped as he spoke.

Andrew walked over to him and signaled for Linda to join him. "Nick. So nice of you to join us."

Ah, Nick. The flake. He definitely looked the part.

"Linda and I were just about to leave. Dad—huh, Senator Morris—" He stopped when he saw his guests' stunned faces.

"He's not my real dad. I have a dad. Sort of. Hardly ever see him or know him. The senator felt sorry for me, so he adopted me." He put air quotes around the word *adopted*. He cleared his throat. "What I was trying to say is that he's giving one of his fund-raiser parties. It's rude to be late." He turned to Bronson. "Mr. Bentley, please fill Nick in on what was discussed. We will meet again tomorrow to finalize the details." He looked at Mike. "Nice seeing you as always." Hand-in-hand, Andrew and Linda made their exit.

Eric shifted his weight and wiggled out of the chair. "I need to go, too. But Larry will be here."

Great. Bronson and Mike would be left with the two cowboys.

Eric shook hands with Bronson and Mike and departed.

As soon as the door closed, Larry began speaking. "You know, Senator Morris considers Andrew to be as much of a son as his own kid."

"Interestin'," Bronson said. "That's not goin' to create a problem."

"No, of course, not. The senator is oblivious about Andrew's going-ons."

"I agree with Larry," Mike said. "I've been working with Andrew on and off for a while. He's very careful to keep this part away from the senator's attention. In fact, I wasn't even aware there was a connection. I know Andrew would never jeopardize the senator's chance of becoming our future president."

As Bronson and Larry chatted, Bushy Texas Mustache stared at Bronson and the air shifted. Or maybe Bronson was reading something out of nothing. Nick's eyes widened as though remembering something. Then they went dark. A dull, black glass as if there was no life in them.

Bronson blinked and the moment passed.

Nick flopped down on the couch and stroked his mustache as he continued to study Bronson.

The tension in the room could be cut with scissors. Something had changed and Bronson wasn't sure what it was.

"Mr. Bentley, do you want me to summarize our meeting, or do you?" Larry asked.

Nick moved his lips forward and back as though trying to figure out what to say. "If you excuse me for a minute, I have an important call to make." He walked out.

Bronson busied himself returning the medallion back

to the backpack. When he finished, he looked at Mike. "Ready?"

Mike nodded.

Both stood up to leave.

The door opened and Nick stepped in. "Leaving already? Surely, you're not in a rush. I know about the treasure we're supposed to help you bring in, and I've been busy making arrangements. In fact, that's why I was late."

Both Mike and Bronson remained quiet. Neither headed to the door.

"Please, I'm eager to show you what I've done," the mustache Texan said. "Mr. Bentley, you must follow me." He turned to look at Mike. "You don't mind if I steal Mr. Bentley for a moment, do you? You and Larry can work out the details while we're gone. We won't be long."

"Where are you going?" Mike asked.

"Just to the backyard. Behind this mansion is the guest house. That's where I'm staying. I want to show Mr. Bentley the details I've been working on."

Bronson cleared his throat. "Mike works with me. If you have somethin' to say, you can say it in front of him."

"There's no doubt in my mind that's true. But what I have to show you is very sensitive. If you approve my plan, I'll call Mike to join us." As he spoke, his eyes went darker.

Bronson shifted, buying time.

Nick forced a smile and his mustache bounced up and down. "It really won't take long. Please do me the honors."

Bronson nodded and Mike sat back down.

Bronson handed Mike the backpack before joining Funny Mustache.

Nick led Bronson down a series of hallways that weaved their way outdoors. Through the floor-to-ceiling windows, Bronson could see the guest house that rivaled the best house in any fancy neighborhood. A bricked walkway led to the guest mini-mansion. "Quite the house," Bronson said.

"Oh, yes. Andrew doesn't cut corners when it comes to taking care of us."

"I can see that." Flowers accented both sides of the path. Once they reached the front of the house, Nick said, "We use the side entrance. It's more convenient."

Bronson followed him around the corner to a sliding door entrance.

Nick stepped back and remained behind Bronson. "Go on in. It's open. I'm sure you'll find it quite comfortable, Mr....Bentley. Or should I say, Mr....Bronson?"

Bronson froze.

FORTY-SIX

Nick shoved Bronson's back.

Bronson gasped. Even though he felt as if the blow had come from a chunk of granite, he did his best to maintain his balance. The edge of the couch in front of him prevented the fall. He staggered and used the following mini-seconds to access the situation as best as he could. A giant stood by the open sliding door and another man, although smaller than the giant, would make any bouncer proud. This man with short-cropped hair and beady eyes stood on the other side of the couch, and worse, he held a gun pointed at Bronson. Nick lurked somewhere behind him.

Bronson prayed Nick remained far enough behind so as not to interfere with his plan. In one quick stride, Bronson closed the distance between him and the bouncer.

Before the beady-eyed man could shoot, Bronson trapped his attacker's wrist with both hands. That forced the stainless pistol to fall against his belly. Using the full force of his legs, Bronson lunged forward, snapping the wrist and causing the bouncer to drop the weapon. At the same time, Bronson met him with a fierce head butt that sent a spray of blood spewing out of the newly formed gap where the bouncer's nose met his brow. The pain forced him to his knees.

The giant wasted no time in coming to his friend's

aid. He hit Bronson in the side of the head with a staggering left hook. Bronson fought off nausea and forced himself to remain standing. He threw a quick elbow to fend off his attacker's oncoming powerful blow.

Roaring like an enraged bear, Bronson pivoted and drove forward, shoving his opponent backward. He pummeled the giant's midsection with all his might. The giant absorbed Bronson's punches as though they were nothing more than annoying mosquito bites.

Nick, on his hands and knees, located the discarded pistol.

To his right, the bouncer regained enough strength to stand. His features twisted and his eyes narrowed. He became a charging bull. At first, he staggered toward Bronson, but with each step he took, he regained strength and speed.

Bronson continued to dodge the giant's punches and even managed to land a couple of his own. But no matter how hard he tried, it seemed he was swatting mosquitoes in a jungle infested with them. No matter what he did, the punches kept coming.

From the corner of his eye, Bronson saw Nick raise the pistol. An evil-looking grin spread across his face as he cocked the weapon and pointed it at Bronson.

The bouncer continued his charge. Bronson braced himself, grabbed him, and drew him toward Nick.

The bullet intended to kill Bronson instead met its mark in the bouncer's heart.

Nick's eyes widened and his lips quivered, but he didn't hesitate. He raised the gun, steadying his shaking hand. He aimed for Bronson's head.

Snarling and growling, Honey dashed past the open sliding door and threw her weight against Nick. For a fraction of a second, Nick hesitated before moving the aim from Bronson to the attacking dog.

But that second had cost him. Honey landed on his chest throwing her full weight against him. A loud *thunk* resonated as Nick's head hit the edge of the glass table shattering it to pieces. The marble-and-onyx sculpture that had graced the coffee table catapulted through the air. As Nick tumbled backward, he fired a bullet into the air.

Honey launched herself toward the giant. He raised his leg to kick the attacking dog. Bronson grabbed the raised leg and twisted it. The giant screamed as he tumbled backward. He did not get up.

Bronson patted Honey's head as he regained his balance and fought for air. He was too old for this. "Thanks, gal. You did good. You're a good dog."

Honey's tail wagged.

From behind him, Bronson heard a voice. "What the hell happened here?"

Bronson pivoted to stare into Larry's narrow eyes. But it wasn't the eyes he focused on.

All he could see was the gun pointed at him.

FORTY-SEVEN

BRONSON RAISED HIS ARMS.

Honey growled.

"If you don't want that dog dead, you better control it."

"Settle." Bronson tapped the side of his leg. Honey sat quietly by Bronson's side but kept an alert eye on the man threatening her master.

"Care to explain what happened?" Larry asked.

Bronson straightened his shirt and stared at Larry. "I'm not too sure. Texas Mustache brought me here and—"

"Texas Mustache?" Larry's eyes widened in recognition. "Oh, you mean Nick."

"Yes, Nick," Bronson corrected himself. "He led me here, and then these two duds were waiting for us. I think Nick planned it all."

Larry squinted as though attempting to piece the puzzle together. "He planned what?"

"On the way over here, Nick tried to talk to me about givin' them my business. Andrew could easily be eliminated, he said."

Larry's features hardened. "What did you tell him?"

"I said Andrew had been the one who had been recommended. It'd be best if you all talked it over. Then all hell broke loose. One wanted to take over the deal. The other one said he was the ring leader. Angry words were used and soon after that, weapons appeared. I ducked and the three of them fought it out." Bronson cleared his throat and flopped down on the couch. He didn't know how long it would be before Nick or one of his men woke up. Bronson wanted to be gone by then.

Mike popped in. His eyes were huge and his skin was aflame as if he wasn't getting enough oxygen.

Larry lowered the gun. "You! I thought I told you to stay in the living room."

Mike shrugged. "I must have missed that part."

"Where's Wally?"

"Wally? The guy you left to guard me? Let's just say that he met with a small accident, but he'll be fine when he wakes up."

Larry smirked. "I should have known."

"Did you expect anythin' else?" Bronson stood, his eyes telling Mike it was time to get out and get out fast. "He is a trained police officer."

Larry's head bopped once, as though acknowledging and dismissing Bronson's comment all at one time. "Back to business." He stared at Bronson. "You say Nick wanted to take over Andrew's business, and these two clowns are part of his team?"

"Looks that way to me."

"Are they dead?"

"Don't know." Bronson massaged his temple. "They roughed me up a bit, so I hid. They fought."

With stoop-shoulders, Larry trudged to where Nick lay. "As long as Andrew is my boss, nobody betrays us." He raised the gun and pulled the trigger. "Nobody."

Bronson bit his lip, hoping he looked scared instead of shocked.

Larry headed for the bouncer's body and even though he looked dead, Larry still shot him. He did the same to the giant. "That solves that problem." Larry put the gun down and faced Bronson. "Do we still have a deal?"

"Yeah." Bronson was quick to answer. "I definitely plan to use Andrew's services."

"Good. Let's keep it that way."

Bronson straightened up. "Mike and I—we better get goin'. Looks like you have other business to tend to tonight. Maybe tomorrow, we can work out the details."

Larry nodded. "Yes, definitely tomorrow."

Bronson and Mike headed out the door, but Larry blocked their way. "About tonight, what just happened…"

"I didn't see a thing. Don't know what you're talkin' about." Bronson looked at Mike. "And you?"

Mike shook his head. "Did something happen? I was over there." He pointed to the main house. "Our lips are sealed."

Larry stepped aside. "Good. Make sure it stays that way."

FORTY-EIGHT

THE EVENING SUN had dipped down to kiss the horizon, turning the valley mauve. The sky shined with shades of bright reds mixed with streaks of orange, fading yellows, and deep blues. Under normal circumstances, Bronson would have admired the sunset. But for now, all he wanted was to get far away from the mansion. He inwardly said a small thank you as Mike left the long, winding driveway and merged onto the two-lane road which led to the main highway heading back to Austin.

Once they had made that first turn, Mike accelerated. "Do you want to tell me what happened?"

Bronson told him.

Mike listened quietly. He stopped at the stop sign and turned left, merging with the heavy traffic heading to Austin. "Continue."

Bronson did.

As Mike listened, he glanced at the rearview mirror. "That's one heck of a dog you have there. You said she's got police training?"

"The previous owner, now dead, was a hermit. There's no way to know, but I'm pretty sure she must have."

Mike's glance once again drifted to the rearview mirror. "You lucked out."

"In more ways than one."

Mike slowed down as he approached the red traffic light. They had reached the city limits. "Meaning?"

"One, Honey saved me, and two, Nick made me but failed to tell Larry. I have no idea how he figured it out, but I'm sure if he had told him about his suspicions, we'd both be dead now."

"True. Maybe even Honey too." Mike readjusted the rearview mirror.

Honey barked.

Mike's sight drifted her way. "I thought you said she was a Basenji, and Basenjis don't bark."

"She skipped that chapter in the Basenji instruction book."

Mike shook his head and half-smiled.

"Maybe she's not a full-blooded Basenji," Bronson said. "All I know is that she seldom barks."

Mike remained quiet as he focused on the rearview mirror.

Bronson looked out the side mirror. A pair of headlights glowed behind them. "Do you think we're bein' followed?"

"We'll find out in just a second." He made a right turn and drove around the block. The car followed at a discreet distance. "Looks like we have a tail. What do you think we should do about it?"

Bronson's site remained glued to the car. As it went under the street light, Bronson caught a glimpse of it. To Bronson's right, he saw a sign for a liquor store. "Pull in there."

Mike slowed down. "What? Why?"

"Whoever is driving behind us has a fancy car. A red Porsche, I believe."

"Yeah, so?"

"Chances are it's one of Andrew's men. That bein' the case, we don't want them to think we're suspicious of anythin'. If we stop at the liquor store and buy a bottle, they'll think we had meant to do that all along. They won't know we spotted them. Let them follow us to the motel. We can deal with them there if necessary."

"Makes sense to me." Mike turned into the small parking lot. "I'll stay in the car and watch them. You go in and make the purchase."

"What do you want me to get?"

Mike shrugged. "Couldn't care less."

Bronson nodded. Behind them, the Porsche parked across the street and turned off its lights. Bronson stepped out of the car and without looking back headed inside. He purchased two beers and returned to the car.

Mike opened the package. "Two beers. I thought for sure one would be a cup of coffee."

"Very funny." Bronson climbed into the passenger seat but not before checking on the Porsche. "They're still there."

"Yep." Mike pulled out of the parking lot and headed directly to the hotel.

The Porsche pulled in behind him.

"Now what?" Mike asked Bronson once they had stepped inside their hotel room.

"Now we take Honey and our beers and sit outside on those benches I saw in the entryway and drink our beers."

"That's a good way to unwind." Mike grabbed the beers. "But knowing you, this has nothing to do with unwinding. What's going on?"

"If I'm readin' this right, the Porsche guys were sent to toss our room. They want to make sure we are who we say we are, and if we are, we have no plans to betray them. That means they're getting suspicious. If we're goin' to pull this through, we'd better hurry. We're runnin' out of time."

FORTY-NINE

THE SOFT SWISH of the wind brought on a cool breeze that chilled both Bronson and Mike, but still, they sat sipping their beers. The last thing they wanted was to head back to their room and catch the men snooping through their belongings.

Honey had rolled herself into a ball and rested by Bronson's feet. "Smart dog," Bronson said. "At least she's warm."

"Wish we could do the same. Or maybe the wind could stop blowing." Mike rubbed his arms.

"Me, too, buddy. Me too." Bronson wished he had thought to bring a light jacket.

"We need something that is going to set the ball rolling," Mike said.

"How about we tell Andrew that I got a call from one of my men back in Columbia? He told me the Columbian government is moving extra fast, and if we want to get any of those treasures out of Columbia, we need to do it like yesterday."

Mike set his beer down and nodded. "That should ignite a fire under them. Soon as the deal goes down, we, along with Antonio's help, will arrest them all, and this thing will finally be over." He picked up his beer and took a long gulp. "At least this part will end. The hard part—facing Adela and everyone else…" His voice faded as he drew a deep breath.

Bronson patted Mike's shoulder. They both knew what lay ahead. The best thing was to change the subject. Bronson took a swig of beer and wished it was coffee instead. At least that would be warmer. "It's settled, then. First thing tomorrow mornin', we'll make the call."

"Do you think it's safe to return to the room now?"

Bronson glanced at his watch. Almost an hour had passed. "Yeah, but you realize the room might not be safe anymore."

Mike set his beer down and frowned. "What are you talking about?" His forehead furrowed as though he were thinking. "I get it. You're thinking they probably planted a bug, aren't you? Do you think they'll really do that?"

"I would if I were them."

"I agree. Let's sit here a bit longer while I report to Special Agent Antonio. I need to catch him up."

Bronson leaned back on the seat and reached for the beer.

BRONSON EXPECTED TO find a mess in the room: drawers emptied, bed covers pulled down to the floor, suitcases emptied and its contents scattered all over the floor. Instead, he and Mike walked into a room that was just as they had left it.

Bronson glanced at the top dresser drawer. It was open a fraction of an inch. He switched his sight from the dresser to Mike who was staring at him. "Dang! I must have left my phone downstairs. I'm goin' to get it. Want to tag along?" Bronson showed him that he had his cell.

"Yeah, sure. I can use the walk." Once out in the hallway, Mike said, "Were we wrong? Do you think they actually came?"

Bronson nodded. "They were here all right."

"What makes you so sure?"

"I left the top dresser drawer opened exactly one inch. It's still open, but not the entire inch."

Mike nodded. "Smart move."

"On my behalf or theirs?"

"Both, I guess. You for thinking of that, and they for leaving everything just as they found it—including a partially open drawer."

They reached the elevators. The opposite wall had a door that led to the stairs. "Which do we use?"

Mike pointed to the stairs. "We need the exercise."

"I was afraid you'd say that."

Mike shrugged. "Just thinking about our health." He opened the door and started down the stairs.

Bronson followed. "Do you realize what this means?"

"That we're dealing with a bunch of smart outlaws?"

"Yeah. Normally, we deal with morons, the bottom of the barrel. Andrew's men are well educated. That presents some new problems. We've got to make sure we always keep one step ahead of them."

Mike stopped halfway down the stairs and slapped his forehead. "That made me realize one thing. Andrew isn't the leader. There's someone above him."

"My thoughts exactly. Any idea who?"

Mike resumed the descent. "I have a candidate, but I want to hear what you think first."

"The guy following us drove a Porsche. Obviously a rich guy. Andrew is tight with the senator's son. From what we heard, Andrew spends a lot of time with him. My bet is on the senator's son."

"That's exactly what I was thinkin'."

"If that's the case, what's our next step?"

They reached the bottom floor. Mike opened the door that led to the lobby and stepped through. "I'm a police detective, which basically means that I'm pretty far down the ladder. If I go against these people, things can get real messy real fast. It can very easily get out of control."

"Are you sayin' you're quittin'?"

"No, far from that. I'm saying I don't want to drag you through this. You're free to go home."

"No way, buddy. We're partners."

Mike's grin spread from ear to ear. "You sure?"

"Never been more sure in my life."

"In that case, our priority is to confirm our theory. Any ideas how?"

"Yeah, let's find the driver of the Porsche. That will tell us a lot." Bronson looked at the door leading to the stairs. "Let's take the elevator back up."

"Ah, an elevator. The lazy man's priority."

"Whatever," Bronson said, dismissing Mike's comment. "First thing we do when we get back to our room is search for a bug. But even if we don't find one, let's assume there's one and not say anythin' we don't want them to hear."

"I'm with you."

Bronson headed toward the elevator.

Mike grabbed his arm. "Uh uh. We're using the stairs."

"You and your exercise."

MIKE AND BRONSON searched the room twice before Mike found the bug hidden on the inside of the lampshade. They had missed it the first time because of the unique way the intruder had concealed it.

They gave each other the thumbs up symbol.

"Where's the dog going to sleep?" Mike asked.

"In bed with me."

"Good thing we have a room with two beds."

"Wouldn't have it any other way."

FIFTY

BRONSON USED THE mirror in the main room rather than the one in the bathroom to shave. This way, whoever was at the other end of the bug could hear him better. "I tell ya, Mike, Manuel wasn't a happy camper when he called last night."

"So you said, but you didn't say what he was so uptight about."

"He thinks I'm takin' too long to set things up. Seems the Columbian government is movin' at incredible speed to retrieve those treasures. Manuel thinks it might be too late for us to sneak any out."

"If that's the case, what's our next move?"

"That's just it. We don't have an alternative. We either get this done within a day or two or we lose everythin'. I certainly don't want that to happen." Bronson paused for a brief moment. "You know Andrew a lot better than I know him. Do you think he can expedite things fast enough to meet our deadline?"

Mike gave Bronson thumbs-up. "He has a lot of power. I know that for sure. But enough to pull this through? We'll see."

"If he doesn't, we'll need to find someone else. Someone who can deliver." Bronson returned the thumbs-up symbol. "Why don't we get some breakfast and then contact him? If we're lucky, he can start makin' the arrangements. See how long it takes him to set things up. Then dependin' on what he says is what we do."

HALFWAY THROUGH THEIR MEAL, Bronson's phone bleeped. He looked at the caller I.D. then up at Mike. "It worked. That's Andrew on the phone."

"Go for it." Mike dipped a piece of toast in the egg yolk and ate it.

"Bentley here."

"It's Andrew—Andrew Beauregard."

"Good to hear from you. How can I help you?"

"I have wonderful news. I just got off the phone, and I've made all the necessary arrangements. We are good to go."

"Oh really? That is indeed wonderful news." Bronson flashed Mike the okay symbol.

Mike nodded and smiled.

"When is this goin' down?" Bronson asked.

"We can do it as early as five PM tomorrow, but we need to finalize the details first. You and Mike should come over so we can work things out," Andrew said.

"Sounds like a plan. We'll be there in what? An hour? Forty-five minutes?" Bronson sought Mike's approval.

Mike mouthed the word *sure*.

"I'll see you then." Andrew disconnected.

Bronson returned the cell to his pocket. "Andrew said he could be ready to go tomorrow as early as five PM. What do you think?"

"I'm thinking that working under such a tight deadline might cause Andrew to be a bit careless. If so, he'll let his guard down. If he's the real leader, we'll find out soon enough. But if he isn't, hopefully his carelessness will lead us to the true head *hancho*."

"Can we rely on Antonio to help us?"

"Not on this. He was clear about that. Once we're sure we know who is who, we set up the time and place, and we make sure all of the big wheels are there. That's when Antonio and the rest of the FBI agents come storming in like the true heroes of this scenario. But for now, all Antonio is asking of us is to keep him informed."

"Which you have."

Mike nodded. "Which I have."

Bronson crossed his fingers. "Hopefully, the next time you call him is to report that all is set."

"Which means that we have a little over twenty-four hours to try to find the true ring leader if it's not Andrew."

"In that case, let's get movin' on this." Bronson pushed his plate away and stood up.

Mike followed him.

AT THE OPPOSITE end of the restaurant's dining room, two men each wearing Windsor Base Sharkskin three-piece suits sat quietly eating their breakfast. Neither looked at Bronson nor Mike or made any attempt to draw attention to themselves. In spite of the extra-expensive suits, they seemed to blend into the crowd.

As soon as Mike and Bronson went to pay their bill, the two men wiped their mouths, set the napkins down, left a one-hundred-dollar bill on the table, and followed the detective and his friend out.

FIFTY-ONE

"One of my household staff will bring pastries and coffee any minute now." Andrew perched on the edge of the couch. "Would you care for anything else?"

Bronson took a seat on one of the twin beige leather chairs Andrew indicated. "Yes, the details please, so I can call my men back in Columbia. They are gettin' rather nervous."

"All in good time. Let's enjoy some refreshments first." Andrew's glance drifted toward Mike. "Would you care for anything else?"

Mike flopped down on the other beige leather chair. "No, that's plenty. We just got finished eating."

The maid entered, carrying a tray filled with various flavors of Danish, a pot of coffee, plates, cream and sugar, spoons, and napkins. She set it down on the chrome-and-glass coffee table.

"Close the door behind you," Andrew told her as she headed out.

"Yes, sir."

"Before we get down to business, do either of you gentlemen have any questions for me?"

They were interrupted by another knock on the door.

"Larry, is that you?" Andrew raised his voice.

"Yep." The door whisked open and Larry stormed in. He nodded at Mike and Bronson and occupied the space next to Andrew.

The coffee's rich aroma enticed Bronson's nostrils. Even though he had had two cups of coffee during breakfast, he poured himself a cup. After all, there was no such thing as too much coffee and as long as Carol didn't find out.

"I hope you're enjoying your stay here, Mr. Bentley." Andrew reached for a Danish and took a bite.

"I am, except for one thing."

Andrew's eyes widened. "And what is that?"

"I have this thing for luxury sports coupes." Bronson stirred his coffee. "I thought when I got to the rich part of the Texas hill country, I'd see plenty of them. But I haven't seen even one. You wouldn't have one locked in the garage or some other place, would you?"

Andrew threw his head back and laughed. "I have a gorgeous Lamborghini locked in my garage. Would you care to see it?"

"I've always appreciated the beauty of a Lamborghini, but silly as it sounds, Porsches are more my style."

"And why is that?" Larry leaned back on the couch, his arms thrown around the cushions' back. He seemed in no hurry, and Bronson assumed he was used to Andrew's way. A little chit-chat first, then business.

"My wife, Amy—she always nagged me about bein' an underachiever. I promised her that one day I'd make enough money to buy enough Porsches to match every outfit she wore." Bronson looked down at the floor and lowered his head. "Cancer took her before I could make good on that promise. Now when I see one zooming down the street, I imagine she's there, smilin' and wavin' at me." He slowly looked up. "Silly, huh?"

Andrew's smile brightened his face. "No, actually

it's very sentimental, and I like that. When we finish our business deal, I'll take you to see a Porsche."

Bronson brightened. "Yeah? Where?" He hoped it wasn't the dealership.

"My friend—he has one. A real nice shade of red."

Bingo! "Your friend? I like his taste. He must be rich."

Andrew huffed. "He most definitely is. He is, after all, our senator's son."

Double Bingo. "Wow. You keep good company." Bronson opened his eyes extra wide to show how impressed he was.

"I try." Andrew took the last bite of his Danish and wiped his mouth. "Now, should we get down to business?"

"That's what we're here for." Mike folded his hands on his lap and leaned forward.

All eyes focused on Larry.

He cleared his throat. "We have a plane, ready to go. The earliest it can leave is five today."

"I'm very pleased that you've expedited matters." Bronson paused and pouted. "But that's a bit too soon for me."

Larry frowned. "Why is that, Mr. Bentley? I thought you were in a hurry to get those treasures out."

"I am. But my men are goin' to have to find a safe place for the plane to land. But now that I know you're ready at this end, I'll immediately contact my men. Soon as I hear back from them, I'll get back to you."

"How long will that take?"

"Less than twenty-four hours. They are very efficient."

Andrew stood up. "Then that part is settled. Now, all we need to do is discuss the payment. Larry, what figure are we looking at?"

"Before we get to the specifics, there's another matter we need to settle," Bronson said.

"Oh? What's that?" Andrew's eyes narrowed as he tilted his head just a bit.

"You know I'm the head of my organization. I have no secrets to hide, and that's what I demand from you all. In a previous case, I dealt with the second-in-command. That turned into a nasty fight. I don't ever want to do that again." Bronson paused. "So, Larry, no offense, but I want to deal with Andrew. You can make whatever arrangements you want or do whatever you do, but in the end, it's Andrew I deal with. Fair enough?"

"It don't bother me none." Larry threw his arms up in surrender. "That's the way it's always been."

Bronson smiled. "Good. That's what I was hopin' to hear. As such, Andrew, you do plan to be at the airport when the plane lifts off."

Andrew shrugged. "I wasn't planning on it, but if that's the only thing that's going to cement this deal, I'll be there. Guaranteed."

"Good. I'll see you there." Bronson paused. "Unless you're not the real leader."

Larry looked down and a small spark lit up in Andrew's eyes, but the flash came and left in a microsecond, and Bronson wasn't sure if he saw it at all.

Andrew straightened up like a proud peacock, cleared his throat, and attempted a weak smile. "Why would you even ask that? Do you think I would give you a raw deal?"

"No, not at all," Bronson said. "I hope you didn't take offense, but I had to ask. I hate surprises. So are you the leader? There's no one you have to answer to."

Andrew's Adam apple bobbed, and he looked up and to his right. "There's no one else. I answer to no one."

That's when Bronson knew Andrew was lying.

FIFTY-TWO

When Mike and Bronson approached the car, Honey wagged her tail and came running to greet them. Bronson bent down and patted her head. "You're such a good girl." Bronson opened the back door and Honey jumped in. Mike and Bronson made themselves comfortable in the front seats.

After checking the rearview mirror, Mike drove away. "That was gutsy, what you did back there." He drove slowly around the tree-lined curves that led away from the Beauregard mansion.

Bronson shrugged. "I had to take a chance. We needed answers, and what's better than using the direct approach?"

"The way I see it, that was the only way to handle it. I'm glad you took the chance. I don't know about you, but I think it answered our question. Now the question of the day: is Andrew the real leader?"

"What do you think?" Bronson checked on Honey. She responded by licking his hand.

"Based on his reaction to your question, I think Andrew is second-in-command. He reports to a silent partner. Is that the impression you got?"

"Exactly the same." Bronson wiped his hand.

They reached the intersection where Mike needed to turn onto the two-lane road. "This road creeps me out." Mike stepped on the brakes, checked to see that no cars came from either direction, and turned. "It needs lights. Even during the day, it's in the shadows."

"Some might say that's what makes it pretty."

"Some, but not me." Mike's eyebrows twitched as he grasped the steering wheel, fighting to control it. His knuckles turned white from the effort. The car slowed down and Mike released some of his grasp.

Bronson's glance swept the surrounding area. "What's goin' on?"

The car came to a stop.

Mike turned the ignition key.

Nothing.

"Car trouble?"

Mike slammed his open hand on the steering wheel. "We're out of gas."

"You forgot to fill her up?"

"We had over two-thirds of a tank when we arrived at the mansion. Now, nothing."

Bronson reached under the seat for the Glock and stuffed it in his pocket. "I'll check it out." As soon as he opened the door, a strong smell of gasoline filled his lungs. He bent down. "Looks like somebody cut the gas line." He straightened up and dusted the dirt off his pants.

Mike stepped out and bent down to see if there was anything he could do. He carried his Glock in his hand.

Bronson went around the car and headed toward Mike. Honey jumped out of the car and joined the duo. The three stood silently, listening, wondering. Bronson reached into his pocket and took out his gun.

Honey's head jerked up.

Seconds later, Bronson heard the squealing of tires as a car headed toward them. From the sound of it, it must have been doing at least seventy on this narrow, dangerous road.

Honey growled.

Bronson could now make out the outline of the approaching car.

A Porsche.

Bronson threw his weight on Mike, knocking him down, just as a single shot from a high-velocity rifle whizzed by. Bronson dropped, landing on top of Mike.

Immediately, he rolled away from Mike, raised his semi-automatic pistol, and fired at the speeding car. Probably didn't even make a dent. Bronson cursed himself.

Honey licked his face and Bronson hugged her.

He sat up. "You okay, buddy? Sorry about knockin' you down."

Mike didn't respond.

"Mike?" Bronson held his breath.

Silence.

Bronson touched Mike's shoulder and felt something warm and soggy. He removed his hand and saw the bright red from Mike's blood.

Bronson gently rolled Mike to his side. He needed to assess the damage and render aid, if possible. As he did, all he could think of was 9-1-1, Officer down.

Mike down.

FIFTY-THREE

COLD AND HELPLESS.

That's how Andrew felt. He'd been in the business since he was a teen, and what did he have to show for it? Nothing. Absolutely nothing. No matter what kind of a decision he made, he had to report to his superior. If he liked it, he'd approve it.

If it went well, who got the credit? Certainly not him. His superior, his friend. Always his friend.

Andrew smirked. As it turns out, he wasn't much of a friend, was he? Andrew sank on the couch, sweat covering his face. His hand held a rum-and-Coke, the third one in the past hour.

He gulped down his drink. Somehow he needed to prove himself so that someday soon, he'd take over the business. Eliminate his "boss." But how? His friend... he'd be impossible— Besides, he's the one who financed the deals.

As long as he held the financial strings, Andrew was trapped in this vicious circle of having to always report to him.

Andrew's phone beeped and Andrew jumped up, spilling his drink. The caller I.D. read Thomas Morris. *The* Thomas Morris. The senator's son. His best friend. Ha!

Andrew knew the call would come. He had failed to report on the latest development. His friend must be furious because he hadn't received an update. Andrew's trembling fingers swiped the answer key. "Yeah?" He wasn't about to play nice.

A long silence followed.

Andrew waited it out.

Finally, "Mike's dead."

Air fled Andrew's lungs in harsh gasps. "What?" He liked Mike.

A small pause followed. "I guess I shouldn't have said that, since I'm not sure. He did go down, but there's no way to confirm his death. At least, not yet."

Mike went down. That meant he had been killed. "What happened?" Andrew gulped down the last of his rum and Coke.

"I guess everything went according to the plan. Drive-by shooting and a lucky shot."

"But why? Why kill Mike?"

"Here's how I see it. We all know Mike's a dirty cop. Sooner or later, the police are going to find out. When they do, they'll see he's been associating with us. We can't have that happening. So now Mike is out of the equation."

Andrew stood and headed to the bar. Why hadn't he thought of that? As the organization's future leader, he should have realized that. But there was a flip side to that coin. Mike's death would lead the police back to them. "The feds are going to investigate Mike's death. They will see the obvious and continue to dig until they find the truth. That'll lead back to us—or at least, to me."

"Don't be a fool. We've got you covered. For the past few days, Larry has been calling the police, claiming there's been illegal hunting going on in the woods surrounding your house. Unfortunately, today, a stray bullet found the wrong mark." He paused for a second and cleared his throat. "You knew about this going down, didn't you? You're acting like this is the first time you hear about the plan."

A small detail someone had conveniently failed to mention to him. Anger burned in his eyes. Andrew poured rum into his glass, added ice cubes, and just a touch of Coke. "Of course I knew." He spoke too fast, too soon. "It's just that I'm really concerned. The police are going to dig and keep digging and that will open a can of worms."

"I doubt that."

"Why?" Andrew flopped down on the couch.

"Because they know Mike's a dirty cop. They'll be glad to sweep everything under the rug. The sooner forgotten the better. They will rule that his death was a result of an unfortunate hunting accident."

"What about Bentley?"

"What about him?"

"Won't the police want to question him?"

"If Bentley is as smart as I think he is, he'll stray clear across the other side. Remember, Bentley isn't exactly on the right side of the law either. He's not going to be a problem. You can proceed with the plan."

Andrew emptied half the contents of his drink in one swallow. "I hope you're right."

"Of course I am. Have I ever let you down?"

No, he hadn't, but there's always a first time. "In that case, I'll make sure the deal with Bentley goes down soon."

"Looks like you're going to need some moral support. When Bentley calls you with the details, let me know. I'll either pick you up or meet you there. Either way, we'll both see the plane take off."

Andrew's world brightened. "Yeah? You'll do that?"

"For you, I'd do anything."

Andrew smiled as an idea started to form in his mind. *You're in for a great surprise.* "Thanks. As soon as I hear anything, I'll contact you."

"You do that." The line went dead.

Andrew punched the end button and stared at the cell. His fingers lightly drummed the phone. Slowly, a smile as insincere as it was ugly spread across his face.

FIFTY-FOUR

Bronson sat hunched forward. He had pulled open his shirt and tie in an attempt to feel better. It hadn't worked. The lower part of his arms rested on his lap, and his hands dangled between his legs. His eyes focused on the plain tiled floor as though he could find some hidden answer there.

The door to the interrogation room opened and Special Agent Antonio Corbalan stepped in.

Bronson straightened up. "Mike?"

"He's in surgery."

"Is he...will he..."

"The doctors wouldn't commit. It's touch and go." He walked toward Bronson and sat next to him. "I'm sorry. I know you two are close."

"Yeah, and I couldn't save him."

"If you hadn't pushed him down, the bullet would have lodged in his heart. He'd be dead by now."

"You weren't there. You don't know that."

"True, but I was at the scene and studied the angles. I'm pretty sure you saved his life."

"I'd like to go to the hospital. Be there when he wakes up." *If he wakes up.*

"That can be arranged."

Bronson's sight bounced from one wall to the other in the small interrogation room that had been his cell for the past hour. "What about—"

"The police? You don't need to worry about them. This is now strictly an FBI case, and I'm in charge."

"Does that mean I'm free to go?"

"Yes, of course." Antonio stood up. "By the way, I'm heading to the hospital. Would you like a ride?"

Bronson bolted to his feet. "Where's Honey?"

"Honey?" Antonio's eyes narrowed then widened as he made the connection. "Oh, you mean your dog."

Bronson nodded.

"My friend Kay has a very big backyard and an even bigger heart. Honey is fine. You can pick her up anytime you want." Antonio took out his car keys. "Are you ready to go?"

"More than ready."

"Good. You can fill me in on all of the details on the way to the hospital."

EVEN THOUGH BRONSON wasn't familiar with the area, he felt that Antonio took too many side roads, thus prolonging the trip to the hospital. Bronson was desperate to be with Mike, but he knew better than to complain. Instead, he addressed each question with as much detail as possible.

Antonio slowed down as they neared the stop sign.

Wouldn't the freeway be faster? Bronson bit his tongue to keep from screaming at the FBI agent.

"Are you sure that the senator's son—what's his name anyway?" Antonio looked at both sides of the street before proceeding.

"Thomas Morris."

"Ah, Thooomas Morrisss."

The way Antonio pronounced the name told Bronson that Antonio had already known that fact. Did that mean that Bronson had passed some kind of a test? It didn't matter. Let Antonio play his games.

For a moment Antonio remained quiet as though focusing on his driving. Then, "Are you sure that Thomas owns a red Porsche, and the passenger in that car was the one who shot Mike?"

"I know Thomas owns a red Porsche, but I'm sure you already knew that. As to who was drivin' the car, that I can't really say. It was too dark and it happened too fast. But I can say that the shot came from the speedin' car."

"I realize it was dark, but can you tell me anything about the driver or maybe even the possibility of a passenger?"

Bronson wished he could. "No."

"The senator's son owns a red Porsche but not all of the red Porsches. Are you willing to testify that the car you saw is the same one that belongs to Morris?"

"I can't verify that. I never saw a license plate."

"Right now, I've got men trying to establish where Morris was and whether he was driving his Porsche at the time of question."

A sign reading Memorial Hospital with an arrow pointing to the right caught Bronson's attention. "Is that it? Is that where Mike is?"

Antonio nodded. "Relax. We're almost there."

"I can't relax until I know Mike's okay."

"I may not act like it, but I'm also concerned about Mike. In spite of the situation he's in, I know Mike is a good man. I'm sure he's innocent."

"He's as straight an arrow as they come."

By now, the hospital, a multi-level u-shaped structure, was visible. Antonio turned into the crowded parking lot. "I realize you can't prove anything, but what do you think Morris' involvement is in all of this?"

Bronson took a deep breath. The parking lot was full. Why couldn't Antonio let him out while he continued to search for a parking space? "Mike's determined to expose the ring leader. That's the only way this organization will fall. For a while, we assumed that Andrew was the man, but we came to believe he was only second in command."

"And Morris is number one."

"Maybe."

Antonio glanced at Bronson. "Maybe?"

"There's Larry Webb, the guy who makes all of the arrangements. Maybe he's the one. Maybe Morris is. All we have to connect him to this case is the red Porsche."

"Keep talking."

"It just seems to me that if you're goin' to kill someone, you wouldn't drive a Porsche."

"Unless there wasn't supposed to be any witnesses left."

Bronson shrugged. "Maybe. That's what Mike and I were goin' to do before he got shot. We were plannin' to establish a connection between Morris and Andrew and see just how and if he's involved."

An elderly couple headed for a car. Both Bronson and Antonio watched them. "Looks like we might have found a parking space."

It's about time. Bronson reached for the door handle, ready to jump out as soon as Antonio turned off the ignition key.

"Before you bolt out," Antonio said, "there are two things we need to agree on."

"I'm listenin'."

"One, you do nothing without first consulting me."

"Okay."

"That means not notifying Mike's wife about the accident."

"Not a wife."

"What?"

"Her name is Ellen Biebesheimer."

"I see. Not a wife."

"It's complicated. Why not contact her? She'd like to be with him, and he would like to see her there."

"In order to keep Mike safe, we're going to say he's dead. If Ellen comes, then we'll have two to protect. That's one too many. And the secret is more likely to get out."

"I can understand that." Ellen was going to kill him. "And number two?"

"You'll continue as though nothing has happened. You'll make all of the arrangements, and you find who that leader is, and everything we discussed before about you reporting to me stands. Can you do that?"

Mike would want him to see this through. "Yes, of course."

"One more thing," Antonio said.

This was going to take a while. Bronson released his grip on the door handle.

"We don't know if Mike is...dead. If he is, you won't allow that to interfere with your work. Your number one priority is your job, not Mike."

A cold chill covered Bronson's arms. He nodded and bolted out of the car.

FIFTY-FIVE

THE STARK WHITE walls and the tiled floors screamed at Bronson. *Mike had been shot. He was here, fighting for his life. Or maybe...*

Bronson trembled as he turned down another wide corridor.

The hospital was spotless, gleaming—just the way hospitals were meant to be. *But Mike shouldn't be here. He shouldn't have been shot. Bronson should have done something to prevent that. He had failed him.*

Again.

Oh, Mike. Please hang on. For Ellen's sake. For your sake.

For my sake.

Bronson swallowed hard to keep the tears from falling. He entered the empty operation waiting room and headed straight for the phone. His peripheral view caught a glimpse of Antonio as he joined Bronson in the waiting room.

"How can I help you?" the chirpy voice over the phone asked.

"I'm here for Mike Hoover's status report. Can you tell me anythin' about how he's doin'?"

"Are you a relative?"

Bronson didn't hesitate. "I'm his brother."

Antonio rolled his eyes.

"Just a minute, sir." Bronson heard her set the phone

down followed by muffled voices in the background. She returned to her place. "The doctor will see you in a few minutes."

Bronson's grip on the phone handle tightened. That couldn't be good news. "Thank you."

"Anything else I can do for you?"

"No." The word was barely audible. Bronson replaced the handle on its cradle and let his hand linger there for the moment. He lowered his head and whispered a prayer.

Antonio stepped forward and put a comforting hand on Bronson's shoulder.

Minutes passed and time stretched into eternity. Each second that ticked by thickened Bronson's burden until he felt he was swimming in a pool of syrup.

Mike.

The doctor walked in. Sorrow washed out his face, blurring his features. His eyes were sunken.

No!

Bronson and Antonio approached the doctor.

"Are you here for Mike Hoover?" The doctor's hands were clasped tightly behind his back. His stance suggested tension.

Bronson swallowed hard and nodded.

The doctor's eyes widened. "Oh, God, no. I'm so sorry. I just came from telling some parents that their two-year-old didn't make it." Without taking a breath, he hurried on. "Mike's fine. The operation went smoothly. We removed the bullet with no major damage to Mike. He's awake now if you want to see him."

Bronson stood numb. The relief he felt drained his energy.

Antonio showed the doctor his FBI credentials. "I'm

Special Agent Antonio Eduardo Corbalan. The bullet. Where is it?"

"As instructed, I put it in a safe place. If you follow me, I'll hand it to you."

Bronson took a step forward. "Can I see Mike?"

"You're the brother?"

Bronson nodded.

"Then follow me. I'll take you to him and Special Agent Corbalan can come with me to retrieve the bullet."

DESPITE BEING IN obvious pain, Mike's face broke into a grin that spread from ear to ear when he saw Bronson. "Hey, Buddy. Why do you look like you've seen a ghost?"

"Very funny." Bronson walked over to the bed. "How are you feelin'?"

"Like I've been shot. I have this pounding pain in my chest that won't go away."

"It will. Just take it easy." Bronson couldn't believe how good it was to see and talk to Mike. "Antonio doesn't want me to contact Ellen, but I'll do it if you want me to."

Mike considered the possibilities for a moment. "Nah, no need to worry her, and let's not antagonize Antonio. He's the only one who might help me get out of this mess."

"As you wish."

A bolt of pain struck Mike and he grimaced. "I owe you a big thanks."

"How's that?"

"The doctor said if the bullet had landed just a few centimeters to the left, I'd be a dead man. By pushing me, you saved my life."

"Maybe I should have pushed you sooner and made the bullet completely miss you."

"You tried. That's what counts. But if you're looking to make amends, there's something you can do."

"Oh?"

"You can finish this for me. Looks like I'm out of the equation, but you still have a shot. No pun intended."

Mike didn't need to have asked. Bronson had decided a while back, he was going to see this to the end. He nodded.

Mike continued, "Do me a favor. If, as we suspect, the senator's son is involved, that's going to get messy fast. I'm sure the senator will do everything in his capacity to keep his son's image squeegee clean. That's going to cause heads to roll, and I don't want yours to be one of them."

"I can take care of myself."

"That's what concerns me. Those who deal with upholding the law are often reluctant to take on certain kinds of people—like the senator's son, who will definitely have certain kinds of power. You, on the other hand, will push forward, regardless of your personal safety. Promise me, you'll be careful. Don't take any extra chances. You can rely on the FBI to back you up. Promise?"

"I promise."

Mike's lips formed a weak smile. He closed his eyes.

Bronson stood by his friend's side until Mike fell asleep. Even then, Bronson felt reluctant to leave. The nurses had told him that soon Mike would be moved to a private room. Bronson would wait until Mike was settled and was reassured that the FBI was present to protect him. Antonio had promised him that the place would have better security than Ft. Knox.

Bronson flopped down on the chair beside Mike's bed and stared at the machine that announced Mike's statistics. The blinking lights helped Bronson concentrate. He needed a plan that would trap the senator's son if indeed he was the culprit. His mind digested and threw out one scenario after another and worked like a runaway engine, spitting out details, absorbing new ones, and re-hashing old ones. Bronson closed his eyes and focused on the problem.

Minutes later, he had a plan, but Antonio would have to approve it. For Mike's sake, he planned to do this by the book. Bronson picked up his cell and talked to Antonio. Once he had his approval, he'd contact Andrew and set up a meeting.

FIFTY-SIX

ON THE WAY to the hotel, Bronson stopped by Kay's house. "Hi," he said to the elderly woman who answered the door. "I'm Bronson, Antonio's friend. He gave me your address and I'm here to—"

Honey bolted from the back of the house, yipping and bouncing all the way. She stood on two paws as she greeted Bronson. Her tail wagged faster than a tumbling leaf on a storm.

Kay smiled as she stared at the excited dog. Small creases formed on her forehead and on the side of her eyes. "I guess I won't have to ask for an I.D. If that isn't your dog, then she doesn't belong to anybody. I've never seen a dog get so excited."

Bronson bent down and Honey licked his face. She bounced from side to side, excitement written all over her face.

"I missed you, too." Bronson hugged her. He gently patted her and she continued to whine.

Kay stepped back and watched them interact. A big smile spread on her face.

Bronson stood up. "Time to go," he told Honey, then turned to Kay. "Thank you for watchin' her. How much do I owe you?"

Kay waved her hands. "Not a penny. She's such a pleasure. I'm sorry to see her go."

"I bet you are. I'm really lucky to have her."

"That, you are. You take good care of her, you hear?"

"Loud and clear." Bronson headed back to the car, Honey following close behind, her curly tail wagging back and forth.

ONCE BRONSON HAD settled in the hotel room, he contacted Andrew and requested to meet.

"By all means," Andrew said. "As far as I'm concerned, we can meet immediately."

"Glad to hear that," Bronson said, "but I have a special request."

"What's that?"

"I want this meetin' to be just between you and me. We can meet somewhere other than your house if that helps."

"Name the place."

"The Four Seasons Hotel has a fantastic lakeside restaurant that serves a mean cup of coffee."

"I'm not one for coffee, but I'll see you there in an hour."

Bronson tapped his forehead. "I don't have reservations."

"Not to worry. I'll get us in."

Of course.

"One more thing." Bronson spoke quickly before Andrew hung up.

"Yes?"

"Do you know about Mike?"

"I heard. I'm sorry. I know you two are close. What happened?"

"Some hunter mistook him for a deer. Supposedly, it was a freak accident. But still I have to ask, could that have been one of your men?"

"No, no way." Andrew's voice was loud and clear. Bronson believed him.

Andrew continued, "I like Mike. I have no reason for harming him. How's he doing?"

Bronson waited several seconds before answering. "I'm afraid he's...dead."

The intense quiet that followed seemed surreal.

Bronson broke the silence. "Maybe Thomas ordered his death."

The seconds filled with silence stretched, causing Bronson to wonder what Andrew knew.

Bronson was about to speak when Andrew answered, "I can't see Thomas involved in something like this, but the thing is, I don't know about Thomas anymore. Maybe. He and Mike might have had some kind of a deal that went south. But I couldn't tell you that for sure."

THE MAITRE D' LED Bronson to a table with a clear view of the lake. "This is Master Beauregard's favorite table. Is this satisfactory to you, sir?"

"It's perfect."

"Very good, sir. Can I get you anything before I go?"

Silly question. "Yes, please, a cup of coffee."

The maitre d' tilted his head and stared at Bronson.

What was wrong with coffee? Bronson sat down, unfolded the napkin, and placed it on his lap. "Make that a cup of *café au lait*."

The maitre d' didn't crack a smile. Tough audience. The employee acknowledged the request with a single nod of his head and left.

Bronson's glance drifted toward the lake. The gentle waves filled him with a sense of peace. Maybe the breath-taking view would work the same magic on Andrew—and speaking of the devil, Bronson saw Andrew approach.

But he wasn't alone.

FIFTY-SEVEN

THE MAN ACCOMPANYING Andrew was not only elegantly dressed, he was also classically handsome. Bronze-gold hair framed the almost perfect oval-shaped face. His smile radiated warmth and friendliness. He walked a few steps ahead of Andrew.

When they approached Bronson, Andrew cast his eyes down. "I know you asked me to come alone, but I wanted you to meet my best friend. He's always so busy, and he had an opening now. So I grasped this wonderful opportunity. Mr. Alex Bentley, allow me to introduce you to Thomas Morris."

The senator's son!

Hot diggity dog.

Bronson's luck had just multiplied faster than rabbits. He had set this meeting specifically to talk Andrew into introducing him to Thomas. Now, he didn't have to. He was here, in the flesh. Bronson stepped forward and offered his hand. "A pleasure, I'm sure."

Thomas flashed a one-hundred-kilowatt smile. "I'm sure the pleasure is all mine." Deep-set blue eyes dominated his features while thick, well-shaped brows hinted at a touch of intelligence.

No sooner had they sat down than a swarm of waiters descended on them. Thomas addressed the head waiter, "I'll take care of the check and make it three of my usual."

The frown on Andrew's face didn't escape Bronson's attention.

The waiter nodded while another poured wine into three crystal glasses. Bronson had no idea what Thomas had ordered. He hoped it was eatable. As the server poured, Bronson wondered if it'd be possible to trade the wine for a cup of coffee. Nah, better not rock the boat. Bronson reached for the wine glass and took a sip. Not bad.

"Tell me, Mr. Bentley—"

"I'm not a formal man," Bronson said. "Call me Alex."

Thomas smiled. "Very well, Alex. I'm Thomas."

Bronson acknowledged him with a nod.

"On our way over here, Andrew and I were talking about you. We wondered how you got into this business."

Bronson looked away and half-smiled. "My dad's to blame. When I was little, he always hid my Christmas and birthday gifts and hand me a paper with hints to follow until I found my treasure, basically my gift." Bronson put air quotes around the word *treasure*. "Ever since then, I've been fascinated with locating treasures."

Thomas threw his head back and laughed. "That's a good story. Wonder where you'd be now if your dad hadn't done that."

Two waiters arrived carrying what Bronson hoped was the appetizer. He had never seen anything like it—or even food that small. It looked like tiny, chopped burritos smothered in some type of sauce and green stuff on top. Two bites and it'd be all gone. He hoped it would be two good bites.

They were. Bronson had no idea what he ate, but it

was oh, so heavenly. Would it be insulting if he asked for seconds? Nah, better not.

"Now's your turn." Bronson wondered why the waiters hadn't brought him his coffee. "What is it that you do?"

"I'm afraid my life is boring compared to yours. I'm what you would call a professional student. I'm studying law and hope to one day follow in my father's footsteps. I want this great nation of ours to once again trust its politicians. I'm seeking to bring honesty, hard work, and dedication to the job. One day I'll represent my people, and they'll know they can rely on me." Thomas reached for his wine but didn't drink any. "I'll get off my high horse now. What I really do is a lot of volunteer work—mostly research—for my dad."

Andrew snapped his eyes shut and tightened his features as tight as a fist.

Bronson made a mental note of Andrew's reaction but otherwise ignored it. "That must be challengin'. What kind of research do you do?"

"Just about anything. My father is considering voting for or against a bill. I search out the ins and outs of the things that affect the bill, the economy, and the people. I check with the voters to see on which side of the bill they stand on." Thomas shrugged. "That sort of thing."

"Fascinatin', but there's not much money in that."

"None at all. Otherwise, it's called nepotism."

Andrew fidgeted in his chair.

Bronson made another mental note. "I can see that. It's nice of you to do this on a volunteer basis."

Thomas leaned back on the chair. "The way I see it, I'm gaining experience that will be useful in the future.

Besides, I don't need any money. My grandfather left me a substantial trust."

Their conversation was interrupted by another herd of waiters.

"Ah, the chicken roulade is here. Our favorite." Thomas pointed to himself and Andrew.

Chicken! Bronson's world brightened. He liked chicken. A waiter set the dish in front of him. Bronson stared at it. This didn't look like any chicken he'd ever eaten before. It looked like, well, small, light brown tires standing up which he supposed were really two pieces of meat. A variety of what may be vegetables adorned the roulade. This was a piece of artwork, not food. He waited to see how Andrew and Thomas attacked the entree.

Bronson summoned up his courage and took a bite. Best chicken ever. Even its aroma, sweet and with just an edge of spice, enhanced his appetite.

Andrew cut one of the vegetables and ate it. "Thomas has a Porsche, and I said that because I know how you love them."

Bronson looked up from his food and met Thomas' eye. "Yeah? You're a Porsche man? You're my kind of person." Bronson pushed the vegetables away from the meat. Fancy or not, they were still vegetables. "Tell me about your car."

"What's to tell? It's a 2022 Porsche Panamera E-Hybrid Sport Turismo. The color is gentian blue metallic. I keep it in good shape. In fact, for the past three days, it's been at the mechanic's for a tune-up."

Interesting. Blue, not red. Hadn't Andrew told him he had a red Porsche? Not that it mattered. He didn't have access to the car. "Your car is not red?"

Thomas' eyebrows wrinkled. "No, not red. Why would you think that?"

"No particular reason. It's just that red's my favorite color. I've been considerin' gettin' me one. A red one, that is. Do you know anyone who wants to sell a red Porsche?"

"I had one, but that was last year's model. I traded it in a week ago for the blue one."

Andrew shrugged. "I didn't know that."

"Is the red one for sale?" Bronson asked.

"I have no idea if the dealership has sold it or if it's still in the lot. However, if you really want to see a red Porsche, there's—"

Andrew snapped his fingers as though eager that he was finally part of the conversation. "I know what you're going to say. You were going to tell him about the Porsche convention going on."

Thomas smiled and raised his wine glass. "Yes, that's exactly what I was going to say." He turned to Bronson. "It's a different kind of convention. Porsche owners like me take their cars and leave them there. People who can't afford the car are allowed to take it for a spin."

"Oh really?" Bronson temporarily stopped eating so he could focus on Thomas. "Wouldn't that create unforeseeable problems?"

"People who attend this event aren't your everyday thieves. Lots of precautions are taken. In all of these years, there's never been a single report of damage to a car or report of a stolen one."

A ghost of a smile touched Andrew's mouth. "Remember how you and your gang used to attend this convention so you all could drive those Porsches and pretend they were yours?"

A portion of Thomas's body's blood supply churned in his cheeks. "Let's not mention that again, and we weren't a gang. We were a group of teenagers who hung around together. Most of us didn't even have our licenses."

"And they still let you drive the cars?" Bronson asked.

Andrew leaned forward and lowered his voice. "Money speaks and so does power. You're forgetting that Thomas here is the senator's son."

More blood rushed to Thomas' cheeks. "Enough of that. The main thing is that you, Alex, should find the time to attend this convention. I bet you could find a lot of red Porsches. That seems to be everyone's favorite."

"But not yours?"

"Not mine. I like mine blue. I'm an individual thinker."

Bronson smiled and let that one go. He finished the chicken part of the roulade. All that was left were the vegetables. Not his favorite, especially those he had never seen before.

Andrew and Thomas further quizzed Bronson about the life of a treasure seeker. When they finished, both seemed satisfied with his answers. Desert arrived—arches of chocolate with tiny pieces of fruits on the top. Hope it tasted as good as it looked.

Bronson wasn't disappointed. The meal enticed his senses, but it wasn't accomplishing what he had set out to do. Bronson decided to take a gamble and ease the conversation toward the idea that Thomas was the man on the top. He was about to speak when Thomas shot to his feet.

"I'm sorry, but I don't have the luxury of time. I'd like to hear more of your stories, Alex, but I'll be late for my appointment if I don't leave now. Please feel free to stay and enjoy a cup of coffee. That's always a relaxing thing to do after a good meal. I wish I had that luxury." He excused himself and walked away.

Bronson studied him as he headed out. He walked like a man who was sure of himself. Someone in control. Bronson had yet to make up his mind about Thomas' position. It was likely he was the leader, but an edge of doubt dwelled in his gut. All Bronson knew was that if Thomas was the ring leader, he would be a hard man to bring down.

FIFTY-EIGHT

"You seemed to enjoy the food and Thomas' company." Andrew leaned back on his chair.

Bronson waited until the waiters finished removing the plates, swept the crumbs off the tablecloth, set saucers and cups down, and filled them with steaming coffee. Another waiter arrived with all of the coffee fixings and a silver urn. "The food was delicious, and Thomas seems to be a delightful person," Bronson said once the waiters left.

Andrew stirred his coffee. "Don't let him fool you. Looks can be deceiving."

"What exactly does that mean?"

"He's a smooth talker, and that's what's going to make him a great politician one of these days."

"Are you sayin' he's not sincere?"

Andrew shrugged. "Sometimes, I wonder." He poured another Sweet'N Low into his coffee. "Sometimes I think he's up to something and that worries me."

"Somethin'?" Bronson paused. "Somethin' that's goin' to upset our business deal?"

Andrew looked away. "Maybe."

Bronson leaned forward so he was closer to Andrew. "The other day, I asked you if you were the one who made all final decisions. You said you were, but both you and I know you were lyin'. Is Thomas the one you report to?"

"I... I..." Andrew cleared his throat. "I didn't say that. I just meant he's...a politician. Unlike me, he always knows what to say and when to say it."

Bronson poured himself another cup of coffee from the dainty urn. "I like workin' with you, Andrew. But I also told you that I only work with Number One." He eyed the coffee he hadn't even touched. "This deal is off." He started to stand.

Andrew gasped. "Wait!"

Bronson sat back down.

"When the deal goes down, when you're there to board that plane..." He paused as though considering how to continue. "Thomas will be standing by my side."

Bingo! "So he's—"

Andrew looked away.

Bronson made a production out of adding more cream to his coffee and stirring it. "A little while ago when we were on the phone, you mentioned that Mike and Thomas are working on other deals." Bronson made a mental note to talk to Mike about this.

"I remember."

"Is that something I should worry about?"

"Absolutely not."

"Good to hear." Bronson pushed his cup of coffee away. "I best be goin'."

"I'm afraid that's impossible." Andrew slid his hand inside his suit and opened it slightly. Bronson spotted the gun. "Until the deal goes down, you're not leaving my sight."

"I seriously doubt that you'd want to create a scene here at the restaurant."

"You're absolutely right. I don't. But do you see those two men sitting at the table next to us?"

Bronson glanced their way.

They grinned, an evil-looking curvature of the lips, and then they waved.

Bronson returned the same evil-looking grin and waved back.

"Now do you see the men behind us?"

Bronson looked at them.

They stared at him.

He stared back.

"You won't make it too far before one of those men grabs you, and they like to play rough. Best if you just come with me."

Bronson reached for the cup. "Mind if I finish my coffee first?"

FIFTY-NINE

THE CHAUFFEUR STOOD by the limousine's open door. Three of the four men Andrew had pointed out in the restaurant lined up like good little soldiers and entered the automobile. The fourth one stood behind Bronson, shoving a gun against his ribs.

"Get in," Andrew hissed.

Bronson started to do so.

"No, wait."

Bronson stopped.

Andrew nodded at the guard and stepped back.

The thug frisked Bronson and relieved him of his gun and phone. He pocketed them.

"Now get in." Andrew indicated the open door.

Bronson did. The rich, black velvet seats that stretched from one side of the limo to the other side would have amused Bronson under different circumstances. Behind the driver's compartment, a fully stocked wet bar enticed those entering the limo. As if that wasn't enough, at the other end, a small refrigerator displayed a see-through door. The large television screen at the back of the car was turned off.

The four men from the restaurant occupied the left-hand side of the limo. Soon as they sat down, they reached for their seatbelts, buckled in, and grabbed their earphones. They placed the piece over their ears. Whatever was going to be discussed, they would not be able to hear. These men were well trained. Bad news for Bronson.

Bronson sat facing them, his feet firmly grounded on the royal purple carpet. "Why are you doin' this?" Bronson waited until Andrew lowered his firm body into the rich, comfortable couch-looking car seat next to him.

"Sorry, my friend, you brought this on yourself."

The limo's tiny, white and purple lights and decorations on the inside of the car's roof captured Bronson's attention. "How's that?"

"You're the one who insisted on dealing with Number One. You weren't satisfied with me. You had to see him." He buckled up. "You've got to understand. Because of who he is, he can't afford to have you run around loose. You might accidentally open your trap and ruin him. He can't have that happening. You must remain where we can watch you every second until this deal goes down. You can understand that, can't you?"

Bronson's mind spat one possibility after the other with the speed of a rocket entering Earth's atmosphere. He had to come up with the right answer so he could get away and notify Antonio. "I have a dog to take care of. She's waitin' for me in the hotel room."

"Yeah, I know. Sweetheart."

Bronson cocked his head and stared at Andrew.

Andrew blinked several times. "Ah, the dog. Her name is Sweetheart."

"Honey."

"Oh, yeah. Honey. I knew it was something silly like that. As we speak, there are men in your room, packing your belongings and taking care of Honey."

"Honey would never let them in. If they hurt her—"

"Relax, will ya? If I were you, I'd be more concerned about me than a stupid dog."

"Honey is anythin' but stupid." Bronson folded his arms and stared out the window. At least he wasn't blindfolded. He'd be able to see where they were taking him. He would memorize the streets and use them to hide once he'd be able to make a run for freedom.

He also had to somehow connect with Special Agent Antonio, a problem Bronson didn't quite know how to solve.

SIXTY

BRONSON DIDN'T NEED to memorize anything. He knew where they were heading. In less than half an hour, they'd be at Andrew's mansion. Did he have a secret dungeon hidden behind secret walls? The house was more than big enough to conceal one. Or two.

Andrew nudged him. "Are you still brooding about Honey?"

"I want her with me."

"I don't like dogs in my house. So, sorry, no, she can't be with you."

"Can you at least tell me where they are goin' to take her?"

"Once you come back with the goods, we'll tell you where you can pick her up."

Bronson wasn't handcuffed, and Andrew sat next to him. Bronson stared at Andrew's Adam Apple and down at his own hand. He formed a fist and released it. He returned his gaze out the window.

Twenty-five minutes later, the limo came to a smooth stop in front of Andrew's three-story palace.

"Not so shabby, is it?" Andrew unbuckled his seatbelt.

So did Bronson. "What?"

"Your new prison. My house. You'll have the run of the place. Go anywhere you want, any time you want. But there'll be restrictions. One, you must stay indoors. If you venture out even to sit on the porch, I can't guarantee your safety. Two, no calls. No Internet. When you need to contact your men, let me know, and I'll monitor the call. Two simple rules. Do you think you can abide by them?"

Not for a second. "I'm sure I can manage to control myself."

"If that's the case, everything will run smoothly." Andrew moved his extended index finger in a small circle. The four men immediately removed their headphones and readied to make their exit.

BRONSON SPENT PART of the evening glancing through the titles in the Beauregard library. Every once in a while, a book captured his interest, but he soon returned it to its shelf. Even in this room with floor-to-ceiling shelves filled with book after book, arranged by category and in alphabetical order, Bronson found nothing that could help.

He glanced at his watch: 7:31. He headed to his assigned bedroom. His suitcase had been delivered and rested at the foot of the bed. He opened the suitcase. As far as he could tell, everything was there, including his pair of comfortable pajamas.

Unfortunately, tonight was not a night that called for comfortable attire. Bronson unbuckled his belt, set the alarm clock to go off at 3:00 AM, and flopped down on the bed.

He closed his eyes and forced sleep to embrace him.

AT 2:50, Bronson sprung out of bed. The last thing he wanted was for the alarm to go off and wake up whoever slept in the bedrooms close to his. He stretched, bringing life to his aging bones. He combed his hair and used the facilities. He was ready to go. The only thing missing was his gun. And his phone. And Honey. And Mike. Okay, that was four things missing, but who was counting?

He opened the door, stuck his head out, and glanced down both sides of the semi-dark hallway. Just as he had hoped, it stood empty.

He crept out.

He brought no paper and no pen with him. Anything worth remembering, he'd memorize. Every door in this hallway was closed. Bronson imagined each led to bedrooms, but he wasn't about to open any of those doors to verify his theory. Later on in the day, when everyone was awake, he'd check the rooms out.

Bronson worked his way down the spiraling staircase to the second floor. He entered the first room to his right. Another library. Amazing. Was Andrew trying to compete with the Library of Congress? He closed the door and headed to the first floor. If there was any way of escaping from this house, it would be from the ground floor. He'd begin his search there.

He stared at the massive front door. If he'd open it, probably an alarm would announce to the world what he was doing. His sight traveled to the window next to the door. Being so close to the main door, chances are that it would also be wired.

But what about the other windows? The ones away from the vestibule. When he and Mike were in the living room and were talking to Andrew and his gang, Bronson remembered seeing a huge window facing the front of the house. What were the chances of that being wired? He made a b-line for the living room.

He stood in front of the window, his hands clasped

behind his back. He stared at the wall around the window. No wires. No gadgets. He took a step forward and opened the drapes. He looked at the bottom of the window. The top. The right-hand side. The left-hand. Nothing drew his attention. Could it be remotely activated? He placed his hand on the windowpane.

It felt cool, almost as if—

That's when he heard it.

Footsteps heading toward him.

Bronson braced himself.

SIXTY-ONE

"WHAT DO YOU think you're doing?" the stern voice behind Bronson demanded.

Bronson lowered his arms and pivoted on one foot to face Andrew. "You might not understand." He looked around, hoping he looked embarrassed instead of startled. "I live in the great outdoors. This is a beautiful place, but it's suffocatin' me. I need to breathe the fresh air. I thought if I touched the window, part of the outdoors would come in. Silly, I know."

Andrew's penetrating eyes crawled over Bronson like beetles on a carcass, probing and examining.

Bronson offered Andrew a weak smile. "I'll clean the window. Probably has my fingerprints all over."

"That won't be necessary." He continued to stare at Bronson. "You really miss the outdoors that much."

Bronson nodded. "More than you know."

"We can, if you want, go sit outside for a few minutes."

"Thought you said somethin' horrible would happen to me if I went outdoors."

"It will, I assure you, but that's only if you venture there by yourself. As long as you're with me, the do—" He stopped.

Dogs. He was going to say *dogs.* "I've slept in the jungle where lions and tigers call the place home. I suppose I could venture out to the porch and face the dogs."

Andrew smiled. "As long as I'm there, you won't even see them."

"That's good enough for me." Bronson followed Andrew out the main door.

Andrew opted to sit on the swing while Bronson chose a comfortable-looking wicker chair with its seat covered in a bright green and yellow cushion.

"Is this better?"

"Much better. I appreciate you losing sleep to spend time with me on the porch."

"I won't make it a habit. Besides, you will be leaving soon. Tomorrow—or should I say today?—you will contact your men and give me a firm date."

"I'll need my cell for that."

"You'll get it back, and you're going to put it on speaker."

Bronson's mind screamed for ideas on how to accomplish that. None came. "I can do that." Bronson looked around. "Your house is brightly lit, inside and out. But beyond these lights, it's awfully dark. Don't you have neighbors?"

Andrew grinned. "That's what I like about living here. It's very private. The nearest neighbor is more than fifteen miles away."

"And they don't turn their lights on?"

Andrew glanced to his right, then quickly away. "I'm sure they have their lights on. We just can't see them from here."

"They? It's more than one home out there?"

"Sort of. The senator and his wife live in the main house, but behind it, Thomas occupies the guest house."

"Nice arrangement."

"It works for them, but enough chit-chat. Tell me what your men are waiting for."

"You mean what I'm waitin' for. I needed to know I had the full cooperation of the man in charge. After talking to Thomas earlier today, I believe I do. You did say he'd be at the airport when I take off."

A small grin formed at the edges of Andrew's lips. It came so fast and just as quickly disappeared that Bronson wasn't sure he saw anything at all. "That's what he told me."

"Then later on today, we'll finalize the plans."

"That's what I wanted to hear." Andrew looked at his watch. "It's late. Let's go inside to sleep. I'm not used to this night thing. Normally, I'm a heavy sleeper."

Good to know. Bronson stood and followed Andrew.

SIXTY-TWO

Bronson waited almost half an hour before he dared venture out of his room again. He had no men to contact and yet he was supposed to make that call today. Things might go south at that point. He needed a weapon. Finding his gun would be impossible, but a knife could work. He'd bet that the Beauregard's kitchen would be equipped with a wide selection.

As before, he inched the door to his room open and peeked down both sides of the hallway. Keeping in the shadows, he worked his way down to the first floor. He was familiar with the front layout of the house, but not the back which was probably where the kitchen was located. He headed that way.

Down the hallway to his left, he encountered two closed doors. He placed his ear against one. When he didn't hear anything, he turned the knob and stepped into a glamorous dining room as big as the front half of his house. Across the room, his sight landed on a closed door. That had to lead to the kitchen.

He was right.

As soon as he stepped in, he heard a gasp followed by a click as the refrigerator door closed. The night light cast shadows on the man frozen next to the kitchen appliance. Bronson inched his way toward him.

"I'm so sorry," the man said. "I let my curiosity get

the best of me. I'll never do this again. Please. I need the job. Please." He lowered his head.

"Relax. I have no plans to turn you in."

The man looked up and searched Bronson's face as though searching for assurance. "You won't?"

Bronson placed his index finger over his lips. "I won't. Just tell me, what were you doing?"

The servant looked down again. "I know. We have our own refrigerator with our own food. I have no business going through yours. I am so sorry."

Bronson focused on the food thief while his peripheral vision searched the area. "It doesn't bother me if you take some of the stuff to the servants' quarters."

"Oh no! It's nothing like that. I don't even live here. I have my own apartment. I was just here to…to…"

Steal some food. Didn't Andrew feed them properly?

Paco lowered his head. "It's for my little girl."

Bronson's throat constricted, and he cleared it. "Are you saying you don't have enough food for her over there?"

The man's eyes widened. "That's not it at all. We have plenty of food, but we don't have fancy food like you do here." He paused and smiled. "She's turning ten and she's never eaten any of those things we serve you. I thought this once…" He swallowed hard. "I'm sorry. I'll leave now."

Bronson's sight zoomed in on the knife rack hanging on the wall. "No, wait. I don't even know your name."

The stranger gasped. "No one has ever asked that before. We are invisible. We serve and clean. We are the faceless people."

"Not to me," Bronson said. "What's your name?"

"My friends call me Paco." He stepped forward and

although he was a good six inches shorter than Bronson, he locked his sight on Bronson's eyes. "I've never seen you before. I know you must be one of the Beauregards, as you are a guest in this house. But you're kind. You're different from them. Who exactly are you?"

Bronson chose his knife. One small enough to hide in his pocket, but large enough to do some damage. He made sure the shield wouldn't come off before he pocked the knife. Paco watched him through hawk-like eyes.

"I got some food in my room." Bronson placed his index finger over his lips. "Don't tell on me."

Paco shook his head.

Bronson continued, "My name is Alex Bentley. I'm the bad seed in the family. I don't normally see eye-to-eye with the rest of the family."

"Which is good news for me, but it must not be for you." Paco stepped away from Bronson. "Thank you for your silence. I'll leave now."

"Paco, wait."

He stopped and turned.

"Have you bought your little girl a gift?"

Paco pointed with his head. "The food. It was going to be her gift."

Bronson pulled out a twenty from his wallet. "Get her something special. You only turn ten once."

Paco's face lit up.

"And choose what you want from the refrigerator. I'll help you carry the food to your car."

Paco's lower lip dropped and his eyes glistened with tears. "Alicia—that's my little girl. She'll be so happy. How can I ever repay you?"

"Just be quick about it. We don't want any of the Beauregards to come stormin' in and spoilin' our plans."

"That's not likely to happen. They wouldn't be caught dead in the kitchen."

"I know that," Bronson said with all of the authoritative tone he could muster. He wondered why they wouldn't be caught dead in the kitchen. "But we still should hurry."

Paco nodded and opened the refrigerator door. He took out enough for a small banquet. Bronson and Paco packed the containers in two boxes. Bronson carried one and Paco the other. As soon as he'd helped Paco, he planned to return to the kitchen and reconsider the knife situation.

"This way," Paco said and led him down a labyrinth of hallways, deep into the outer part of the house.

"I really want to repay your kindness," Paco said. "What can I do?"

That's when an idea started forming in Bronson's thoughts.

SIXTY-THREE

THE JINGLING OF the cell woke Andrew up. He fumbled for the phone. When he saw the caller ID, he rubbed his eyelids and tried to focus. "Yes? Hi! Uh...?"

"Were you asleep?" Came the voice from the other end of the line. "My God, Andrew, it's almost ten. Do you plan to sleep the day away?"

"Uh, no." Andrew's mind was still foggy and he shook his head, hoping to clear the webs away. Last night, after leaving Bronson, he had stopped at the bar and picked up a bottle of rum. Bad move. He should have headed straight to bed. "I had a late night, that's all."

"Oh? Linda and you—"

Andrew smiled. That would have been nice. "No, nothing like that. Business kept me up. But I'm awake now."

A small pause came from the other end. "Business? As with Bentley?"

Good! He sounded pleased. "Yeah. We sat outside and talked."

"Is that so? You're one step ahead. One of these days, you're in for a big promotion."

Ah, sweet music to my ears, but I don't plan to wait that long. Andrew's smile widened. "I told him that today he's going to make that call."

"Excellent! What did he say?"

Andrew attempted to recall Bentley's words. He

closed his eyes but nothing came. It didn't matter. He'd tell his leader what he wanted to hear. "He said that would be no problem. He's as ready as we are."

"You do plan to listen in on the conversation?"

"Of course."

"Good. You'll have all of the details then, and that's exactly what we'll need."

Andrew sat up in bed. "What do you mean? Why should we be focusing on the details?" Was there something he wasn't catching onto? "Won't Bentley be taking care of them?"

"Think about it. Why complicate matters by having a third party? He sets the deal up and we move in."

Andrew swung his legs over the bed and slipped his slippers on. "I'm not following you."

"Really?" He stressed the word so it sounded like *rreallly*. "Do I have to spell everything out for you?"

Andrew rubbed his forehead, wishing the hangover away so he could think clearly. Then it dawned on him exactly what they were talking about. "You're considering killing Bentley."

"Do you have a problem with that?"

"He's a pleasant man, very easy to talk to. He listens to what I have to say." As soon as Andrew said that, he regretted it. In his kind of business being pleasant had nothing to do with the end result. He had to say something else fast before he'd be considered a weak link in the chain. "But I can see how his death will benefit us. That's the important part. No middle man means more money for us and less chance of things going wrong."

"Now you're talking."

He had gotten it right. Andrew beamed with happiness. "What are the plans?"

"Is Bentley still at your house?"

"He comes and goes as he pleases but only within the house. He knows he's not allowed to step outside."

"Which bedroom is his?"

"Third floor. The master guest bedroom."

"Good. As always, you do nothing. Tonight after all the details have been determined, call it an early evening and make sure all of your servants are gone. My two men know their way in. By late tomorrow night, Bentley will be dead."

SIXTY-FOUR

ANDREW AND BRONSON sat in the sunroom located on the left-hand side of the Beauregard mansion. They had been tweaking the plans each had made for the delivery of the goods. Andrew drank the last of his homemade lemonade, set the glass down, and looked at Bronson. "Do you have any questions before we finalize the deal?"

"Just one."

"Go ahead."

"I want to make sure your boss agrees to our plans. That's why I want him there tomorrow. I want to hear him say it before I leave."

"That's a reasonable request."

A few seconds passed before Bronson asked, "Are you and Thomas as close as everyone says?"

A faraway look came over Andrew's eyes. "Yes, of course. You saw us at the restaurant."

What Bronson had seen was an unspoken edge between them that united and separated them. "And the truth?"

Andrew's eyebrows rose in an arch as though a giant tree had been shattered. "What—what do you mean? We were always close."

"Were? Past tense?"

Andrew opened his mouth to speak. Then closed it. His eyes wandered around the room. "Was that what you'd call a Freudian slip?"

"You tell me."

Sorrow washed out Andrew's face, blurring his features. "We used to be very close when we were kids."

"What happened?"

"His dad—the senator—was always hard on him and kept comparing him to me. Eventually, Thomas got fed up and blamed me. He said I was more of a son to his dad than he was." Andrew's cheeks turned red and he looked away. "I didn't help matters either."

"How's that?"

"My father and I were never close. Sure, he provided for me, but he was never there. I heard from him two times a year, at Christmas and on my birthday. So if Thomas' dad wanted me to be his son too, I encouraged him." Andrew squirmed in his chair. "But enough about me. In spite of our troubles, Thomas and I are still friends." He looked at his watch. "We've been sitting here for almost an hour. Are you ready to make that call?" He offered Bronson the cell.

Without hesitating, Bronson accepted the phone and turned it on.

"Remember to put it on speaker. We don't want to be in for any surprises."

"I have no problem with that." Bronson punched in the corresponding numbers. He knew he would have to make the call today, and in the middle of the night, he had come up with an idea. He hoped it'd work and if it didn't, he had the knife in his pocket. Just in case.

Even before the person at the other end of the line answered, Bronson blurted out, "Hey, Manuel. It's me, Alex Bentley. You're on speaker, so the connection might not be all that good. Can you hear me?"

At the other end, Special Agent Antonio Corbalan

picked up on the code. "Hey, boss. I was getting worried. I thought maybe you had run into trouble."

"Not unless you call being kept prisoner in a millionaire's house trouble."

"Doesn't sound too bad. Or is it?"

Bronson looked at Andrew and smiled as his hand swept the area around him. "Nothing I can't handle."

Andrew nodded.

Antonio continued, "How long are you going to be held there?"

"Only long enough to finalize the arrangements."

"Which are?"

"Before I answer that," Bronson said. "Is everything set at your end?"

"My men are sitting around waiting for the command."

"Tell them that tomorrow at nine A.M. Central Time, we—that's me and all of those involved with this deal—will be at the Beauregard's private airstrip. There, I'll board a gray twin-engine Beechcraft plane. It's a sweet little thing with the Texas star painted on the tips of the wings and two more on each side toward the back of the plane. The wings also have a blue and white stripe pattern. It should be easy to spot."

"We'll be looking at the sky for that twin-engine Beechcraft plane. Tell the pilot to head for Bogota. To the south side, he will spot Parque Nacional Natural Chingaza. That's where we'll be. You know the place."

Bronson searched his brain. Was that some form of code? "I do."

"Then you can guide him, and when you get close enough to make contact, have him call us, and I'll give him specific directions." The FBI agent temporarily paused. "You will be safe in the plane, right?"

"I hope so," Bronson said and cast his eyes on Andrew.

He looked away.

SIXTY-FIVE

ANDREW LOCKED HIMSELF in the main library, one of the few soundproof rooms in the mansion. Even as he closed the door, he speed-dialed Morris' private number. He used the business number, the one that gave him direct access.

"How did the call go?" Morris wasted no time with friendly chit-chat, not that Andrew had expected any.

"That's what I'm calling about." Andrew's stomach turned. Anything that called for a change of plans was bad news, but he had no choice. "You can't kill Alex, or at least not yet."

"Arrangements have already been made. Why must I change plans?"

Andrew knew he would be drilled about the details of the call. He had carefully listened and memorized the key points. "Bentley's contact is a man named Manuel. He specifically said that Bentley had to be on that plane to point out where the pilot had to land. Without Alex there, how's the pilot going to know where to land?"

"What else did he say?"

"He said that we are supposed to head to Bogota, and at its south side, the pilot will spot Parque Nacional Natural Chingaza. That's where they would be. Then that's when he said that Alex had to be there to guide the pilot as to which way to head."

"Anything else?"

"Manuel said that when they get close enough, Alex is to contact him and he would give him specific directions."

"I'll call you back." Morris disconnected.

ANDREW SUNK RATHER than sat on the recliner facing the backyard. Books surrounded him, but what good were they if they couldn't give him the answer he sought? He shifted into a full reclining position. Might as well be comfortable.

The seconds dragged like thick molasses running uphill. Still, he waited for the call. He closed his eyes.

The cell vibrating in his hand startled Andrew awake. "I'm listening."

"Relax, will you? We got it covered. The pilot is familiar with the area. He said there are only two places he could land, and they're not that far apart from each other. When he's close enough, he'll make contact and get specific directions."

"What if Manuel demands to speak to Alex?"

"He will tell him that Alex is asleep in the back of the plane and there's no way he can be reached."

Andrew nodded even though he knew Morris couldn't see him.

Morris' demanding tone spoke loud and clear. "That takes us back to our original plan. Empty the house out and call it an early night."

"I will." Andrew rubbed the bridge of his nose. There was nothing he could do. As much as he hated it, Alex had only a few hours left to live.

SIXTY-SIX

Dinner that night was a quiet affair, filled with long, awkward conversational pauses. The silence was magnified by the gentle sounds of silverware, crystal, and china. Bronson sat across from Andrew at the long dining table. As he slurped his soup, he locked his gaze on Andrew.

Andrew looked everywhere but at him.

Maybe Andrew felt embarrassed at having revealed so much about himself. If so, that would explain the lack of eye contact. "Good soup." Bronson took another spoonful.

A long pause followed, then, "Yes, it is."

"You're lucky, having great cooks. Each night must be a feast."

Andrew nodded but didn't look up.

What was bothering Andrew? Bronson wished he knew. His alert button turned on.

Both focused on the rest of the meal.

At long last, the meal was over and Bronson felt relief. He set his napkin beside his empty plate. "As always, thank you for dinner. It was very good." He faked a yawn. "I'm tired and tomorrow will be a long day. I'm goin' to head to my room and have a good night's rest."

Andrew looked at his watch and a wave of relief

washed over his face. "It's only seven. You're calling it quits this early?"

"I may stop at the library and read for maybe half an hour, and then I'm off to my room. Is that all right?"

Andrew nodded. "Of course, it is. In fact, that's not a bad idea." He signaled for the head waiter.

"Yes, sir?"

"Mr. Bentley wants to have a good night's rest. I want you to gather all the servants and have them out of here by nine. Is that clear?"

"That's not necessary," Bronson said.

Andrew ignored Bronson and zoomed in on the head waiter. "Is that clear?"

"Yes, sir." He turned and headed toward the kitchen.

Bronson stood. "I've changed my mind. I need to pack, so I'll head to my room instead. Then I'll read and get some shut-eye."

"I'll do the same—except for the packing part."

Bronson smiled. "Goodnight, then." He headed out of the room.

"Alex."

Bronson stopped and turned.

"I just want you to know that it's been a pleasure working with you. I wish… I wish things didn't have…" He cleared his throat. "What I meant to say is that I wish we had gotten to know each other a bit better."

Bronson digested and made a mental note of every word Andrew spoke. "We will. Next time."

"Next time." Andrew spoke so softly that Bronson hardly heard him.

That had been the warning signal. There would be no next time. Of that, Bronson was sure.

MIGHT AS WELL PACK, Bronson thought. He gathered his few personal items and stuffed them in the suitcase. He placed the open valise on the floor by the door.

He set the alarm clock for two forty-five AM and forced himself to fall asleep. He would need all of his strength for the events he knew would soon unfold.

Right before he turned off the light, he placed the knife under the pillow next to his. It'd be easy to reach just in case he needed it.

SIXTY-SEVEN

Gerry stood six-foot-five and was all muscle and no fat. He preferred trucks because they reminded him of a manly vehicle. They were big and strong, like him.

He drove his Ford truck to the back of the Beauregard mansion and parked in front of the door normally reserved for deliveries.

"We're already here, and you haven't said a word." Jack, who often teamed up with Gerry to do odd jobs, said. He was a bit taller than six feet and like his partner, pure muscle. "What gives?"

"I've been considering various ways to eliminate Bentley."

Jack wiped the sweat from his forehead and took out his subcompact semi-auto .380 ACP. "This would be the easiest and fastest." He kissed the barrel of the gun. "Always reliable." He allowed it to rest on his lap.

Gerry turned off the engine. "Put that away. The gun is to be used only as a last resort. We don't want anybody to see or hear us. I want us in and out at the snap of a finger."

Jack frowned and returned the gun to its holster. "You're thinking of doing the deed with a knife?"

Gerry shook his head. "Too messy. The staff would call the police as soon as they saw all of that blood and realized Bentley was missing. We want Bentley to simply disappear. No police. No mess."

"What then?"

"A pillow."

"Huh?"

"We sneak into Bentley's room and since it's past midnight, he should be sound asleep. I'll grab a pillow and smother him. You hold him down."

Jack bit his lip. "What if he's awake?"

"Then we apologize and say we're guests and we got the wrong room. We'll ask him to show us where the other bedrooms are. When he turns around, we grab him. I don't like snapping necks, but I've done it before."

Jack shook himself as though attempting to erase a memory. "That should work, but I'm taking my gun just in case."

Gerry opened the truck door and slid out. "That's a wise move." He headed toward the back door, the one reserved for deliveries. Jack followed close behind.

Gerry turned the doorknob and the door opened, just as he had expected. He knew Andrew would leave it open for them.

Gerry and Jack stepped into the entryway and darkness bathed them. Gerry had thought to bring a flashlight, but he was so familiar with the Beauregard floor plan, he knew it would be unnecessary.

"Ready?" Gerry mouthed the word. He didn't want to take a chance of waking anybody.

Jack nodded.

Gerry led him past a large room that served as the pantry, then into the kitchen, and down the series of hallways that led to the stairs. At the bottom of the staircase, Gerry paused and listened to the silence. He wasn't expecting any problems, but he had always leaned toward the side of precaution. After he was satisfied no one was around, he signaled for Jack to follow.

Soon as they reached the third floor, Gerry zoomed in on the first door to the right, Bentley's master suite. He looked at the bottom of the door. Only darkness came from the other side. He pressed his ear against the door. Quiet as a grave. Gerry's lips curved upward in an awkward smile. He liked that comparison.

He reached for the doorknob and gently turned it.

He stepped inside Bentley's room and focused on the bed.

SIXTY-EIGHT

PACO CHEWED THE inside of his mouth. Andrew had ordered all household staff—those who live outside the mansion—out by nine. Those, whose quarters were part of the house, would be restricted to their area. That could only mean one thing: something was going down tonight, and a rock settled in Paco's stomach.

Why of all the nights, why tonight?

That was typical of his luck, Paco thought. Or maybe not. Maybe his luck was changing, and it was due to that nice man, Alex Bentley. He wasn't anything like the rest of his family. Andrew ruled as though he were a god and everyone in the house were peons.

But this Alex Bentley—he seemed to care. He had made his daughter, Alicia, so happy.

When she saw the rich, fancy food Paco had brought for her birthday, she squealed with joy. The two of them had sat and enjoyed the rich man's delights. "I didn't think food could look and taste so good, Papa." She helped herself to another serving. "This is the best birthday ever. Thank you, Papa."

"That's not all." Paco reached into his wallet and handed his daughter the twenty-dollar bill Alex had given him. "This is for you to spend any way you want." He wished he had taken the time to gift wrap the money.

Alicia's mouth dropped open. "Papa, no. That's a twenty. That's too much. We can't afford it."

Paco smiled. "This time, we can."

Alicia threw her arms around him and squeezed him tight.

Paco could still feel that embrace. He beamed with such radiance that it would put the brightest lighthouse to shame.

Alex had made his little girl happy, and that's something Paco would never forget.

When Alex asked him to come tonight to help him, Paco had no choice but to say, "Yes." Paco felt he had to pay back the kindness. He came even though he knew something was going to go down tonight and he knew he should stay away.

The problem was that Alex had asked him to meet him at three. He looked at his watch. It read 12:23. Way too early.

Paco considered his alternatives. He could go down to the kitchen and bring home some more of those fancy dishes. He shook his head. That would be stealing. There was a big difference between celebrating and stealing. Paco wasn't a thief.

The only thing he could do was wait for Alex to join him.

Paco took a deep breath. Waiting was not a good alternative. He had specifically come early because he knew something was going down tonight. He wanted to get done whatever Alex wanted him to do and then be out and gone before the storm hit.

Paco chewed the inside of his cheek and stared at his watch. Only two minutes had dragged by. Right now the house was nice and quiet, but who knew what would happen in an hour or two? Maybe even in ten or fifteen minutes.

If he didn't act now, Alex might not get his wish, and that was wrong. That man deserved the best.

That left only one choice. He'd climb to the third level and wake Alex up.

Paco took a deep breath and began his ascent.

SIXTY-NINE

"Where the hell is he?" Jack asked. They had found an empty, unmade bed. Bentley had been sleeping here not too long ago.

Gerry checked the adjoining bathroom while Jack searched the closet. Their efforts proved fruitless. Gerry signaled for Jack to check under the bed.

"You think he knows?" Jack lowered his voice.

"How could he?"

Jack shrugged and bent down and looked. No Bentley. "Should we wake Andrew up?" He straightened up and dusted the lint off his pants.

"No. That will only complicate matters."

"Then what do we do?"

Andrew spotted Bentley's suitcase. It had been neatly packed and remained opened on the floor by the door. "Andrew told me Bentley likes to roam the house at night. His suitcase is still here. He hasn't left. Chances are he's somewhere out there." Gerry pointed to the door. "Let's find him."

"And if we can't?" Jack made sure his gun was easily available.

"We can always take care of Bentley tomorrow. Our main concern is that Morris is safe. We'll give our search fifteen minutes. If we can't find Bentley by then, we'll head next door and make sure Morris isn't in danger." He opened the bedroom door and waited. When nothing happened, he stuck his head out. The hallway was empty. He let himself out and signaled for Jack to follow.

PACO CLIMBED ONLY three steps when he heard his name called. He froze. He didn't want to lose his job. He slowly turned, his mind formulating lies as to why he was here. His sight landed on a dark shadow. Paco nibbled on his lower lip. "I can see you."

The figure took a step forward, away from the darkness. "It's me, Alex. I didn't mean to scare you."

Paco relaxed his shoulders. "You're up. We weren't supposed to meet for at least two more hours."

"I know. I felt restless, so I got up. Is that okay?" Alex looked around as though expecting someone.

"It's more than okay." Relief flooded Paco's lungs. "Are you ready?"

Alex nodded. "You have no idea how ready I am."

"Then let's do this." He looked at Alex. "What exactly do you want me to do?"

"Take me away from here."

Alex had told him that much yesterday. He had explained how he couldn't leave on his own because he would set off the alarm and once outside, he'd have to fight the dogs. But if Paco came in through the servant's entrance, he'd be able to leave with him. "That's all you want?"

Alex nodded.

Easy enough. "Follow me."

Paco led Alex to the servants' quarters. Under normal circumstances, this was a bright, happy place. But now with all lights turned off and a silence that devoured them, Paco began to sweat.

"How far is your apartment?" Alex asked.

"Not far from here. One of these days, I hope to earn the privilege of living here." He opened the door at the end of the hallway. "This way."

Alex saw the car parked in the servant's garage, an early 2000 Chevy sedan. It was in desperate need of paint. "That's the most beautiful car I've ever seen."

"Liar." Paco smiled. "But it's all mine. Get in."

Alex slid into the front passenger's seat.

Paco started the engine and the car was soon bouncing down the road away from the Beauregard mansion. "Now that you have your freedom, where do you want to go?"

"I want to talk to the neighbors, specifically, I'd like to pay Morris a visit."

SEVENTY

"I appreciate you doin' this for me," Bronson said. "I don't want to make a pest of myself, but I have one more favor to ask."

Paco glanced at the man sitting next to him. "What's that?"

"I'd like to borrow your cell. I have an urgent call to make."

"I use the little money Mr. Beauregard pays me to buy food and clothing for Alicia and pay rent and utilities. There's no money left for luxuries like a phone."

Bronson closed his eyes. All that money Andrew had—what good did it do? "I'm sorry. Do you have access to a phone at all?"

"The apartment complex has a community phone. I use that."

"If I give you a number, can you relay a message for me?"

"Depends. Who am I calling?"

"His name is Antonio Corbalan. He's an FBI Special Agent."

Paco whistled a *wow!* "What do I tell him?"

"Tell him I'm at the Morris mansion and may need back up."

"Back up?" Paco slowed down.

Bronson sat up straighter and glanced around, making sure no one was following them. He remembered the last car trouble episode he and Mike had, and its memory made Bronson feel uncomfortable. "Car trouble?"

Paco pulled off and the car came to a stop. "Look, Alex…Bentley, I don't want any trouble. All I wanted was to repay a favor."

"There will be no trouble, at least not for you." Bronson focused on the dark shadows that surrounded them. Nothing there. He hoped. "Just drop me off at the Morris' house and you take off. You and your daughter will be safe. Just please, make that call."

Paco pocked his keys. "I'm not moving until I hear the truth."

Bronson turned away from the car window and met his look. "Meanin'?"

"I may be poor, but I'm not a fool. No matter what you say, you're not a Beauregard. Who are you?"

"That's not really important." Bronson tossed out the remark as casual as yesterday's lunch.

"It is to me. I don't want any troubles descending on my little girl." He watched Bronson closely with eyes that missed little and revealed less. "Maybe you should get out. You can walk the rest of the way. My debt to you has been repaid. I got you out of the house."

Bronson's sense of foreboding deepened. "You're right. I'm not a Beauregard. I'm sorry about lyin' to you." He took a deep breath. "I just thought it would be safer for you. The less you know, the better."

"That doesn't work." Paco folded his arms and rested them against the steering wheel. "The truth or you start walking."

Bronson frowned and nodded. "Alex Bentley isn't my real name. It's Bronson. Harry Bronson. I'm not an FBI agent but I do work for the bureau. Sort of. I used to be a homicide detective for the Dallas Police Department. But I'm not anymore. I'm simply a man tryin' to right a wrong and help a close friend along the way."

"Bronnnson." Paco said the name as though he tasted the word. "That name suits you a lot better. What wrong are you trying to fix?"

"Sorry. I'm not at liberty to discuss the details. It's an ongoin' investigation."

"So Andrew has dipped his hand into something illegal. I knew it." He started the engine and pulled off into the road. "I'm assuming Mr. Morris is also involved. Is that why you're trying to get to his house?"

Bronson was hoping to find something that would connect Thomas to Andrew's illegal going-ons. He knew Antonio would be furious with him for doing this on his own, but he had no choice. He was running out of time. "What can you tell me about Thomas?"

Paco's eyebrows arched. "Oh, that Morris. I thought you were talking about the senator."

"We'll get to him later. But first, tell me about Thomas."

"Thomas. He's the best in the bunch. He takes care of us. I work for him, you know."

"I thought you worked for Andrew."

"I work for both." He sighed. "I can't spend as much time with Alicia now, but it's only temporarily." Paco beamed as though he had accomplished a great task. "I just started. Two weeks ago. I haven't been paid yet, but the first thing I'm doing with that money is buying me a phone. Alicia would really like that."

"If you work there, then you're familiar with the house's layout."

"My job is to straighten out the rooms. That may not

sound like much, but it does keep me busy. The house is very large, so yeah, I am acquainted with the layout."

"Tell me about it."

Paco did and Bronson made mental notes. When he finished, Bronson asked, "Can you get me inside?"

"Now? At this time? I don't have a key or the code like I do to Andrew's house."

"How can I get in?"

Paco's eyebrows furrowed. "The main gardener likes to work on the yard at this time of night. He sleeps during the day. Tito is my friend. I'll explain things to him. If he's outside working, he'll let us in. If not, you're on your own." Paco turned into the long, sweeping driveway.

"Once you drop me off and talk to Tito if he's there, you can go. I don't want to get you into trouble. I'll find my way back to Andrew's house."

The road formed a *Y* and Paco took a right, past the senator's mansion. Bronson focused on the structure. It loomed before him, giving him the feeling that its dark windows were eyes staring. Watching. Waiting for him.

Further on down the road, Bronson spotted a second dwelling, Thomas' residence. The structure was too big to be called a house. It was more like a mini-mansion, without the mini part.

Bronson wrote down Antonio's phone number and handed Paco the paper. "Please make that call."

Paco studied the paper. "I'm sure Tito will let me borrow his cell if he has one." He accepted the paper, drove to the back of the house, and turned off the engine. "You're a lucky man. That's Tito over there." He pointed to a man pulling out weeds from around the rose vines. "Wait in here while I talk to him."

Bronson watched him as he approached the gardener. Several times, during their conversation, Tito would turn to look at Bronson. He nodded and both headed toward Bronson. Bronson slid out of the car and waited for them.

"He doesn't have his cell, but he can get you in," Paco said.

MINUTES LATER, Bronson was inside the house.

Based on what Paco had told him, Thomas had an office in the house. He'd begin his search there.

SEVENTY-ONE

As Bronson crept down the hallway toward Thomas' office, his heart pounded with such force, he was sure he had swallowed a full marching band complete with a drum line. If Paco had been correct, the pair of light oak doors next to him led to the office. He plastered his ear to the door and listened to silence. He looked under the door. No lights. He turned the knob. It easily opened.

Bronson stepped in and closed the door behind him, thankful that the floor-to-ceiling curtains were open and the full moon lit up the room. The spacious office contained high ceilings and museum-quality furniture. Just as Bronson had expected.

The right-hand side of the room housed two four-drawer wooden file cabinets, a bookcase filled with books, and a mahogany leather top desk. Other than a set of solid-gold Mont Blanc fountain pens, a calendar with flip pages, and a lamp, its top was empty.

At the opposite end of the room, a leather couch faced a Bolivian Rosewood coffee table. Two recliners and a loveseat completed the décor.

Bronson's head jerked up when he heard footsteps in the hallway. He scanned the room and figured that he could if need be, dive behind the couch. Not the best place to hide, but for now, the only place. Whoever walked the hallway went past the office and continued down the hallway. Bronson let out the air he'd been holding. He was safe, at least for the moment.

He tried to open the top cabinet drawer. It was locked. Naturally. He'd tackle that later if need be. Chances were that if Thomas was hiding something, it would be hidden in his desk. He opened the top right-hand side drawer. It was filled with office supplies, notepads, and a basket that held odds and ends. Bronson took out the basket and tapped on the drawer's bottom. No secret compartment there. He returned the basket to its original place.

The next drawer held a small box filled with stamps, address labels, and envelopes. Neatly stacked next to this box was a stack of blank stationery. Bronson thumbed through the papers. Other than the fancy letterhead, the stationary held no interest. Just like before, he tapped on the drawer. Again, no false bottom.

He attempted to open the last drawer but found it locked. He studied the locking mechanism. If he had a pick, he'd have it open in less than a second. But without the proper tools, he was out of luck.

He reopened the first drawer and searched through the basket. He saw paperclips—a possibility—a ruler, a measuring tape, address labels, file folders markers, a magnifying glass, and a custom-made leather box. He opened it and encountered miniature screwdrivers, various sizes of files, and—*bingo!*—a set of picks.

Hot diggity dog. He was on a roll.

He chose the largest of the picks and got to work on the lock. The pick was too small to do a proper job. Maybe if he used a steadier one, he'd have better luck. He grabbed it and tried again. And failed. *Focus, Bronson, you can do this.* On the third try, the lock clicked open. He returned the tools to their proper place and slid open the bottom drawer.

It concealed only one item. A ledger. Bronson's heart revved like a squad car in pursuit. Could he really be this lucky?

He reached for the ledger but stopped when he heard footsteps approaching. This time, whoever stood on the other side was turning the doorknob.

Bronson closed the drawer and dashed toward the back of the couch just as two men stepped in.

SEVENTY-TWO

"You're a deep disappointment to me," one of the men who entered the room said. Even though he spoke in hushed tones, his words erupted geyser-like. "Always have been. Always will be."

"I could say the same about you, Dad." Thomas stressed the word *dad*, making it sound dirty.

From his hiding place behind the couch, Bronson was privy to their conversation. One of those men had to be Thomas. Bronson recognized his voice. The other one—dad—had to be the senator.

"How dare you speak that way to me," Senator Morris said.

Someone flipped the light switch and the room lit up as bright as noon.

"And how dare you invite filth into your life and then spread it to encompass mine," Thomas said.

One of them sat on the loveseat across from the couch while the other paced. Bronson's gut told him Thomas was the one who did the pacing.

"I have no idea what that means." The Senator cast the sentence out with as much enthusiasm as one would devote to last week's agenda.

The pacing stopped. "Don't ever play me the fool again. I've known for a while now what Andrew's doing. I also know you're the one he answers to."

Bronson's eyebrows shot up. *Oh really?* He had had

his suspicions, but until now, he couldn't confirm it. Bronson would give anything if he could see the senator's face.

"Again, I have no idea what you're talking about." The senator's tone was steady and calm. A true politician—indeed.

Thomas continued, "The smuggling, the laundering, all those other activities you and Andrew dipped your hands in. I tolerated them. I even looked the other way because we're...family. But I draw the line at murder." He resumed his pacing, then stopped. "Murder. Really, Dad? What right did you have to order Mike's death?"

Bronson clenched his fists so hard his knuckles turned white.

The senator bolted to his feet. "Do you know what you are? You're an ungrateful spoiled brat. You like all that money to do as you want. But did you ever try to earn even one penny? How dare you!"

"No, Dad. How. Dare. You." He resumed his pacing and the senator flopped down on the loveseat.

Tension, as thick and ugly as dirty motor oil, filled the room. Bronson waited for someone to speak.

"You know what, Dad?"

Thomas' quiet, calm tone sent a bolt of lightning through Bronson's heart. He could only imagine what affect it had on the senator.

Thomas continued, "I've had it. For weeks now, I have wanted to call the police. But I couldn't bring myself to do it. Then Andrew unknowingly confirmed you had ordered Mike's execution. That's murder, Dad. Murder." A long silence followed, then, "It's going to kill me, but I will testify against you and Andrew."

The senator laughed. The sound reminded Bronson

of a mink, sleek and cute on the outside, but ready to bite at a minute's notice.

"You can't prove a thing, and you'll come out sounding like a spoiled brat who's trying to discredit his father. I'll make sure I let everyone know that I've disinherited you because of your laziness, and this is just your way of trying to get revenge. You'll be one-hundred percent discredited. Is that what you really want?" The senator spoke with as much emotion as if he were dictating a letter. "You'll become a laughing stock. People will feel sorry for me, and you will be ruined. I, on the other hand, will continue on my path to become president of the United States."

"You'll never get there."

"And what makes you think that?"

"Because I have proof."

The Ledger! That would be his proof.

The senator's voice vibrated with an almost undetected tremor. "You're lying. What evidence could you possibly have?"

Bronson waited for the answer but instead, he heard Thomas' retreating steps as he let himself out and gently closed the door behind him.

Senator Morris remained glued to the loveseat for a few seconds. Then he stood and flipped off the light switch.

Bronson relaxed. As soon as the senator walked out, he would check the ledger, take it with him if need be, and get back to Andrew's house before he was missed. He waited to hear the senator's footsteps telling him he left the room. But instead, Senator Morris flopped down on the same seat he had previously occupied.

Time ticked away and yet the senator remained unmoving, the room's darkness embracing him.

Bronson cocked his head. He was as alert as a bird getting ready to take flight. He heard muffled noises. Was the senator crying?

Moments later, Bronson detected a small light. The senator had activated his cell. He must have punched in some numbers for the phone began to ring.

Someone picked up and Senator Morris said, "Listen carefully. I will only say this once. Thomas is facing some conflicting issues. It always helps him calm down when he takes the Porsche for a drive. He should be doing that in about half an hour. I want you and Floyd to follow him. When he's out in the road, I want you to cut him off."

A silence followed as the senator listened to whomever he was talking to.

"Yes, that's exactly what I mean. He may be my son, but he's become a dangerous threat to us. He needs to be eliminated. Do it fast and efficiently. I don't want him to suffer more than he has to. Just make sure you make it look like an accident."

The senator went quiet as he once again listened to the speaker at the other end.

"Jack and Gerry should be arriving any minute. I sent them to Andrew's house to have them take care of that other business. Soon as they get here, I'll tell them to go help you. Call me when it's done." He disconnected and remained sitting as though he wanted the darkness to swallow him.

Bronson leaned his head back on the couch.

Think. Think. Think! He had to warn Thomas. But how? He was trapped in this room.

SEVENTY-THREE

TIME ADVANCED AT a glacier's pace and still the senator remained in Thomas' office, sitting in the darkness.

Bronson took a deep breath and started to formulate a plan. He knew he could over-power the senator, but he might let out a scream before Bronson was able to knock him out. Alerting the entire house wasn't a good idea.

Maybe he could belly-crawl like a soldier and pray the senator was too focused on what he was about to do and wouldn't see him advance. Once—

The senator stood and headed toward the entrance. He waited by the open door, probably staring at the room. At long last, he gently closed the door and walked away.

Bronson let out a sigh of relief and forced himself to wait for the senator to leave the hallway. Bronson slowly counted. *One*...

Two...

Three...

When he reached thirty-three—his lucky number— he crept out of his hiding place. Bending low, he returned to the desk and retrieved the ledger. He couldn't afford the luxury of looking it over. That meant he'd have to take it with him.

Bronson stepped forward and pressed his ear to the door. No sounds came. He took a deep breath and inched the door open. The hallway was clear.

Now to find Thomas. Where would he go? Bronson searched his brain for an answer. If, as his father said, Thomas derived comfort from his Porsche, then chances were he'd find him sitting in his car.

Paco had given Bronson a detailed layout of the house. So far, everything had been accurate. If he headed down this hallway and up the next one, it would lead to the garage.

The sound of approaching footsteps sent Bronson's heart pounding. He dashed into the room to his right, a game room, complete with a pool table and a television as large as most theaters' screens. He plastered his body behind a bookcase stacked with table games. He held his breath.

He waited.

He heard distinct voices as the men approached. From the sound of them, two men walked side by side. One must have said something funny as both laughed.

Then they stopped in front of the game room door frame.

Another funny thing was said, but this time, only one laughed.

"Let's forget this and hit the sack instead. We're going to be sucking tomorrow."

His partner must have agreed as both turned and left.

Bronson waited and counted. This time he counted only to twenty. He was running out of time. When he finished, he stuck his head out from behind the case. The coast looked clear. As he drifted toward the exit, his elbow hit the case, knocking down one of the games.

Bronson froze.

He listened.

Nothing.

He thanked his lucky stars and dashed toward the door he hoped led to the garage. He turned the knob and let himself out.

He was in the garage, the blue Porsche before him. The empty blue Porsche.

SEVENTY-FOUR

"ALEX?" THE VOICE came out high-pitched and incredulous. "What the heck are you doing here?" Thomas stepped away from the shadows at the opposite side of the garage.

Bronson mentally slapped himself because he had failed to see Thomas. Bronson had been so focused on the car. "You're in danger."

"What?"

"I need to get you out of here."

Thomas headed toward Bronson. When he saw the ledger in Bronson's hand, Thomas' jaw stiffened and his eyes bore into Bronson's. "What are you doing with that?"

"You said you had evidence. I thought this might be it." He handed it to Thomas.

Thomas grabbed it away from him. Anger burned in his eyes. "You better explain yourself."

Bronson realized that the only way to make him move was to spit out the truth. "You told your father you were going to call the police."

Thomas stared at Bronson, wide-eyed. "How did you—"

Bronson didn't let him finish. "After you left your office, the senator called someone and ordered him and Floyd to give you half-an-hour, then follow you when you drove off in the Porsche. They are to cut you off the road and kill you. Your father is also sending two more men, Jack and Gerry, to help them. Now can we go?"

The color drained from Thomas' face, and his blue eyes searched Bronson's face as though he was eager for Bronson to assure him that he'd just told him a bad joke.

"Move it." Bronson used his commanding voice. "If we leave now, we might not encounter them on the road."

Thomas remained still.

"Move it. Now!"

Thomas shook himself and jumped onto the driver's seat.

Bronson climbed into the passenger's side and buckled up.

Thomas started the engine as the garage door opened. "Where to?"

"Just drive. I'll tell you when to stop." Even as he spoke, Bronson's mind spat out various possibilities.

The tires squealed as Thomas gunned the engine and sped away.

"Whoa. Slow down. You don't want them to think you're onto them. Drive like you normally do."

Thomas shrugged. "This is how I always drive."

"Okay, then." Bronson tightened his seat belt. "Can I borrow your cell?"

"I don't have it. It's back home."

Bronson sighed in frustration. He had to believe that Paco had found a way to contact Special Agent Antonio. "This is Texas. Tell me that you at least have a gun."

"That's also back home, next to my cell." The senator's house came to view and Thomas stared at it as though it had grown fangs.

"You okay?" Bronson asked.

Thomas shook himself. "Yeah." He returned his sight to the road. "How do I know you're telling the truth?"

"Listen to your gut. It's tellin' you I'm your only chance."

Thomas' silence gave Bronson hope. "Up ahead, just after the road forms an upside-down *Y*, you'll see a small dip in the road. I want you to pull off there."

"Why?"

"You'll open the hood. They'll think you got car trouble and started walking. They'll start combing the woods. They're not expectin' me. That'll give me an advantage." Bronson focused on the line of trees, unmoving black sentinels in the dark road.

"What do I do?"

"You follow the road, but remain hidden behind the tree line." Bronson focused on the rearview mirror. No lights headed their way. At least, not yet. "You see a car approachin' duck and wait until the lights disappear before you move. With luck, maybe you'll see a line of police cars headin' this way. If so, wave them down."

"How would they know to come?"

"I asked Paco to call Special Agent Antonio Corbalan."

An expression of confusion mirrored in his eyes. "Paco?"

"Paco, like your new servant. I'd give him a raise if I were you."

They reached the dip on the road and Thomas eased off the gas. "It's not right, leaving you here. Four men will be out there hunting for me, and there's only one of you to stop them."

"I'm countin' on takin' care of the first two before the other two show up."

Thomas parked the car and turned off the engine. "Still, they have guns. You don't."

"I have rocks, branches, and a kitchen knife. They don't." Bronson pointed to the ledger. "Aren't you goin' to need that?"

Thomas nodded and reached for it. "You'll need to explain how you got hold of this."

"Another time." Bronson got out and nodded toward the hood.

Thomas opened it.

"That should do it," Bronson said. "Now go get help."

Thomas shook his head. "Alex—"

"Bronson."

"What?"

"My real name is Bronson. Harry Bronson. Now get goin'."

Thomas stood still. "I shouldn't leave you."

"Do you know how to street fight?"

Thomas shook his head.

"Have you ever hit a person with the intent to kill or render him useless?"

Again, Thomas shook his head.

"That's what I mean. I can't fight them and take care of you at the same time. Your intentions are good, but you'd be a bigger help if you could bring the cavalry to me."

Thomas looked down and nodded. He turned and headed down the road.

"Thomas."

He stopped. "Behind the trees, remember? And walk on the other side so you're facing traffic. If they try to abduct you, they're goin' to have to turn around."

Thomas crossed the street and disappeared into the trees.

Bronson sat on the ground and removed his shoes and socks. After putting his shoes back on, he glanced around for the right size rocks. He stuffed them into his sock. Next, he searched for the right size branch.

A beam of lights appeared at the edge of the hill. Bronson dashed toward the darkness. He wished he had had more time to prepare.

Here we go.

SEVENTY-FIVE

From his vantage point behind an oak tree, Bronson watched the car roll down the hill. *They must suspect something. Otherwise, they wouldn't be approaching at a snail's pace.* Bronson's alert button went up a notch.

The car pulled behind the Porsche but its passengers didn't get out. They kept their brights on, making it impossible to see inside the car.

Bronson held onto one of the stuffed socks, ready to swing it at one of the men's head. That should knock him down while Bronson disabled the other man. But he couldn't do anything until they got out of the car. What were they doing?

Time ticked away at a snail's pace. Still, the men remained sitting in the car.

Bronson caught a glimpse of another set of headlights heading his way. Now he knew what they had been waiting for.

So much for fighting two at a time.

Thomas did exactly what Alex—no, not Alex. What had he said was his name? Bronson, that was it—told him to do. He sprinted forward, keeping the trees between him and the road. He wished he could run on the pavement. He could go much faster. What would it hurt? Hardly anyone used this road, especially at three in the morning.

He was about to leave the safety of the trees when at the far distance, he saw the glow of headlights growing bigger as the car approached. He bolted back to the forest where the trees concealed him. He watched as a gray sedan roared past him.

Thomas immediately recognized the company car. Although it had been too dark to see inside, Thomas felt sure that Jack and Gerry were the passengers. They rushed to help Floyd and Ruben so all four could hunt him down like an animal and kill him.

Thomas shuttered as disbelief settled in. Dad—no, not Dad but Father—had ordered his death. What was the purpose of continuing? If his own father didn't love him enough to save him…

A branch scratched the top of his head and he swat it.

A branch.

Bronson had more than just a branch to fight. He had four trained men, not two like he had hoped. Should he turn back and help him?

THE APPROACHING CAR came to a stop and two beefy-looking men got out. The driver's door of the first car opened and a man let himself out. Where was his partner? Had Bronson assumed wrong?

The three conversed in low tones.

Like rapids in a river, Bronson's mind bounced from one possibility to the other. He could fight two at a time, but three armed men? Bronson's job was to protect Thomas. These men had no idea where he was. He was safe.

Maybe Bronson should retreat. Let the authorities round up them up. Bronson looked down when one of them slammed shut the Porsche's hood. They had probably realized that nothing was wrong with the vehicle. They must be growing suspicious.

Best if Bronson made his exit while he still could. He stepped away from the protection of the tree. He'd take one tree at a time until he was safely out of their sight and firing range. The next one was about three feet away. He bent low and kept quiet.

He edged his way forward and froze.

The barrel of a gun shoved against the small of his back forced Bronson to stand still.

"Start talking," the voice behind him said.

Bronson raised his arms but didn't turn around.

SEVENTY-SIX

"Is that your Porsche, Mister?" Bronson asked. "I was walkin' when I saw the abandoned vehicle. I thought maybe I could…" He shrugged. "Well, you know. But if that's your car, I'll keep headin' my way. No harm done."

"You were walking on this particular road at three in the morning?" His sarcastic tone told Bronson everything he needed to know.

"Is that what time it is? I'm a drifter, and I don't have a watch." Bronson mentally prepared himself for the next step.

"Very funny." The man gave him a small push. Just what Bronson had been waiting for.

"Start walking." His firm voice demanded to be obeyed.

Bronson pretended to stumble from the push. He used that distraction to swing his elbow backward. It impacted with his assailant's mid-drift.

The man doubled over.

Bronson pivoted, clasped his hands together, and brought them down hard on the man's back.

The man dropped to the ground, face first. A trickle of blood ran down the hill.

Bronson turned him over and as best as he could checked him. He was still alive but unconscious.

If Bronson was to get away, he'd better hurry. But first, he'd locate the man's gun. His search cost him several precious moments. He was about to give up when he spotted the glint of metal on the ground. He smiled when he realized it was the gun he'd been looking for. He picked it up and placed it in his pants pocket.

He glanced down at the three men. They continued with their conversation but soon, their concern would grow for their friend.

Bronson had no time to waste. He turned, heading away from them. He had traveled several yards when he heard his attacker yell in a wobbly voice, "Over here. He's getting away."

Bronson gasped as though he'd been stabbed by a thousand needles. He had thought he'd be unconscious a lot longer.

The man staggered as he attempted to stand. He held on to a tree for balance.

In record time, Bronson reached him.

When he saw Bronson approach, his eyes widened, huge as saucers. He released his hold on the tree and moved forward, away from Bronson and toward his companions. Bronson reached out with a kick. The man stumbled and fell, hitting his head on a boulder. He remained still.

He would no longer pose any problems, but the damage had already been done.

With guns drawn, the three below ascended the small hill, heading toward Bronson.

SEVENTY-SEVEN

Instead of heading away from his attackers, Bronson ran in a horizontal position, hoping to put distance between him and the man furthest to his left. Then he'd do a ninety-degree turn and move downward so that he'd come behind his first target.

Bronson focused his vision downward. A clearer pathway lay ahead, but reaching it would consume valuable time. He'd take the rockier and more direct trail, a trail that would consume most of his energy. He galloped down the path as best as he could. He dodged fallen timber and was forced to climb over rotting trunks, but he kept going. His muscles felt on fire and his lungs screamed. Still, he advanced.

Staying in the shadowy stretch of the woods, he reached his turning point and rested a moment. Here, the trees sat wider apart and the shadows were less concealing. This was where skill stopped and luck entered. He started to descend, keeping several yards between him and his target.

Whispering a silent prayer, Bronson left the safety of a tree and scooted toward the next one.

His pursuer's head pivoted at the sound of crunching leaves. He had caught a whisper of Bronson's movement.

Bronson froze, hoping the shadows swallowed him.

The man cocked his head and stopped. He swept the area with his gun.

An inch at a time, Bronson slid behind a tree. He waited for the sound of approaching footsteps.

He listened.

Nothing.

Bronson relaxed. He stuck his head out only enough to assess the situation.

The thug remained still, his head sweeping the shadows. He shook and then was on the move, slithering his way toward Bronson.

Bronson held his breath. He was the lamb in a den of lions.

The man continued his advance.

Bronson skirted the tree. With luck, the thug would go past the mighty oak and Bronson could surprise him from behind.

The other two men seemed unaware of the drama unfolding around them and continued their climb.

"Over here," yelled the one furthest away from Bronson. "It's Ruben. He's unconscious."

Bronson's intended target hesitated as he directed his attention toward the sound of his friend's voice.

That hesitation was all Bronson needed. He stepped away from the safety of the tree. The man half-turned. His eyes, dark beneath the rim of the baseball cap, widened when he made eye contact with Bronson.

Before he had a chance to warn the others, Bronson grabbed his neck, felt for the right places, found them, and squeezed. That shut down his carotid arteries. To Bronson's relief, the choke-hold worked quickly. The man went limp and passed out.

Bronson bent down, checked him, and removed the

man's baseball cap and his brown jacket with the name *Floyd* embroidered on the upper right-hand side. Bronson swept the dirt away from the cap and placed it on his head. Next, the jacket. It fit Bronson a bit smug, but it'd do.

Bronson picked up the discarded gun and put it in the small of his back, not his favorite place to hold a gun, but necessary.

Casting the man one last look, Bronson's attention turned to the two remaining hoods.

The hills before him stretched out like an accordion. He'd use that to conceal himself as he approached the other two.

Like a stallion evacuating a burning barn, Bronson bolted toward the other men.

One down and two to go.

SEVENTY-EIGHT

As Bronson neared the men who were fussing over their companion's unconscious body, he kept his head low, the baseball cap hiding his face. He shoved his shoulder forward so that the name in the jacket could be seen.

One of the men glanced his way. "Hurry up, Floyd. Help me carry him to the car." He turned his attention back to Ruben's inert body then looked at Jack, his companion who crouched with him. "Floyd and I can take care of this. Why don't you go search for the senator's son? He can't be far away."

Bronson increased his pace and further lowered his head. He slipped his right hand inside his pant pocket.

Jack rose and pointed west. "I'll go find him. I'm thinking Thomas is heading that way, toward Austin. Get Ruben in the car then hurry back to help me search. I'm going after Thomas. We can't let him get away." He focused on the darkness around him.

Bronson now stood a few feet away from the man crouching next to Ruben. An easy target. He closed the gap.

"Maybe we should leave Ruben," the intended target said. "We can get him later. What we need to do is our job. Let's find and kill Thomas. What do you say?" He looked up again, and this time, he zeroed in on Bronson.

His eyes widened and he gasped as though he wasn't getting enough oxygen. "What—who—"

The man searching for Thomas doubled back in a flash. He faced Bronson head-on and raised his gun. "You're not Floyd!"

Bronson hurled the sock filled with rocks. It hit Jack in the face. He dropped the gun as he tumbled down. The scream died even before he hit the ground.

The man who squatted by Ruben's body bolted to his feet, his hand reaching for his gun.

Bronson kicked his opponent's hand and the gun went flying through the air.

Bronson eyed the gun that had landed by Jack's body as he fell. He had to get it before his opponent did. He moved toward it.

The hood's lips spread in devilish anticipation of the fight. He bent his knee and viciously jacked it upward thus blocking Bronson's attempt to retrieve the gun.

Bronson was familiar with this classic street brawler's move. He side-stepped him.

They circled each other like a pair of snarling wolves.

The man threw a left hook, which landed on the side of Bronson's head.

Bronson staggered back. The blow had felt as if he'd been hit with a chunk of iron. But he kept his balance. Bronson threw a quick elbow to fend off another powerful hook. This time he was successful, but that did nothing to keep the other blows from coming.

Roaring like an enraged mama bear, Bronson grabbed him and met him with a fierce head butt. His opponent bellowed, spewing a spray of blood from the gap formed where his nose met his brow.

Bronson snap kicked, administering a crippling blow to the side of the thug's knee.

Much to Bronson's horror, the man wobbled but still managed to throw a staggering right to Bronson's face, sending a wave of nausea through his gut. He exhaled hard and closed the distance in one quick stride. He slammed the flat of his left hand into his opponent's damaged nose.

The man yelped and put both hands to his face.

Bronson hit him three times in the belly. The man folded over. Bronson pushed the back of the man's head down and at the same time, Bronson brought his knee up. The impact was solid. The man stood dazed as though his body didn't know if it should straighten up or fall down.

Bronson shoved him hard, and he plummeted to the ground.

Bronson had won the round, but at what cost? The pounding inside his head crushed like waves against a sea wall. He tried to keep from grimacing as the throb in his brain increased. The pain shot like bullets ricocheting in his head. He sank to his knees.

Focus! Clear your head and focus. Why? The culprits were down. He could let it go.

It's not over. It's just beginning.

Bronson's peripheral vision barely registered that Jack had regained consciousness. An image formed in Bronson's brain. Jack had picked up the discarded gun and he was steadying his hand as he raised it, pointing it at him.

Bronson tried to reach for his gun, but his punch-drunk mind couldn't coordinate his hand movements fast enough. He dropped to the ground just as Jack cocked the gun. The gun followed Bronson's movement. The barrel loomed large.

Bronson was a sitting duck.

SEVENTY-NINE

A WAVE OF nausea attacked Bronson's body as he rolled on the ground, making his body a smaller target.

Snap out of it! Get up! The man has a gun.

Pain shot up his arm in sharp flashes as he dragged his hand to his back. The gun was there. He knew it. He could reach it. All he had to do was find it. Reach for it. Grab it.

His arm, his hand couldn't obey the sample command.

Too late. You're not goin' to make it.

Jack reared up and aimed for Bronson.

A small shadow like a bolt of lightning swept past Bronson and toward Jack. It jumped on him, forcing him back to the ground.

Honey!

Honey sprung toward Jack. He kicked the dog. A loud *thump* resonated through the woods. She yelped as she tumbled down the hill. Jack sat up and raised the gun.

A single shot rang out.

Jack collapsed back to the ground like a half-empty sack of flour.

Bronson stood over him, the gun still in his hand. "No. One. Kicks. My. Dog." Fearing the worst, he scanned the darkness for any kind of movement. Not even the leaves moved.

He cupped his mouth. "Honey."

He waited for an answer, the smallest indication that Honey was alive.

Through gasping breath, Bronson yelled, "Hoonnney!"

No answer came.

Bronson dropped to his knees.

THOMAS LOOKED UP one side of the road and down the other.

Bronson had given him specific instructions. Head to Austin and get help.

Thomas took a deep breath and returned to his original path. Up ahead he encountered a wall of heavy brush. He pushed past them, tearing his skin on branches and thorns. Still, he plunged on blindly with the speed of an arrow leaving the bow.

He stopped.

He had heard—

What?

He listened.

The shifting of the wind. The deadly silence of the forest.

Then, the sound of approaching cars.

He held his breath and waited.

Seconds later, he saw them. A line of cars heading up the road toward him.

Not just cars, but police cars. No sirens wailing. But they were speeding. He had heard they did that when they didn't want to announce their arrival.

A black sedan led the procession. Was that the agent's car? The one Bronson had told him to contact?

For a fraction of a second, Thomas hesitated. Would they hurt him?

Thomas shook his head. This wasn't the time to think

about himself. Bronson needed help. Without further thought, he jumped out of his hiding place and waved his arms.

EIGHTY

A FIGURE JUMPED out from behind the trees and Special Agent Antonio Corbalan slammed on his breaks. "What the—" He squinted and focused on the man. "Isn't that Thomas Morris?" he asked his partner, Special Agent Sue Hamilton.

"I never met the man, but he certainly looks a lot like the pictures I've seen of him."

Antonio heard the squealing of tires as the cars behind him came to an abrupt halt. He opened the door and stood behind it. "Identify yourself." He heard car doors behind him open.

Thomas hesitated for a moment as he watched the drama unfold in front of him. He shook himself and continued to approach. "Are…you…" He swallowed a deep breath. It was obvious he had been running. "…Special Agent Corbalan?"

"Who wants to—"

Thomas didn't give him a chance to finish. "A bit up ahead, just past that first hill—" He pointed to his right. "Alex or Bronson, rather, is alone and unarmed fighting four armed men."

Antonio cursed under his breath. He had specifically ordered Bronson— He shook his head. No need to go down that road. The irony didn't get past him. It was *that* road that led to *this* road. "You are?" Although Antonio had recognized him, he had to verify his identity.

"Thomas Morris."

Antonio pointed to the car. "Get in. You can fill me in on the way."

They sped down one hill and up the other. When they crested the next one, Antonio spotted the Porsche and two other cars parked at the bottom of the hill. Antonio cruised down the hill. Soon, the area swam with policemen and FBI agents. "Stay inside and stay down," Antonio ordered Thomas as he opened the car door and joined the other law enforcement officers.

"Spread out and stay alert," Antonio told the men. He pointed toward the back seat of his sedan. "Morris says four armed men are going after my informant." Antonio both welcomed and dreaded the silence that engulfed them.

Antonio had climbed over half of the hill when his partner yelled out. "Antonio, over here."

He worked his way to where Sue stood. She was facing downhill aiming her flashlight at the base of a tree.

A man sat on the ground, leaning against the tree trunk. A dog rested on his lap, gently licking the man's face.

"Bronson." Antonio shined his own light on him. "You look like a train ran you over."

"I feel like a train ran me over."

"What happened?" The question popped out of Antonio's mouth before he had a chance to think. He looked past Bronson. He had used belts to tie the three men who looked like quarterbacks who had been tackled and defeated. A fourth man lay on the ground, his hands tied behind him.

"They're alive," Bronson said. "The one on the ground will need surgery to get a bullet removed, but his life is not in danger. The other three, they'll be sore tomorrow but otherwise, okay."

"Looks like you'll also be sore tomorrow."

Bronson shrugged. "It goes with the territory."

Antonio ordered one of his men to request an ambulance. He offered Bronson a hand.

Bronson accepted it and groaned as he stood up.

Antonio pointed to Honey. "I thought Paco told me you and your dog had been separated."

Bronson smiled and grimaced.

His facial muscles must be screaming with pain, Antonio thought.

"Good ol' Paco," Bronson said. "He came through for me."

"He sure did. He was very adamant that I gather a small army and head this way immediately." Antonio bent down and patted Honey. "Looks like we really didn't need to hurry. You've got everything under control."

"Or maybe you didn't hurry enough."

The agent half smiled. "How did you and your dog reunite?"

"I'm not sure. My guess is that whoever was holding her was doing so somewhere around here. When Honey smelled me, she escaped, and it's a good thing she did. She saved my life."

"Is that so? Maybe we should award her a metal."

"She deserves more than that. She deserves a McDonald's hamburger."

Antonio's lips formed a thin smile, but seconds later, he was all business. "You broke protocol, you know that? You're in a lot of trouble."

Bronson shrugged. "Should I turn my badge in now or later?"

Oh yeah. The imaginary badge. "You should have called me before you came here. You know that."

"Sorry. No phone." Bronson straightened himself and stood taller. "At least we've accomplished what Mike wanted us to do. We got 'em. I don't know if Thomas told you about the ledger, but he claims there's enough evidence there to hang 'em all."

"He did mention it, but I haven't had the chance to look at it. Strictly from your testimony, do we have enough evidence to warrant an arrest?"

"We've got enough to convict Andrew Beauregard and Senator Morris of illegal trafficking and a host of other crimes, including attempted murder. The system can lock 'em up and throw away the key."

Antonio opened his mouth to speak but changed his mind when he heard the ambulance approaching at a far distance. "Wait here. I'll have the paramedics look at you, and then you and I are going for a ride."

"Where to?"

Antonio kept his focus on his men who were leading the three thugs down the hill. "You're sure we have enough to arrest Beauregard and Senator Morris?"

"More than enough."

"In that case, let's have the paramedics look at you. Soon as they release you, we'll head toward the two mansions. That is if you want to be there for the arrests."

Bronson beamed. "You bet I do."

"Okay, let's get you looked at."

Bronson didn't argue.

As the paramedics checked on Bronson, a fog of sheer, hopeless misery embraced Antonio. He took a deep breath. He needed to do what had to be done. That was his job.

"Let's go." Bronson approached him. "I'll fill you in on the way to the mansions."

Antonio fished out the car keys out of his pant pocket. "After we finish arresting Beauregard and the senator, there's a third arrest I have to make. I don't know if you want to join me for that one. I'll understand if you don't."

Bronson stared at him through agonized eyes. "Mike." He whispered the word.

Antonio nodded.

"I'll be there, but not as a member of your team, but as a friend."

"I don't see any problem with that. I understand you already turned in your FBI badge." Antonio forced himself to maintain a straight face.

Bronson smiled then grimaced as the pain in his entire body reminded him of what he had just gone through. "I need to retire. Now's a good a time as any."

"Before you completely retire, I have something that I want you to give to Mike. Coming from you, I think it will be a lot more effective and special." Antonio took out his wallet and handed Bronson a neatly folded piece of paper.

EPILOGUE

Three Months Later:
Dallas, Texas

BRONSON CLEANED THE glass on the picture frame. He was expecting Mike to walk in any second, and Bronson wanted the moment to be perfect.

The doorbell rang. Bronson set the framed note down and opened the door.

Mike stepped in. His eyes were vacant and his face ashen. Bronson hugged him. "It's over."

"Not for me, buddy. It'll never be over for me." Mike had just returned from visiting Adela. "She's so sad, but she doesn't hold me responsible. God bless her." He broke the embrace.

"Then you should let it go." Bronson closed the door behind Mike.

"I promised to provide for their son, even pay his college tuition when the time comes. She said that wouldn't be necessary, but for me, it is."

"I understand." Bronson reached for the framed note and handed it to Mike. "Thought this would help."

Mike looked down at Chief Kelley's confession, the last thing he wrote before killing himself. Mike had read the note so many times he probably had it memorized. Still, he read it one more time, this time aloud: *Mike Hoover is working undercover. He's not at fault for killing Detective Herbert Finch. Detective Dave De La Rosa knowingly switched the blanks for real bullets. I suspected as much but I didn't take action. May the Lord forgive me.* The note was signed *Chief Rudy Kelley*.

Mike's smile didn't reach his eyes. "In the end, it was this note that saved my hide." He stroked the paper through the glass. "Thanks for framing it."

Bronson nodded. "Least I could do."

Mike's cell beeped. "It's Antonio." He and Bronson eyed each other. Mike put the phone in speaker mode. "Special Agent Antonio, I wasn't expecting to hear from you. To what do I owe the pleasure?"

"Hello, Mike." A small pause followed. "And Bronson. I'm sure you're there too, listening."

Bronson smiled. "Hello, Special Agent Antonio. As always, you're right. I hope you're not calling about that FBI badge because I know I turned it in."

"I know that if such a badge existed, I'd be looking for it right now, and I'd find it somewhere in your belongings."

Mike nodded and Bronson smiled but both remained quiet.

Antonio continued. "I thought you'd want to know that all of the stolen artifacts have been returned to the National Egyptian Museum."

"That was brought up at my hearing," Mike said.

"You don't get it. All of the pieces are accounted for." He stressed the word *all*. "That includes the two missing Cleopatra statues."

Mike lowered his head and rubbed the bridge of his nose. He closed his eyes and remained quiet for a moment.

"You're still there?" Antonio asked.

Mike nodded even though the only one who could see

him was Bronson. "Naunet's little girl is dead. Naunet said she would return them when…when…" He looked away, but Bronson still saw the tear streaming down his face.

"I figured as much," Antonio said. "That's why I thought you'd want to know."

"I did." He looked at Bronson. "We did. Thanks for letting us know, and double thanks for your support at the hearing."

"You're a good man, Mike, and so is Bronson. He's the kind of man I'd want to have by my side. Just don't let him know I said that. I don't want his head to get swollen more than it is." He paused, and then added, "Both of you take care. Maybe, some other time in a different universe, we can work together again."

Bronson and Mike looked at each other. Both nodded at the same time.

"We'd like that." Mike disconnected and turned to Bronson. "Ellen should be arriving soon. She doesn't know about Naunet."

"It's not my place to tell her."

"Thank you." Mike ran his fingers through his hair. "I realize she needs to know. One day soon when the time is right, I'll tell her, but not now."

The doorbell rang. "That's probably Ellen."

Mike bolted to the door. When he saw her, he wrapped her tightly in his arms. "Oh, Ellie. You're the love of my life."

She looked up at him. "Ellie?"

"That's my new, special name for you. Ellie. Do you like it?"

"Love it," she said.

The back door opened and Honey came bouncing in and greeted everyone. Carol had gone to get pizza, and she had taken Honey with her.

As they sat down to eat, Mike said, "I returned to work yesterday."

Bronson helped himself to another slice of pepperoni pizza with onions. "You had mentioned that. How did it go?"

"Not well. Everyone tried to act normal, but they couldn't. I knew they were talking about me behind my back. I don't blame them. I realized it's never going to be the same. Eventually, it'll get to the point that I either quit or be fired." Mike set his pizza down and focused on Ellen. "I turned in my resignation early this morning before visiting Adela."

Ellen reached for Mike's hand and squeezed it. "Are you okay?"

Mike remained quiet. He nodded. "It was time." He wiped his hands with a napkin. "Now we can get married and live happily ever after."

Ellen's eyes widened. "Mike, is that a proposal?"

Mike shrugged. "A sloppy one, I suppose. But still a proposal." He looked down at her hand that still covered his. He turned his hand so that now he held her hand. "Ellie, would you marry me, again?"

The sparkle in her eyes revealed her emotion. She leaned over and kissed him. "You bet. I'll put all of my stuff for sale in Pennsylvania and move back home."

Mike's face lit up. "Yeah? You'll do that?"

"If you can put your job behind you for me, I can do the same."

Bronson raised his coffee cup and offered a toast.

Honey released a small, happy howl.

Bronson gave her a pepperoni.

* * * * *

KUDOS

PEOPLE SAY THAT it takes a village to raise a kid. They also say that every book is an author's child. Expanding on those two thoughts, it takes a village to write a book. Yes, definitely, the writing process is a lonesome effort. But the creation, the perfecting, and the publishing of a book—that's where the village comes in. Therefore, if you had a hand in this book, consider yourself thanked.

Having said that, there are some folks I'd like to individually thank: First of all, to my Harlequin editor Dana Grimaldi. You are super and working with you is always such a pleasure.

Second, I'd like to thank Ellen Biebesheimer and Mike Hoover for allowing me to use their names; Fran, the best critique partner in the world; Rich, my husband who always supports me, no matter what; and finally Honey—yes, Honey, the dog. She went to wait for us at the Rainbow Bridge and we miss her terribly. But her adventures and tricks continue to show up in this book as well as future Bronson books.

Then there's Shadow, our new basenji. Some of the things I write about in the Bronson books are really Shadow's doings although Honey is taking credit for them.

Special thanks go to the beta readers and the members of my Dream Team, the wonderful folks who offered to read the manuscript in progress and provided helpful information that made this book so much better. Thank you so much for this invaluable service. The book is so much better because of you.

Last, but not least, a million thanks go to all my readers. Without you, I wouldn't have a reason to write. I appreciate your support and loyalty. I couldn't make it without you. I love hearing from you. Contact me through my website at www.lchayden.com. While you're there, sign up to receive my newsletter and get some free goodies.

If you're not my Facebook friend, please befriend me at https://www.facebook.com/profile.php?id=100063732082453 and also please like my author Facebook page at https://www.facebook.com/MysteriesbyHayden/?fref-ts.

ABOUT THE AUTHOR

L. C. HAYDEN IS THE creator of the popular Harry Bronson Thriller Series. Prior releases have won several major awards. What Lies Beyond the Fence was a finalist for the Best Suspense Novel for Killer's Nashville's Silver Falchion Award as well as the Reader's Choice Award. When the Past Haunts You, a thriller that hit the Kindle Police Procedural #2 Best Seller List, was a finalist for Left Coast Crimes' Watson Award for Best Characters. A previous Bronson release, Why Casey Had to Die, became an Agatha Award Finalist for Best Novel and a Pennsylvania Top 40 Pick.

Besides the Bronson Series, Hayden has penned a standalone thriller, Secrets of the Tunnels, and also the Aimee Brent Mystery Series. All of these books contain that edge of the seat suspense and unexpected twists Hayden is known for.

Her non-mysteries include a series about miracles and angels. The books are spiritually uplifting.

Hayden's other works include two children's books and several others in various genres.

Besides being an accomplished author, Hayden is a popular speaker. She has done workshops and school presentations, has spoken to clubs and organizations, and has worked at several major cruise lines speaking about writing while cruising all over the world. From October 2006 to October 2007, Hayden hosted Mystery Writers of America's only talk show, Murder Must Air.

Please check out L. C. Hayden's books at www.tinyurl.com/LCHaydenbooks and visit her website at www.lchayden.com. She loves hearing from her readers.

BRONSON'S HONEY

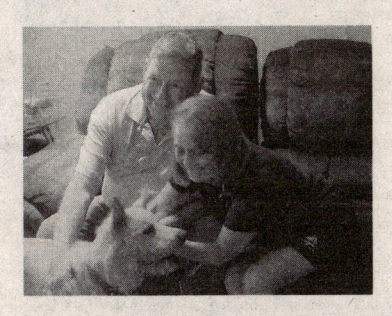

Honey may be Bronson's dog, but she's also ours. Here my husband Rich and I enjoy a time with her.

Introducing Shadow (Honey in the book) doing what he enjoys doing: looking at us from the other side of the couch.

Get 3 FREE REWARDS!

We'll send you 2 FREE Books plus a FREE Mystery Gift.

FREE Value Over $20

Both the **Harlequin Intrigue®** and **Harlequin® Romantic Suspense** series feature compelling novels filled with heart-racing action-packed romance that will keep you on the edge of your seat.

YES! Please send me 2 FREE novels from the Harlequin Intrigue or Harlequin Romantic Suspense series and my FREE gift (gift is worth about $10 retail). After receiving them, if I don't wish to receive any more books, I can return the shipping statement marked "cancel." If I don't cancel, I will receive 6 brand-new Harlequin Intrigue Larger-Print books every month and be billed just $6.49 each in the U.S. or $6.99 each in Canada, a savings of at least 13% off the cover price, or 4 brand-new Harlequin Romantic Suspense books every month and be billed just $5.49 each in the U.S. or $6.24 each in Canada, a savings of at least 12% off the cover price. It's quite a bargain! Shipping and handling is just 50¢ per book in the U.S. and $1.25 per book in Canada.* I understand that accepting the 2 free books and gift places me under no obligation to buy anything. I can always return a shipment and cancel at any time by calling the number below. The free books and gift are mine to keep no matter what I decide.

Choose one:
- ☐ **Harlequin Intrigue Larger-Print** (199/399 BPA GRMX)
- ☐ **Harlequin Romantic Suspense** (240/340 BPA GRMX)
- ☐ **Or Try Both!** (199/399 & 240/340 BPA GRQD)

Name (please print)

Address   Apt. #

City   State/Province   Zip/Postal Code

Email: Please check this box ☐ if you would like to receive newsletters and promotional emails from Harlequin Enterprises ULC and its affiliates. You can unsubscribe anytime.

Mail to the Harlequin Reader Service:
IN U.S.A.: P.O. Box 1341, Buffalo, NY 14240-8531
IN CANADA: P.O. Box 603, Fort Erie, Ontario L2A 5X3

Want to try 2 free books from another series? Call 1-800-873-8635 or visit www.ReaderService.com.

*Terms and prices subject to change without notice. Prices do not include sales taxes, which will be charged (if applicable) based on your state or country of residence. Canadian residents will be charged applicable taxes. Offer not valid in Quebec. This offer is limited to one order per household. Books received may not be as shown. Not valid for current subscribers to the Harlequin Intrigue or Harlequin Romantic Suspense series. All orders subject to approval. Credit or debit balances in a customer's account(s) may be offset by any other outstanding balance owed by or to the customer. Please allow 4 to 6 weeks for delivery. Offer available while quantities last.

Your Privacy—Your information is being collected by Harlequin Enterprises ULC, operating as Harlequin Reader Service. For a complete summary of the information we collect, how we use this information and to whom it is disclosed, please visit our privacy notice located at corporate.harlequin.com/privacy-notice. From time to time we may also exchange your personal information with reputable third parties. If you wish to opt out of this sharing of your personal information, please visit readerservice.com/consumerschoice or call 1-800-873-8635. **Notice to California Residents**—Under California law, you have specific rights to control and access your data. For more information on these rights and how to exercise them, visit corporate.harlequin.com/california-privacy.

HIHRS23

Get 3 FREE REWARDS!

We'll send you 2 FREE Books plus a FREE Mystery Gift.

FREE Value Over $20

Both the **Romance** and **Suspense** collections feature compelling novels written by many of today's bestselling authors.

YES! Please send me 2 FREE novels from the Essential Romance or Essential Suspense Collection and my FREE gift (gift is worth about $10 retail). After receiving them, if I don't wish to receive any more books, I can return the shipping statement marked "cancel." If I don't cancel, I will receive 4 brand-new novels every month and be billed just $7.49 each in the U.S. or $7.74 each in Canada. That's a savings of at least 17% off the cover price. It's quite a bargain! Shipping and handling is just 50¢ per book in the U.S. and $1.25 per book in Canada.* I understand that accepting the 2 free books and gift places me under no obligation to buy anything. I can always return a shipment and cancel at any time by calling the number below. The free books and gift are mine to keep no matter what I decide.

Choose one:
- ☐ **Essential Romance** (194/394 BPA GRNM)
- ☐ **Essential Suspense** (191/391 BPA GRNM)
- ☐ **Or Try Both!** (194/394 & 191/391 BPA GRQZ)

Name (please print)

Address   Apt. #

City   State/Province   Zip/Postal Code

Email: Please check this box ☐ if you would like to receive newsletters and promotional emails from Harlequin Enterprises ULC and its affiliates. You can unsubscribe anytime.

Mail to the **Harlequin Reader Service:**
IN U.S.A.: P.O. Box 1341, Buffalo, NY 14240-8531
IN CANADA: P.O. Box 603, Fort Erie, Ontario L2A 5X3

Want to try 2 free books from another series! Call 1-800-873-8635 or visit www.ReaderService.com.

---

*Terms and prices subject to change without notice. Prices do not include sales taxes, which will be charged (if applicable) based on your state or country of residence. Canadian residents will be charged applicable taxes. Offer not valid in Quebec. This offer is limited to one order per household. Books received may not be as shown. Not valid for current subscribers to the Essential Romance or Essential Suspense Collection. All orders subject to approval. Credit or debit balances in a customer's account(s) may be offset by any other outstanding balance owed by or to the customer. Please allow 4 to 6 weeks for delivery. Offer available while quantities last.

Your Privacy—Your information is being collected by Harlequin Enterprises ULC, operating as Harlequin Reader Service. For a complete summary of the information we collect, how we use this information and to whom it is disclosed, please visit our privacy notice located at corporate.harlequin.com/privacy-notice. From time to time we may also exchange your personal information with reputable third parties. If you wish to opt out of this sharing of your personal information, please visit readerservice.com/consumerschoice or call 1-800-873-8635. **Notice to California Residents**—Under California law, you have specific rights to control and access your data. For more information on these rights and how to exercise them, visit corporate.harlequin.com/california-privacy.

STRS23

Get 3 FREE REWARDS!

We'll send you 2 FREE Books plus a FREE Mystery Gift.

FREE Value Over $20

Both the **Love Inspired®** and **Love Inspired® Suspense** series feature compelling novels filled with inspirational romance, faith, forgiveness and hope.

YES! Please send me 2 FREE novels from the Love Inspired or Love Inspired Suspense series and my FREE gift (gift is worth about $10 retail). After receiving them, if I don't wish to receive any more books, I can return the shipping statement marked "cancel." If I don't cancel, I will receive 6 brand-new Love Inspired Larger-Print books or Love Inspired Suspense Larger-Print books every month and be billed just $6.49 each in the U.S. or $6.74 each in Canada. That is a savings of at least 16% off the cover price. It's quite a bargain! Shipping and handling is just 50¢ per book in the U.S. and $1.25 per book in Canada.* I understand that accepting the 2 free books and gift places me under no obligation to buy anything. I can always return a shipment and cancel at any time by calling the number below. The free books and gift are mine to keep no matter what I decide.

Choose one: ☐ **Love Inspired Larger-Print** (122/322 BPA GRPA)   ☐ **Love Inspired Suspense Larger-Print** (107/307 BPA GRPA)   ☐ **Or Try Both!** (122/322 & 107/307 BPA GRRP)

Name (please print)

Address   Apt. #

City   State/Province   Zip/Postal Code

Email: Please check this box ☐ if you would like to receive newsletters and promotional emails from Harlequin Enterprises ULC and its affiliates. You can unsubscribe anytime.

Mail to the Harlequin Reader Service:
IN U.S.A.: P.O. Box 1341, Buffalo, NY 14240-8531
IN CANADA: P.O. Box 603, Fort Erie, Ontario L2A 5X3

Want to try 2 free books from another series? Call 1-800-873-8635 or visit www.ReaderService.com.

---

*Terms and prices subject to change without notice. Prices do not include sales taxes, which will be charged (if applicable) based on your state or country of residence. Canadian residents will be charged applicable taxes. Offer not valid in Quebec. This offer is limited to one order per household. Books received may not be as shown. Not valid for current subscribers to the Love Inspired or Love Inspired Suspense series. All orders subject to approval. Credit or debit balances in a customer's account(s) may be offset by any other outstanding balance owed by or to the customer. Please allow 4 to 6 weeks for delivery. Offer available while quantities last.

Your Privacy—Your information is being collected by Harlequin Enterprises ULC, operating as Harlequin Reader Service. For a complete summary of the information we collect, how we use this information and to whom it is disclosed, please visit our privacy notice located at corporate.harlequin.com/privacy-notice. From time to time we may also exchange your personal information with reputable third parties. If you wish to opt out of this sharing of your personal information, please visit readerservice.com/consumerchoice or call 1-800-873-8635. **Notice to California Residents**—Under California law, you have specific rights to control and access your data. For more information on these rights and how to exercise them, visit corporate.harlequin.com/california-privacy.

LIRLIS23

HARLEQUIN PLUS

Try the best multimedia subscription service for romance readers like you!

Read, Watch and Play.

Experience the easiest way to get the romance content you crave.

Start your **FREE TRIAL** at
www.harlequinplus.com/freetrial.

HARPLUS0123